# KINGS OF MERLIN

PRIYA ARDIS

VULCAN INK

Published by: Vulcan Ink Media, LLC
http://www.vulcaninkmedia.com/
Visit the author website: http://www.priyaardis.com/
ISBN-13: 978-1-952767-12-9
E-BOOK ISBN-13: 978-1-9517671-5-0
First Edition, April 2020
Juvenile Fiction / Legends, Myths, Fables / Arthurian

# ACKNOWLEDGMENTS

Thank you fans of Merlin for continuing to support the stories. The best part of writing the series are the notes I get from you about your favorite parts. This next chapter is a little spicy but you know, if it stayed the same, where would be the fun?
Enjoy!

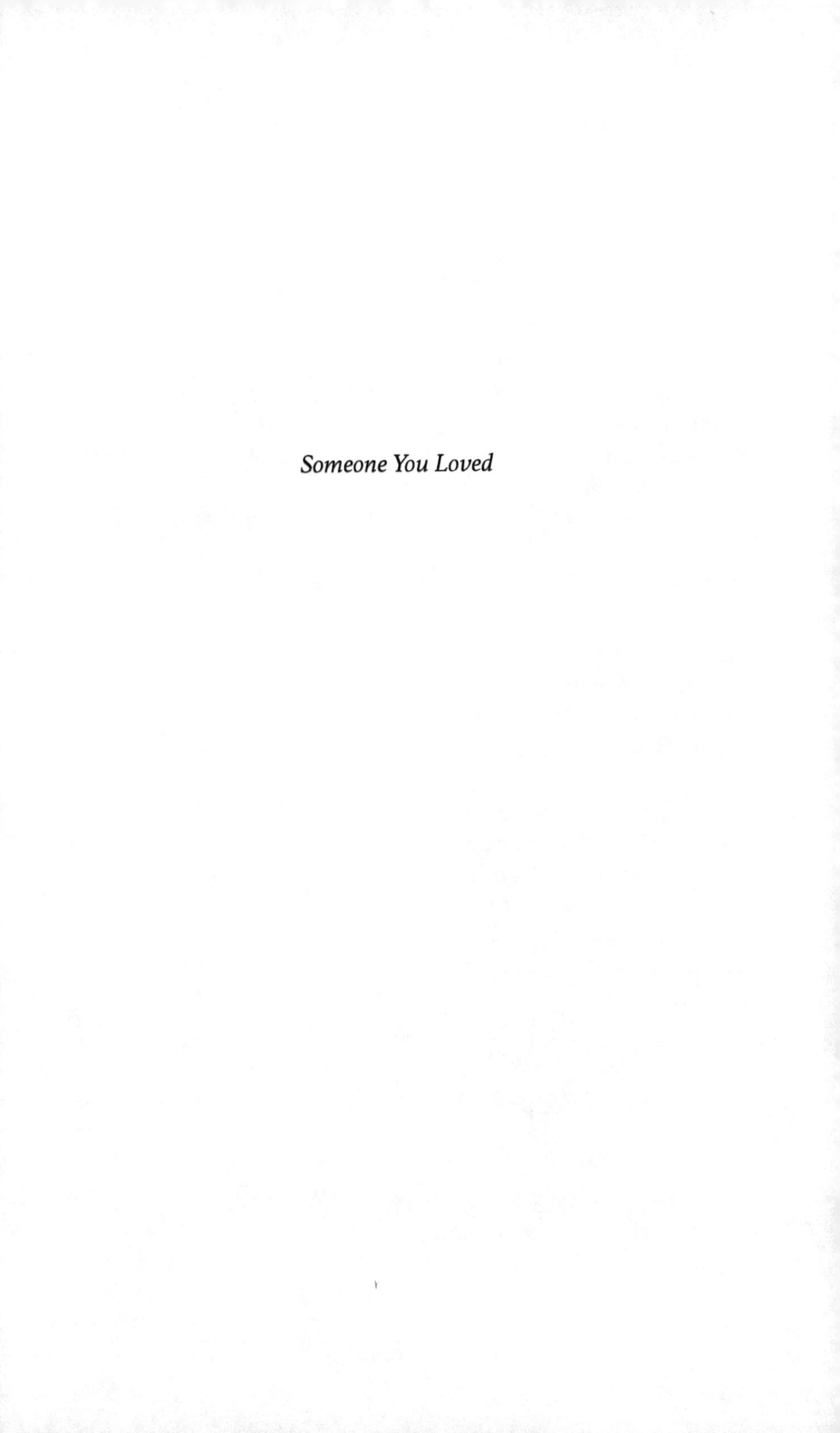

*Someone You Loved*

# KINGS OF MERLIN

Gods of Merlin, 2

PRIYA ARDIS

# CONTENTS

# PROLOGUE

**Eowlyn - Three Years Ago**

The boy lay on the bed sprawled like a sacrifice to an ancient god. Blood splattered white-flowered sheets. His mother screamed hysterically at a police officer. Another man in uniform drew a plain white sheet over the gutted body.

I sat in the hallway just outside the room, but I could still see inside. People in suits and uniformed policemen buzzed around here and there. Another uniform stood over me. He'd put a jacket over my shaking shoulders. I huddled in it, keeping a death grip on my shirt, holding the torn bits together. I'd been sleeping when the boy creeped into my bed. I couldn't even remember grabbing the knife. I always kept it under my pillow. Habit. I couldn't sleep without it.

"She has scratches all over her. He fought her as she sliced him up," a man in a suit, Detective Something-or-other, said. He stood inside the room, but my hearing had always been really good.

A second detective, one with kinder eyes, stared at the

bloody mess on the bed before me. "This isn't his room. He attacked her. He was trying to assault her. She fought back. Someone's trained her to defend herself."

"She gutted him like a piece of meat with a fraking steak knife," the detective spat. "Can you imagine her with a real one?"

The kind one smiled. "She's pretty impressive."

"You're sick." The detective shook his head. "Just look at her. She looks catatonic. Crazy."

The kind one gave me a long look. His eyes lingered on my huddled form before he turned back to his partner. "She looks scared. Those cuts she gave him—the strike pattern—they aren't vicious. They're practiced. Someone trained her with extreme precision. She could very well have been asleep when she killed him." He said quietly, "No, she's not crazy."

Detective Something snorted. "Then what is she?"

"Someone who was loved. Once upon a time."

*But not anymore.*

～

## Merlin - 523 A.D.

I cried on the steps as my older brother, Vane, stomped up into the cottage. The Lady wore white. A gold brooch tied her toga on one side and showed bare shoulders. She turned when I walked into the small space. The cottage wasn't big. On one side, two cots lay behind a curtain partition. Another partition at the opposite end of the cottage hid a third cot, where the Lady slept.

She sat at the table with her son. He didn't stay with us. A parade of sons and daughters came through the cottage. All of them had the same golden eyes and all of them made me itchy, as if just looking at them made my insides beat against my skin.

I gave another wail.

The Lady jumped up. "Merlin is crying. What happened, Vivane?"

Vane didn't move. "He needs to learn to take care of himself." He pointed to a bag on the floor next to the son. A small bag sat under the table. Vane nodded at the two cots where he and I slept. One cot had been stripped of its blanket. A muscle ticked in one side of his jaw. "He can't count on me any longer."

My wail cut off, as real fear replaced the pain. I took slow steps forward. My gaze went to the bag. A bit of the blanket stuck out from its top. *Vane's blanket. What is happening?*

The Lady sighed. "You could always read a situation well."

I went up to the Lady. My head almost hit the top of the table. Vane stood back, trying to be brave. His face was still but I knew him better. His fisted hands betrayed his fear.

The Lady's son rose. His eyes glowed gold, with a hint of blue. The deepest blue, which became deeper the longer I looked.

The son leaned down and picked up the bag at his feet. He stood. "It is time," he said in a full, deep voice. "Are you ready, Vivane?"

Resignation filled my brother's face. He gave a small nod.

As the Lady's son walked to Vane, a hint of salty water emanated from the son. Instead of cool and refreshing, his scent reminded me of briny fish and blood. A gold brooch of a fish held together his toga. He towered over the Lady with big, hulking muscles. His face was eerily beautiful, even with a short beard covering it.

Vane betrayed nothing in his voice as he said in a flat tone, "What do you expect of me?"

"Our mother has declared you are to be trained." The son glanced at the Lady. "It will not be easy, but you will come out a warrior."

The Lady walked to Vane and put her hand on his head. "You will come out a protector."

The son made a noise of dissension. "You are meddling, Mother."

"I am not meddling. I could not. I cannot interfere directly. But these boys are of this world. They can decide its fate."

The son gave her a skeptical look. "You're skirting the line."

The Lady's lips twitched. "That is why the line is there." She patted Vane's head. "Remember, Vivane. It is Merlin's destiny to save your world. It is your destiny to help him."

My ears perked. *Vane would help me? Usually he just cuffed my ear.*

Vane's chin rose. "As he will help me. He is *my* family."

"We are all family." The Lady glanced at her son. "Do not worry. The love between brothers is strong and true. No one can come between it. Not even gods."

# 1

## A GARGOYLE COLDCOCKED ME

"I hate Merlin so much right now," I muttered from my position crouched behind a garbage bin. Like anywhere in London, a thick smog degraded my lungs with every breath I took. But the polluted air layered the dirty alley like a blanket.

Ryan DuLac chuckled as she leaned over my shoulder to peer at the back door of the dilapidated pub. "That's what I say about Vane all the time. You've got it bad, Eowlyn Patience."

"I don't do anything bad anymore," I groused.

"Well, don't sound so disappointed about being part of the good-guy team now," Ryan said. After a pause, she asked, "You don't like to call him Matt?"

"I'm calling him by the name he really is, not the name he'd rather hide behind."

"I wouldn't describe Merlin as someone hiding." She pointed at the quiet back door. "He's out here tracking gargoyles, instead of locked away at the school. I've barely seen him since we got Excalibur."

*That's part of the problem.* "For all his pretty words about being a team, he's just the same. Secretive and too stubborn to ask for help."

Ryan let out a snort. "I might say the same of you."

The back door cracked open. I hissed, "Get down."

Ryan ducked, coming down on top of me, her elbows landing on my back. "Do you see the boys?"

I shrugged her off. "They are going to be pissed we snuck out."

"They weren't telling us anything about anything," she said. "If they had, we wouldn't be here."

The back door closed, but no one came out. I glanced around the empty alley. No degenerates or gargoyles lurked. So far.

"How do you know anyone's going to come out from the back door?" Ryan whispered, chatty like. The petite blonde did not look like an all-powerful, sword-toting warrior, but she was.

"The bad guys always come out the back," I whispered. "Haven't you watched any TV?"

"I'm not into all that superhero stuff."

Typical. *Because you are a superhero.* Well, the Merlin version of a superhero anyway.

"Eowlyn"—Ryan put a dainty hand on my shoulder—"I'm glad you're here."

I flinched and she let go.

"Sorry," she said. "Does it still hurt?"

I grunted. "Training should be relabeled to torture."

She chuckled. "Vane is bad enough. But you've got the most advanced sword trainer the school has to offer."

"That isn't it. Merlin also has me training with Blake on magical defenses. I got this one when he threw a crystal hexing bomb at me." It had burned my shoulder and the hex immobilized me for a whole hour. I stood. The empty alley remained quiet. "All right, if there were any gargoyles in the club, the boys would have driven them out here by now. I say we go in just in case."

"We can't go in," Ryan hissed. "You said it yourself—we're just backup."

"Time to go be backup." I marched to the pub. "What if they need help in there?" Reaching the door, I took a deep breath before I flung it open.

Loud music slammed my ears. Thumps, grunts, and the distinctive crash of furniture breaking came next. I rushed through a short corridor to the main part of the bar and stopped at its threshold.

My jaw dropped open.

A melee had broken out inside the dank bar. Rock music blared as bodies flew here and there. Men and women crashed into high tables and broke barstools. Ryan came up behind me.

I pointed a finger to the middle of the mess. "Look."

Merlin and his brother, Vane, fought with what looked like broken barstool legs as sticks. Against fifty or so opponents. Merlin threw a small blue fireball at one man. The man took it in the stomach, stumbled, then, shaking it off, charged again.

"Gargoyles," Ryan hissed as she pointed to a few faces in the fight. Their foreheads protruded like Neanderthals, their faces transformed and set in angry lines. Gargoyles did not go down with one hit. Sometimes it took fifty.

"I thought he was going to try to talk," I said.

Ryan snorted. "There's no talking to those beasts."

As attackers kept charging, Merlin and Vane turned in a circle. A third man appeared in my line of sight, out from behind Merlin. The third man also stood with his back to the brothers and held a sword, which he thrust and parried as if he'd been born to it.

Ryan declared, "I should have brought my sword."

Her sword. Excalibur. I had yet to see if a magical sword was really worth the number of dead bodies it had piled up.

A broken barstool leg rolled to our feet. Ryan picked it up. "But this will do."

She moved to lunge into the fight.

I put a hand on her arm to stop her. "Together."

She nodded. We ran into the melee.

Keeping Ryan at my back, I slammed a fist into a gargoyle. Another came at me and I ducked and punched. One got me in the gut. Tears stinging my eyes, I grabbed his arm and held it. With my other hand, I drew out a charm from my pocket and slammed it into his chest. He screamed as he went flying back.

"That's new," Ryan commented as she whacked an attacker who ran at her.

"Merlin's fault," I said as another attacker came at me. I front-kicked the charging girl in the stomach. "He's been gathering all sorts of magic." Now that he couldn't do his own.

"Hmm." Ryan hit another guy.

She didn't have to say it. Guilt rolled off my back. *You lost Merlin his magic. You sacrificed him, the lamb to a god-slaughter.*

As if hearing my words, Merlin's head jerked up. "Eowlyn."

He spreads his hands out. He hissed in a magical tongue, "*Nidra.*"

*Sleep.* Blue fire burst out of his hands. It hit a circle of attackers around him. Then, the blue fire petered out, fading when it should have spread.

Merlin put his hands on his thighs and panted.

Across the room, I wanted to rush to him. His exhaustion was my fault.

Vane and the third man covered him, coming to stand in front and behind Merlin like bodyguards, as more attackers rushed them.

"We need to get closer to the boys," I ducked around an attack.

She didn't answer as another gargoyle charged her. He managed to get in a punch and knocked away her makeshift chair-leg weapon. The gargoyle drew out a knife and thrust it at her.

I ran and side-tackled him, knocking away the knife. A hard punch came at my face. I ducked but my body reeled as his fist connected with my shoulder. I fell.

Ryan moved to get to me. Another gargoyle ran at her.

I backed up on the floor. My hand brushed the gargoyle's fallen knife. I picked it up and everything changed. My nostrils flaring, I leapt up and attacked, slicing at him without even seeing him. The crowd became a blur—and only by instinct could I tell friend from foe.

Ryan beat back the other guy. We quickly fought our way to the others though the herd thinned out as fewer and fewer attackers managed to get back up. When we finally made it to Merlin and Vane, only a few remained.

As soon as Ryan neared, Vane uttered, "*Nidra.*"

The utterance spread out in a small red wave. It hit half of the remaining attackers and they dropped, falling unconscious to the ground. It took mere minutes to beat the rest into the same unconscious state.

A gargoyle coldcocked me. With a yell, I recovered. The steel of a knife flashed as he attacked. My hand swung. The small knife brought the gargoyle down. The gargoyle's beast face blurred. It settled back into its human form. Golden-Hainey. The gargoyle had the face of my old physics teacher. My hand trembled. Rage surged, I leapt on top of the fallen body and stabbed him again.

"Gwenhwyfar, stop."

An arm hauled me away from the fallen gargoyle. Blond hair and kind grey eyes stood too close. *He's too bright.* My eyes squinted. It hurt to look at a soul so bright. I struggled in his hold.

"Her name is Eowlyn, Arthur," a serious voice said.

Merlin's words washed over me like a cold bath. It cut

through the intoxicating haze of battle and the pub came back into view. A prickle went down my spine as time changed from frenzied to normal. *What have you done now?* My head whipped back to the gargoyle I'd just gutted. The dead gargoyle had a surface resemblance to my old physics teacher, Hainey, but I'd never seen him before. My head began to throb as if I'd been forced into sudden sobriety.

Putting his hands on my face, the blond asked, "Are you all right?"

I shrugged out of his hold. "I'm not Gwenhwyfar."

He smiled. "Of course, I apologize. It was mere instinct."

Merlin scowled. "I told you to stay at the academy."

"I'm not good at being told. You should know that."

"I know," Merlin murmured, a hint of heat filling his tone.

The heat hit me like an arrow, piercing quickly and burying deep. My heart slowed at the sight of his stubbled jaw, broody amber eyes, and lean, muscled body. He wasn't quite the underwear model with rippling abs like his brother, but I could still taste his mouth on mine even though it had been over a month. *Get a grip, Patience. One kiss and you want to haul him off to a dark corner.* Looking away, I spread my arms wide. "You asked me to be part of your team. This is what it looks like."

"I agree with Merlin," Arthur interjected. "I am not sure you should put yourself at such risk. Women should be protected—"

"Is that so?" I hooked a thumb at Ryan, who stood with Vane. Ryan was pushing a barely conscious gargoyle's bruised face against the wall while Vane lounged behind her and watched. I said dryly, "We women seem to have taken care of ourselves."

Merlin grumbled, "It's not safe to have Ryan out. The gargoyles won't hesitate to go after the rightful heir."

"Like I could stop your precious rightful heir," I said. "She jumped on the back of the bike."

Merlin's face darkened. "You stole my motorcycle."

"Borrowed," I corrected quickly.

"Bickering again?" Vane walked up, dragging a half-conscious gargoyle behind him. "You two need to get a room."

Arthur frowned. "Why do they need more room? We just cleared out this tavern."

"We're in a pub," Vane corrected. "Put it together, Your Majesty. Why would anyone need a separate chamber?"

As both Arthur and Merlin turned red in the face, Vane chuckled.

I elbowed Vane.

He let out a grunt and dropped the gargoyle to the floor. Vane swept a hand over his face and wiped off a streak of blood.

On the floor, the gargoyle's head lolled back. A brand had been seared into his neck. The brand was unmistakable.

I gasped. "Oliver's mark. You found Oliver's hideout?"

The gargoyle had headed up the group to challenge us for Excalibur.

Merlin glanced around at the pub. "Not much of a hideout. But yes, we got a tip."

I tensed at the thought of my former schoolmate. "Is he here?"

Merlin shook his head. "But the fact they bear his mark confirms these men have broken from the king and shifted allegiance to his son."

*Shifted allegiance to Oliver.* Every gargoyle was connected to the king, who could force his will on them and make them act like mindless automatons. I grimaced. "How is that possible? A disloyal gargoyle? I thought they couldn't go against their king. Last time, Oliver went behind the king's back, but getting another's mark? Isn't that open rebellion?"

"I don't fully understand it. Something's happened. These gargoyles seem more loyal to the son than to the king. That should be impossible. They don't have a choice in following their leader." Merlin looked down at the unconscious gargoyle. Power emanated from his eyes, but it only hinted, rather than burned, as it should have been.

Guilt choked me. How did I destroy everything I touched? *Especially the things which you care about the most.*

Vane kicked the limp gargoyle's arm with a boot heel. "This one has it out for Ryan, in particular. I have no problem putting him down."

The gargoyle king's son wanted Excalibur. Even though it belonged to someone else, he thought he could take it. Vane sauntered up and put an arm around my shoulders. He dropped a kiss in my hair. "Good timing, tiny. We needed a little backup."

I beamed and poked a muscled ab. "I thought so."

Merlin glowered. "Don't encourage her."

Arthur Pendragon, more famously known as King Arthur of Camelot, also glowered. "You haven't changed, Vivane."

"I never planned to change." Vane's expression darkened, reminding me that, a thousand years ago, he'd been a Roman legionnaire. "You, Arthur Pendragon, could never go far enough. Never do what needed to be done. That's why you lost."

Arthur's grey eyes shaded. "As I understand it from what Merlin said, you turned my son—a son I can't remember even having—against me."

Vane's hands fisted. "Camelot wouldn't have fallen if you hadn't turned your back on those who helped you build it. You wanted to only please those you favored. You stopped listening to *all* your people. You became weak."

"Stop." Merlin put up a hand. "Arthur can't remember anything past first meeting Guinevere and the first days of Camelot." Merlin looked over the younger king. "They somehow preserved him so he's aged backwards."

"Convenient," Vane said under his breath.

I sighed. "This argument has nothing to do with what is happening now."

"What is happening now?" Ryan walked up. Sweat darkened her blonde hair.

On the floor, the gargoyle Vane had dropped took a shallow breath as he woke.

Merlin marched to him and knelt down. He took a crystalline-orb the size of a golf ball out of his pocket and put against to the gargoyle's face. "Get a message to your king. Tell him Merlin wants to speak to him. Tell him if he wants his men back, he will come to me."

Merlin smashed the orb on the gargoyle's forehead.

The gargoyle gasped, writhed, and passed out again.

Ryan raised her eyebrows. "You didn't have to hurt him, Matt. I don't think he was getting away."

Merlin stood. "I don't want him to hear anything else."

Vane crossed to Ryan, though he didn't put his hand on her shoulders as he'd done with me. In fact, his expression was stone. I knew him well enough to see through it—he was worried.

With carefully blank eyes, he said, "We need to know why the sword came to you."

"We need to know why I've been awakened," Arthur said.

Merlin shook his head. "The only way to get those answers is to restore my powers. I haven't had a vision in months."

*Because you served him up like meat on a platter.* My stomach twisted. "All your answers are tied to one source—the gods. Why are we hunting gargoyles when we should be hunting them?"

Arthur bent down and hoisted an unconscious gargoyle on his shoulders. "Merlin's plan is to trade these captured gargoyles for information."

Merlin gave him a fond smile. "You've been paying attention."

Vane snorted, eyeing Arthur with misgiving. "What information?"

Merlin shook his head. "I'll tell you when the time is right."

Vane and Ryan scowled identically.

I crossed my arms. "Exactly what do you intend to do with *these gargoyles* until they get traded?"

"The school has a basement," Merlin said.

I gawked. "Avalon Preparatory Academy has a dungeon?"

To my shock, straitlaced, do-right Merlin stared over the litter of gargoyles with determination. "Yes, we do. And I intend to enjoy this."

Arthur frowned. "I do not think we should enjoy hurting people."

Vane laughed and slapped his brother on the back. "There's hope for you yet, brother."

2

# KING ARTHUR HAS GREY EYES

y arms strained to hold the heavy sword, bending backwards and twisting into a torture position Arthur Pendragon had tricked me into as we sparred. My fingers tightened around a wooden practice weapon, the only thing blocking Arthur's wooden stick from whacking me in the head.

Locked in a stalemate, I tried to step back. My foot slipped on grass and I went sliding into mud. My bottom hit the ground. Mud oozed into the stretchy skintight fabric of my athletic pants.

"Victory, at last." Arthur raised his hands in gleeful triumph.

I swiped his leg with mine and he went tumbling into the grass beside me. Mud splattered his face. I laughed as he sputtered and spat out mud.

"That was not fair," he said, getting up. "I already defeated you."

I met his grey eyes. *King Arthur has grey eyes.* It still startled me to know it. Mud covered his shirt, making it cling to tight abs and broad shoulders. Wavy blond hair curtained his eyes, and yet when the god-like specimen smiled, his face shone with kindness.

No wonder an entire kingdom once pledged loyalty to him.

As it was, we'd spent the last three months getting him to understand he'd woken up a thousand years later and needed to acclimate into modern society, or at least our little protected pocket of it at magic school.

Arthur stood. Sunlight shone like a bright halo behind him.

I tried not to be dazzled. If we'd been at my former school in Boston, he would have definitely been a ballplayer—any kind of ball.

He smiled as he held out his hand, offering it to me.

Something about the love in the smile created shy flutters in my stomach. *He's looking at her, not you,* I reminded myself. My palm slid into his. His Majesty's hand was surprisingly rough with calluses. He was no paper-pushing ruler.

Arthur pulled me up. "Have they forgotten the rules of engagement in this future world?"

"The rule is no surrender," I said.

Arthur's eyes flickered. "You are really not like my Guinevere, are you?"

I blinked. "Is that okay?"

"Of course." He frowned. "It's just that she was not so... confusing." He stared at me for a long second before concluding, "She never cared to try her hand at swords." He twirled the wooden sword in his hand with the ease of a man who'd held it all his life.

I put my sword in the dirt. "I'll never be as good as you or Vane...or Ryan."

"No one could beat Guinevere at the bow. The way she made an arrow fly, sharp and true..." He smiled fondly. "Once she sliced an apple I held in my hand from across the Great Hall."

I smiled. "What did you do to upset her?"

Instead of smiling back, Arthur frowned. "It was but a dare on her part, I think. On behalf of one of the knights."

"That doesn't seem nice."

"A harmless jest. She did have a unique sense of humor."

How did one say, *Your queen sounds like an ass?* But I didn't voice the thought. Instead, I lifted the sword and swung the wood in a practice form. My movements weren't as natural with a bow, but I was getting better. "I thought you didn't remember being married to Guinevere."

"I do not. My memories go up to the last great battle for unification. We hadn't even formed Camelot." He blushed. "Though I must confess I have had the name in mind for quite some time. Guinevere and I have been courting for some time. She is—" He paused and swallowed. "*She was* the king's daughter of one of the kingdoms I united. She fought alongside us with Merlin and Vivane."

"You were courting? Like dating?"

"Dating," he said slowly, as if he was tasting it. "I have seen some of your moving pictures. Dating seems...very fast. A relationship without many assurances. It is quite shocking ladies agree to it."

My lips twitched. "Men agree too. They can get hurt from a lack of assurances too."

He cleared his throat. "Are you dating?"

*Am I? I wish I knew.* I aimed the sword at him. "How about another go? This time remember—duty before honor."

"Unsurprising. Honor seems to be in short supply in this time period," a low voice said from behind.

My head whipped around and I met rich chocolate-colored eyes. My insides immediately melted. *Merlin.*

He stalked toward me, purpose defining every bit of his lean, taut body.

"This time takes getting used to," Arthur murmured. Lifting

his shirt, he sniffed. "Though even dirty, I feel cleaner. I cannot believe you bathe every day."

"Believe it and live it," I said with feeling. A thousand years asleep in a rock couldn't fix habits. I shuddered. "Vane still runs around without a shower for days at a time."

"I don't have a problem," Merlin muttered.

No, he didn't. I eyed him, wondering how he'd ever survived in the Dark Ages. I'd never seen him without a perfect shave. Today, his sweater vest and dark jeans looked straight out of a rich-boy polo-cardigan-wearing catalog.

A bell from the tower rang as the hour turned. Students ran out the classrooms and rushed around the green square set at the center of campus. The sun shone high in the sky, even though the evening approached. Classes at Avalon Preparatory Academy were winding down as spring break neared, and everyone ran around in a mad rush to finish tests before break.

Merlin's gaze fixed on Arthur. "How are you getting on?"

Arthur shrugged. "As well as the last time you asked. You may be older now, but I am not a child."

"I never said you were," Merlin said steadily. "However, it takes time to adjust. You've had a big shock."

Arthur's lower lip stuck out ever so slightly. "I'm stronger than you give me credit for."

"Be grateful you have this time. We have a lot to figure out and you are part of the question."

Arthur stood stubbornly without acknowledging Merlin's reprimand. I wondered if he would stomp his feet as Merlin mothered him.

Before the two could actually start yelling at each other, I interjected, "What bad news do you have for us now, Merlin?"

A lone eyebrow rose. "I don't always have bad news."

"Yes, you do," Arthur and I said together.

Our eyes met and we both grinned.

Merlin gave us an unamused look. "Arthur, may I talk to Eowlyn alone?"

Arthur blinked. He gave Merlin a charged look but inclined his head. "Of course." Taking my hand, he lifted it up and bowed over it. "You are doing well. Next time, milady. We shall see who is victorious."

An unfortunate giggle escaped me. I clamped down on it but not before Merlin sent me another glare.

Flashing another handsome smile, Arthur tucked his wooden sword at his side and walked off down the central green lawn of the school. He disappeared in a crowd of students as they hurried back into the buildings before the next class began.

I sighed, stretching and soaking in the rare bit of sun in rainy England. "I'm being trained to be a knight by King Arthur himself. How awesome is that?"

Merlin looked down at my feet. "You're bouncing."

"Arthur is more patient than Vane. I'm learning a lot from him."

"The way you sliced up the gargoyle in the pub, I'm not sure you need more learning to become a killer."

*Killer.* The word hit me in the gut. I said lightly, "Ryan and Vane still kicking your butt in training, grumpy?"

"I'm worried about you."

Unbidden warmth heated my insides. "You don't need to be. I might have some PTSD issues after Golden-Hainey. Surely you can understand that."

"You sacrificed my magic. Yes, I understand all too well. But this isn't just internal. You are aggressive. Very aggressive." He reached out a hand and put it on my mud-soaked arm. Not on the fabric of my long-sleeved shirt but on an exposed wrist. His thumb pressed into bare skin. "You can come to me if you want to talk."

A short breathiness overtook me. I nodded. *Too eager, Patience. Have some self-respect.*

He sighed. "I know you like Arthur, Eowlyn. But be careful. He may look like a naïve boy. He is not. He may not have all his memories, but it only makes him more deadly. When he was this age—handsome and seductive—he was unstoppable. He's used to getting his way. He's always sure he's in the right, and he has a grudge against Vane."

My lips twitched. "Are we talking about Arthur or you?"

"I'm serious. You are the spitting image of the woman he wanted to make his wife. The one he did make his wife. The one he loved like no other." Merlin's thumb pressed deeper, in an almost painful caress. "But you are not her."

"Got it," I snapped. I tugged at my wrist. "I'm not Her Royal Majesty, Guinevere. The Helen of Troy of her age. Arthur knows that. I know that. Happy now?"

"No." Merlin's hold on my arm tightened. "What happens when he learns all the stories? He doesn't know Guinevere betrayed him. He hasn't felt the pain yet. But he will."

He glanced off in the direction Arthur had walked. The boys' dormitory, Monmouth House, stood higher up on a hill. It was one of the tallest buildings of the campus. Its bottom floors housed teachers as well as the greatest wizards in the world and one legendary king. When Merlin had told him where and when he was after he'd woken, he'd just stared at me with the most befuddled look. Arthur's exact words had been, *The gods are playing with me.* Considering the manner in which he'd been woken from eternal slumber, they were playing with all of us.

Merlin let go of my wrist. "Believe me, you don't want to be her. Now, are you ready to focus on what's going on in the here and now and not on someone who's been dead a thousand years?"

I bowed deeply, mimicking Arthur as closely as I could. "What can I do for you, dear sir?"

"Wouldn't you like to know," Merlin said in a low murmur.

I stilled. Was he flirting with me? Merlin didn't flirt, did he? The tips of my ears turned red, but I thrust up my chin. "I would like to know. For real. You've got the hot-and-cold routine nailed."

He frowned. "Eowlyn, what do you mean—"

"Nevermind." Seriously, he was clueless. I made an impatient sound. "Pray tell, what pulls the mighty Merlin from his tower?"

# 3

## HE WANTS MY THRONE

"You mean my tower the library?" he asked dryly. "I thought you liked it there."

I shrugged. All right, I loved the library. Last night, I'd fallen asleep in the stacks, researching ways to restore Merlin's magic, and woken to find myself drooling not on a table but on Merlin's chest. My eyes went to the body part in question. Getting over the embarrassment of leaking saliva all over his shirt, I hadn't missed how ripped his body had become since he'd begun training with Vane on swords.

Merlin smirked. "A moment of silence from Eowlyn Patience. Should I be afraid?"

"Why don't you tell me what's got you bothered?"

"Many things have me bothered," he said softly. "But the one that concerns me at the moment is the one waiting to kill us."

My head snapped up. "What now?"

"Rourke and his team are in Glastonbury."

"Right. Let's go then." I turned on my heel and began walking off the lawn.

He moved to get in front of me. "Why are you so mad at me?"

"Why do you think?" I exploded. Marching up to him, I lifted my chin and glared. "We kissed, and then you took off for a month without telling anyone. After you told me you wanted me to be on your team"—I double quoted the air—"for the past three months, you've barely told me anything except all the leads didn't pan out. I get to avoid you for as long as I want."

"I went to chase a lead in Greece." He waved his hands in the air. "It is the home of the gods. I thought it might be worth looking for the Lady's temple there."

"You went without telling anyone."

"Yes."

No apology. I sighed. "And? Did you find anything?"

"I lost money to the cab drivers. Apparently, I am not good doing currency conversion."

"Vane happens to be very good at math."

Merlin glowered. "My brother doesn't want to help. He just wants glory."

"Still upset the world thinks *his* name is Merlin?"

"No, because I'm not looking for notoriety."

"Just glory," I said, tongue-in-cheek.

He gave me a furious look. Then, he took a breath. "You're trying to bait me."

"Is it working?"

Another glower told me...yes. A rush of satisfaction went through me. He deserved it for being...Merlin. I ground out, "The point is, they have these things—a quaint invention called phones. You could have easily called or gotten in touch. But, no, you always have to be on your own." I stepped closer to him, getting in his face. "I thought we'd both learned secrets hurt us. Tell me, why call us Team Merlin if the only member is Merlin?"

His breath whooshed into my face, annoyingly clean, with a hint of mint.

He smirked. "Because I said so."

*I SAID SO*. I PICTURED KICKING HIS BACKSIDE. UNSURPRISINGLY, A picture didn't give much satisfaction. I needed the real thing. A march down to the front of the campus didn't alleviate my need. Yet I eyed his backside all the way to the manor that served as the academy's administration building. Maybe I was beyond help.

We entered the regal building through the back. Inside, men and women in different-colored robes roamed the open floor plan. Most of the teachers had their offices in buildings where they held classes, but the administration building housed the headmaster and all of the Wizard Council. Most of wizard-kind, the *Keltoi*, took orders from their headquarters at the school. Merlin led me to the large gathering room where the Excalibur candidates had taken their trial to get into the school. We'd all drunk water from a magical pond, which the Lady of the Lake had once blessed a thousand years ago. Instead of being empty, however, the room boasted a fire in a giant hearth I hadn't even noticed on the day of the trial. Sofas had been placed in a welcoming arrangement around the fire. As we entered, Vane and Ryan rose from a sofa.

Vane hooked a thumb at Ryan. "She shouldn't be going."

"I'm going," Ryan said. "Merlin asked me here."

Merlin took out a pouch from his pocket. He blew at the top of it. Blue dust flew into Ryan's face. Merlin uttered, "*Nidra*."

Ryan's jaw dropped. "No—" She broke off as her eyes shut.

Vane caught her as she crumpled. He laid her down on a sofa. "I could have done that."

Merlin shook the small brown pouch. "I wanted to see if it

would work. I have to practice and conserve what little power I have left."

"That was high-handed. She is going to be pissed," I said, but he'd impressed me. He wasn't taking the loss of his power lying down.

"It's for her own good." He crooked a finger at two mages who hovered, watching us from the hallway. "Claudine sent you?"

The two nodded.

"Watch her."

The mages went to stand by the sleeping Ryan.

Grey walked into the room. "What did you do to my sister?"

"Good, you're here," Merlin said. "Let's go. You'll be standing in for her."

A black SUV waited outside at the front of the school. I rode in silence with Merlin, Vane, and Grey. We were the core of Team Merlin. Most of the Excalibur Program, the candidates who'd been recruited to try to pull out the sword from the stone, had been repurposed to help the Wizard Council figure out why Excalibur had fallen after a thousand years.

We reached the small town of Glastonbury in less than twenty minutes. The SUV wound through narrow streets and rowhouses. A small crowd lingered in front of a pub at the center of town, marked by an obelisk-looking statue. As the SUV came to a stop, an older woman in a stylish suit broke from the crowd of middle-aged adults. Her heels clattered on the ground as she rushed forward. "I'm so glad to see you."

"Mom," Grey said, startled. He pulled her into a bear hug.

Sylvia clung to him for a long minute before pulling back. She cradled his face. "You look tired."

Actually, he looked terrible. Since the time he'd been reawakened, it was as if the world wore at him. He barely ate or slept. His roommate had confided in Ryan—and therefore her roommates, me and Gia—that he barely seemed interested in anything. He wasn't the same Grey as before the terrible night spent on the trial. Sighing, he disentangled himself from his mother. "What are you doing here, Mom?"

The older woman looked around. "Where's Ryan?"

He hooked a thumb at Merlin and Vane. "They wouldn't let her come."

"That's probably for the best." Sylvia glanced back at the other adults who sat at the outdoor tables. Some wore the robes of the Wizard Council and others had on high-quality suits to match Sylvia.

Merlin looked around. "Well, where is he?"

"Certainly not here," Sylvia snapped. "You shouldn't have gotten me involved. You know I can't stand them."

"That was Marla," Merlin reminded her. "Not Rourke. The king didn't order the strike."

"He made her queen. That was his choice," I said. "Also, he ordered the kill on the Boston boy who pulled the fake sword. Rourke's hands aren't clean."

"That boy didn't live far from Concord," Sylvia muttered. She turned big eyes on Merlin. "I made the mistake of trusting them once. I worked with them. Look where it got me. Alexa is gone, and if it hadn't been for Ryan, I would have lost Grey in the trial."

Another SUV pulled up. An older woman in white got out. Marilynn, the school's administrator, stepped out after her. Determinedly keeping her eyes averted from me, Marilynn came forward, wearing an eager smile directed mostly at Merlin.

I rolled my eyes. Marilynn had a crush on Merlin since I'd come to the school last year.

The woman in white came up to Sylvia. She extended a hand. "Ms. Ragnar, I am Claudine. I have taken over from Ambrose as Second Member of the wizard council. You are welcome at Avalon Academy. Thank you for helping us with Merlin's problem."

Claudine glanced at Merlin and grimaced.

I lifted one eyebrow. Not a fan of Merlin. That was a first. It made me like her better.

Beside me, he bristled. "It's not just my problem. Everyone's problem. We need to prepare for why Excalibur has landed *now*. In your time. But first, we need to—"

"Let me guess. He didn't answer to your hostage demands, so you had to come begging to me." Sylvia folded her arms across herself. She turned soulful eyes on him. "How could you ask it after you know what the gargoyles did to my baby girl?"

"I understand who the gargoyles are. So you should know I wouldn't be doing this without a purpose, Sylvia." Merlin took a step closer and put his hands on her shoulders. "You know why I have to resort to you."

"Absolutely not," Grey thundered. Athletic and a little bulky, he could have passed for a linebacker. "You're not going to give those murdering bastards anything—"

"Grey," Sylvia protested. "You must trust Master Merlin."

Grey shook his head. "You shouldn't have involved her, *Matt Emrys*."

Merlin had used the alias Matt Emrys at my high school in Boston before we'd been recruited to Avalon Preparatory. In fact, I'd tried not to think about Matt Emrys at all. Matt had always been Ryan's.

Vane said smoothly, "Sylvia was uniquely suitable. Her past—"

"—isn't relevant." Sylvia paled under spray-tanned skin.

Merlin cleared his throat. "Sylvia's bank and gargoyles have done business for many years."

"Rourke is inside," Sylvia said stiffly. "He's followed every protocol you asked. Only a handful of his security came."

Claudine said, "He's dangerous without any security guards. Are you sure about this?"

"We'll find out." Merlin marched to the pub.

I went after him. So did Vane. Everyone else followed at a more hesitant distance.

Inside the small tavern, a middle-aged man with an austere face and dark hair streaked with grey sat surrounded by four hulking bodyguards. Rourke, the king of the gargoyles, stood as we approached.

I stomped out ahead of the others, my hand rising as I went. A red fireball crystal lay on my palm. "You're the one killing us."

"Yes and no." Rourke eyed my hand. But he didn't laugh at it. "But that stops now. I need your help."

I took another step toward him. "What makes you think we would help you?"

Merlin came up beside me and lowered my arm. "We will hear you out."

Vane harrumphed. "If what you say isn't amazing, we get to kill you."

The bodyguards moved to tighten around him, but Rourke waved them off. He stood, his eyes fixing on Sylvia. "I am sorry. You have my deepest sympathy on your daughter Alexa's death. Marla and my son were able to exert control over the clan who killed her—"

"Don't lie," Grey thundered. "The gargoyles are like a pack and you are the alpha. You have complete control."

"Not if another alpha—as you say—can exert himself and displace me. Which is what my son was able to do."

"All you lot know is how to take and take," Grey growled in frustration. Despite the bodyguards, he tried to lunge at the king.

Rourke's bodyguards moved in a blink. They caught Grey.

"Release him," Merlin said. "Or we walk out."

Rourke gave a small nod and the bodyguards let a

squirming Grey go. Vane caught him before he could charge the king again.

"Grey," Merlin said sharply. "Stand down."

Rourke gave Grey a pained look. "You have a right to your anger. Believe me, I would have never harmed Sylvia's family. I didn't think it possible for my son to usurp me with his kinfolk, but it has happened." The dark-haired king stared down at the floor. "There is a war going on within our ranks." He waved to his bodyguards. "These clans are loyal to me. However, my son has taken over his mother's kin and other clans who are close to them. He is expanding clan by clan. My own son rallies against me."

"Just like Mordred against Arthur," Merlin murmured.

I glanced at him. He'd been off ever since his best friend from the past had awakened, his behavior angry and brooding.

"Mordred had cause," Vane remarked.

Merlin glared at him. "A cause you instigated and fostered in him."

Vane shrugged. "Justice doesn't care about familial ties."

Rourke laughed. "Oliver isn't looking for justice. He wants my throne."

My hands squeezed into fists. Golden-Hainey had accused me of wanting power. He hadn't been entirely wrong. "We understand the lure very well."

Vane squeezed my shoulder. A look of understanding passed between us. Those who'd been reduced to nothing could understand the need to cling to something, despite the right or wrong of that something.

"What you don't understand is my son will have it." Rourke sighed. "Oliver will win this war."

Claudine and the other council members shifted uneasily.

"Why think that?" Claudine asked.

Merlin stepped in front of her. "How is he winning?"

I studied Rourke. "Because the king is dying."

# 4

# IS THIS WHAT WE DO NOW? TORTURE PEOPLE?

Rourke sat down heavily on a chair, his face taking on a wan, tired expression. Still, sharp eyes locked on me as if suddenly noticing me. His head bobbed in a small nod. "Yes."

Vane cursed. His hand went to his trouser pocket where he'd hidden a magically shrunken sword in his coat pocket. "We should have killed him when we had the chance."

Sylvia gasped, putting a hand to her mouth. "H-How?"

"Poisoned." Rourke smiled. "My son was responsible."

Merlin stepped forward. "What do you want with us, Rourke?"

"I want a cure," Rourke said bluntly. He walked forward, coming out from behind his bodyguards. "I think it's in both our interests if you help me."

"Why would we be interested in helping you?" Merlin asked with a slight sneer. "You've killed so many innocents. You've killed *Keltoi*, all for your gain—"

"For our kingdom," Rourke corrected, shaking his head. "I don't do this for personal gain. That is the difference between me and my son. If he wins, which he will now that he's poisoned me, you will have to deal with a gargoyle king who is only concerned with using the kingdom to serve him."

Merlin shrugged. "That's bad for your kingdom, not for us."

"It is bad for everyone, if Oliver decides to break the first rule."

First rule? I eyed Claudine.

"He wouldn't dare," Claudine said. "The reason we have survived is because we have been hiding from the Regulars for over a thousand years. Nothing has changed. If the world found out about us, the battle at Mount Camlann would happen again and again. Oliver would not court such chaos with open hands."

"He would," Rourke said. "He has forgotten what it means to be among the Regulars. He has been raised in a privileged world. He doesn't understand we are outnumbered by the Regulars. He only understands he can beat one."

"Not this one," Vane said. "He can't beat Excalibur."

Rourke nodded. "Even so, it is only one sword. You need help on a global scale. Help me, and I will help you."

"And if we don't?" Merlin asked.

"Then you'll be as dead as I am."

"You need us to find the cure," I said. "What do you want us to do?"

"There is an ancient kingdom, lost and buried long ago. Oliver gave me this poison because he believes there is no cure. He is mostly right. It doesn't exist in our known world. I need you to find the lost kingdom for me and dig up what we need."

Merlin snorted. "You want us to dig for buried treasure? We're not archeologists or treasure hunters."

Rourke's lips quirked up. "This requires magical help to uncover. If I didn't believe in this, I would not be wasting the precious bit of remaining strength I have on you. If anyone can do this, it is you."

I eyed Rourke, a little apprehensive to confirm he was who

he claimed. He didn't seem to have golden glowing eyes like the mysterious Greek god who'd tried to kill nearly everyone in the Excalibur Program.

The king stared back steadily. "I need to find the Healing Cup of the immortals."

My heart thudded. Could this be the answer to what we'd been searching for—a way to fix what I'd broken in Merlin? I exchanged a glance with him.

His eyes glittered in suppressed excitement.

"In gargoyle lore," Rourke said, "the Guides safeguarded a cup that if drunk from could cure anything, or so it is said."

"A cup that heals," Vane said slowly. "You mean like the Holy Grail? The legends of Arthur going after the Grail are wrong. We know nothing of it."

"Maybe we should ask before declaring it nothing," I said.

Merlin interjected quickly, "We'll *research* later."

Apparently, the newly awakened King Arthur was not a public topic.

Rourke's lips twisted into a smile. "I don't know if it is the Grail, but I do know this—the cup I seek exists." He added slyly, "If you are interested."

Claudine, the head of the Wizard Council, stepped forward. "What if we don't need it?"

"You do need to find out why Excalibur has fallen. The path to the Healing Cup and the path to finding out what's happening are one and the same. It is the biggest reason I came to you. After all, it is you who have a connection to *her*. The answer to our problems lies with her." Rourke paused. "The Lady of the Lake."

"How do you know about the Lady?" Vane demanded.

The king snorted. "Do you not think we know everything about you, *Keltoi*? We have been around as long you have."

Merlin stepped forward. "What is your price?"

"First, I'd like my men back," Rourke said. "I will need all my men to fend off my son until I am better."

Merlin gave a small nod. "Fine."

Rourke held up two fingers. "Next, we go with you. We work together."

Vane snorted. "You've been trying to kill us for months, ever since Ryan pulled the sword. And now you dare ask us to work with you?"

Merlin stepped forward, putting Vane behind him. He met Rourke's gaze directly. "Agreed."

When Vane sputtered, Merlin walked forward. He asked, "What lead do you have?"

"There is an artifact we need. We need to get the map showing the way to the Lady's temple. I believe the Healing Cup as well as the answers you seek about Excalibur are there."

"Wait," I said. "Now there's a map?"

Vane lit up. "You're missing the point. This is a treasure hunt."

Merlin sighed. "One we can't afford to give up."

"Exactly," Rourke said. His enthusiasm became subdued when Merlin gave him a critical glance.

Finally, Merlin faced Rourke. "Where do we begin?"

Rourke shook his head. "Do I have your word we will work together?"

"You have a truce until we reach the Lady's temple." Merlin slammed his palms down on the pub table Rourke sat behind. "Now, where is it?"

"Patience," tsked Rourke. He met my eyes and winked at his own pun. Turning his gaze to Sylvia, he smiled. "We need to go back. To your home. The path to the Lady's temple begins in Salem, Massachusetts."

~

AN HOUR LATER, WE SAT OUTSIDE THE PUB, WAITING FOR A VAN full of gargoyles.

"He's playing us," I exploded. "We can't trust him."

"It's done. No use fighting about it." Vane said. "The Great Merlin has decided."

This last bit was clearly sarcastic.

Merlin scowled. "What else was I supposed to do? Rourke is right. The Lady of the Lake will help us." He lowered his voice. "So will the Healing Cup."

"Your interests are aligned for now," I said. "But the minute they are not, he will turn on you."

Merlin threw up his hands. "Then, we will be prepared. But this is the best lead we've got right now. This is what we're doing, unless you have a better idea."

I stared at his scowling face. *So hot.* I blinked. *Oh. My. Gods. Get your mind out of the gutter, Patience.* Quickly, I turned away, only to find Vane smirking at me.

Lifting my hand, I gave him the middle finger as a small box truck pulled up. Wizards, sans robes, climbed out of the cabin. They went to the back of the truck and opened the cargo door. One by one, a group of gargoyles streamed out. The gargoyles had a few bruises, but the vacant listless look in their eyes bothered me. I stepped toward one.

It was a mistake.

He whipped around and lunged with fists raised. I blocked the punch, but his hand glanced my arm. I punched with my other hand, and to my surprise, he staggered back as if I had super strength, and fell to the ground. He screamed, curling into a ball and clutching his head.

My eyes went to Merlin. "What did you do to them?"

"They've been spelled to feel ten times the pain they would usually feel." Facing the mewling gargoyle, he put out a hand. Then, shaking his head, he closed it. "Better to let him ride it out."

When the gargoyle finally stopped shaking on the ground, two other prisoners bent down and helped him up. They staggered along with him into the pub. Claudine blew dust into their faces as they walked past her.

"Claudine is very gifted," Merlin said.

My eyes went to Vane. The same surprise showed in his eyes. At least I wasn't the only one. I turned on Merlin. "You had her do this to them. How could you?"

Vane said, "He did what he had to."

"I can speak for myself." Merlin sighed. "They're unharmed. Mostly."

My hands clenched. "Is this what we do now? Torture people?"

Vane grinned. "I'm liking this dark turn."

"They're gargoyles," Grey said from where he sat at a small circular table. "They don't deserve your sympathy, Eowlyn. They certainly haven't shown any to us."

I let out a huff. "Then how do you plan on working with them?"

Movement came from the front seat of the truck. Arthur slid out. "You work with them how you would work with any enemy—trust them until you have reason not to."

Merlin strode to him. "What are you doing here? You're not ready—"

"I brought him." Ryan climbed out of the truck behind Arthur.

Vane strode toward her. "Are you crazy? It's not safe for you to come traipsing right up to the very people who are trying to kill you."

"If you don't think I can handle it, then maybe you haven't been training me as well as you should have," she snapped. "I'm here and I'm staying. Don't leave me out again."

"I'll do what it takes to protect you," Vane retorted in a near shout.

I cleared my throat. "Ryan is right."

Vane rounded on me. "Stay out of this, Eowlyn."

I didn't flinch. "You trained me, Vane. You thought I could handle being here. If you've done half as good of a job with her, she can handle it too. You shouldn't be leaving her out of decisions that clearly impact her."

"You and she are not the same," Vane said.

"Right," I said. "Because I'm expendable."

Vane cursed. "That's not what I meant."

"Haven't you learned anything after Golden-Hainey? No more secrets." I turned on Merlin. "And I won't be a party to outright torture."

"You're a Vandal. From our time. You should be used to it," Vane said.

My hands fisted. "Exactly. I have enough blood on my hands."

Merlin laughed. He turned and waved his hands wide at the quaint town square. People were bustling here and there, an occasional one giving us the odd look. He pointed to one. "Take this picture and put it in your mind. Do you know how many of these roads are built upon Roman construction? It's startling to see the foundations the empire laid come to fruition. Do you know how they did it? Do you think they talked and negotiated? No, they took. They killed. Blood and war. Submission or death." Merlin turned back. His eyes fixed on me. "Peace doesn't come without sacrifice. Your ideals are all well and good, but we're going to need more to figure out what threat is coming for us. If we have to work with Rourke to get the Healing Cup, you should get used to getting your hands dirty."

I shook my head. "There must be a better way."

Ryan walked to my other side to face off against Vane. "I agree."

Arthur stepped up beside me. "You seek the Healing cup? You never told me you were looking for immortality."

Merlin raked a hand through his brown hair. "Healing, not immortality."

"If you say so," Arthur said quietly.

Sylvia came out of the pub. She walked up. "Should I book flights to Boston?"

"This Rourke may not be right," Arthur interrupted. "I sent Galahad and Perceval after the Holy Chalice. If you truly want to get to it, you should retrace their steps."

"CONCENTRATE, EOWLYN," MERLIN SAID, TAKING A HEAVY breath.

My mind bent to his persuasive voice. I let my guard down and sank under the water of his subconscious. I swam in the murky depths, treading water and staying above the surface. As if losing in myself in a night swim, I drifted in the dark. Then, a splash hit me. I was naked. Nothing protected my skin against the water. It penetrated my pores and weighed me down. The water swirled and pushed. A wave rose in the dark and crashed on top of me.

My eyes snapped open.

The ruby gemstone called the Dragon's Eye gave a tiny spark. A tiny flicker of blue electricity cracked across the gemstone's damaged and broken surface. Then, the spark disappeared.

Merlin let out a frustrated sound. "You have to hold the connection."

"I can't," I said. "It was drowning me."

"Because your mind is resisting mine. Why?"

I stared down at the destroyed charm. I'd given it up to save the world. I'd given up Merlin to the insane god who'd nearly destroyed Excalibur. With a frustrated sigh, I dropped it and set my head down on the table. "We've done this a thousand times. I can't help you fix it. Did you try Blake?"

Blake Emerson with his little black spectacles happened to be the best student wizard at Avalon Prep.

"He couldn't even siphon off this little bit of static electricity to give to me." Merlin shook his head. He leaned back in the chair beside mine. His voice lowered. "The charm is bound to you."

*I am bound to you.* The implication made me want to clutch my head, squeeze my temples, and scream. Trying not to be overwhelmed from the pressure, I rose up on my elbows and inhaled the scent of musty papers. Stacks of leather-bound books littered the low library table. The stacks had yellow legal pads of paper and about a hundred pens here and there with Merlin's notes.

I picked up the closest pen and twirled it between shaky fingers. To distract myself from the pit in my stomach, I stared at the cluttered desk. "This is quite the nest you've made for yourself."

He blushed under dark hair. Amber eyes blinked with shy pride. "I do tend to get a bit involved when I'm working a problem."

"Involved is one word for it." With my pen, I pointed to three dirty plates with varying degrees of crumbs. "Some might use another one."

In a swift move, he grabbed at my pen. Refusing to give it up, I tugged back hard. He fell against me. His chest pushed against my shoulders. Lips grazed my ear as he straightened.

In a low tone, he asked, "What is the other word?"

"Manic." If I turned my face, our lips would meet. My hair curtained my face, but I didn't need to see him to know he stared at me. Waiting. But something inside me couldn't let myself turn. Ever since The One Kiss and his subsequent disappearance, something inside me trembled when he got too close, and I couldn't decide if the trembling was a good thing. I whispered, "Some might say you're obsessive."

"I would definitely say he's obsessive." A loud, cheerful voice broke the quiet of the library. Vane marched up to the table. Ryan, her blonde hair bobbing around her face, strode up with equal purpose. Grey and Blake followed.

"The Scooby gang?" I forced a smile. "This must be important."

"I am not a Scooby," Vane said with an offended sniff.

Ryan snorted.

Ignoring her, Vane wagged eyebrows at his brother. "You two look cozy."

Merlin rose. "Don't you have somewhere else to be?"

Vane put a hand to his chest. "Not at all. You are the most important thing in my life." He grinned at Ryan. "Well, maybe one of the most important."

"I see you're getting a lot of studying done." Grey picked up a book from one of the stacks on the table. He sent me a long look. "For your Latin test?"

"I finished intro Latin," I said. "I'm learning Greek now."

Blake Emerson adjusted black glasses. "You've been here half a year. It took me two to get decent on Latin."

"I'm good at languages."

"And she knew a fair amount already," Vane said. "From actually being there."

"Merlin!" Arthur burst into the library. He stalked toward the table waving a touchpad in his hand. He slammed the touchpad down on the table hard enough for the stacks of books to wobble.

Vane let out a low command and the books righted themselves. He scowled. "What's got you in a twist?"

"You didn't tell me." Arthur turned on him, his face livid. He pointed to the touchpad. "How dare you keep these things from me? You said my son led the battle against me at Camlann. You didn't give me the whole story. I had a right to know how my knights turned against me too. About Lancelot and"—he glanced at me—"Guinevere."

"We gave you a book," Vane said.

"I can't read it! I am not of this time!" Arthur waved his hand in agitation. "I had to figure it out from your little box of moving pictures. This ludicrous thing." He picked up the touchpad.

Before he could slam it down again, Merlin moved swiftly. He got around the table and grabbed the touchpad from Arthur's hand. "Destroying this won't make the past less true. But you need to remember it is over. It is all in the past—"

"Not for me. It hasn't happened yet."

"And it never will," Merlin said flatly. "You are not going back there. But you have been given a gift. You get to restart. You have a second chance here."

"They betrayed me." Arthur slammed both hands down on the table. This time the stacks shook and fell. His eyes met mine. "She betrayed me. This wasn't how it was supposed to turn out."

Such pain filled them, but I couldn't do anything but look back.

"It never is how it's supposed to be. You make do with what life throws at you and try to remember it's a gift to have any life at all." Vane sighed. He bent down and picked up a book. He stared at it. "*On the Trail of the Grail. The Origin of the Holy Chalice.* Clever title." He held it out to Merlin. "We came up here to figure out when we were leaving, and I guess I can see why you haven't made up your mind about Rourke. Tell us, oh, great mage who has lost his powers, what have you found out?"

Merlin stalked to Vane and snatched back the tome. "I have not lost my powers."

We all gave him a skeptical look.

"They are temporarily weakened," he muttered. He opened

the book and flipped through its pages. "I've gone through most of these and the trail of the Healing Cup starts not with Arthur and his knights but in the fifth century BCE. The first mention of it is in Asia, in the Hindu epic, the *Ramayana*."

Arthur shook his head. "I don't understand. What is this place?"

Merlin took a large tome from the top of a pile of other books. He dropped it in front of him. The book fell open on the table with a thud. It showed a map of the world. Merlin pointed to Sri Lanka, the island at the bottom of the Indian subcontinent. "In the *Ramayana*, the monkey god helped rescue Princess Seetha. King Rawana kidnapped her and took her to his home in ancient Lanka. He hoped to woo her into becoming one of his wives. Prince Rama came to rescue her after Hanuman found her. Rama's and Rawana's armies battled across the island until Rama finally defeated the king in battle." He chewed his lip. "Now, King Rawana was said to be a master of astrology. Supposedly, the creator god, Brahma, gave him the nectar of immortality as a celestial gift."

Vane grabbed at the book and, after a sad tug of war on Merlin's end, studied its pages. He flipped through it quickly. "This nectar of immortality might be the Healing Cup?"

"Maybe," Merlin said. "Who conquered most of the ancient world? Alexander the Great. The Cup could have easily gone with him back to Egypt, to Babylon, to Jerusalem, and back to Babylon, which would be Iraq today."

"The Knights of the Round Table found the Cup in the Middle East?"

"In the Waste Lands of the realm of the Fisher King." Merlin tapped the table with a finger. "In some of the texts, Galahad went after the Healing Cup with Perceval and Lancelot. In other texts, it was only Perceval or it was only Galahad. Some call the Cup a grail. In the legends, the knights make it to the castle of the Fisher King. They don't make it back out.

This is where the text fails. The Cup disappears after Perceval's arrival at the court of the Fisher King."

"The court of the Fisher King could be in Iraq," Ryan said slowly.

Arthur said, "But Galahad took the Cup from the Fisher King's court back to its birthplace."

"Back to Asia. Sri Lanka," I said. "But for some reason Rourke thinks he knows how to get to the Cup from Boston?"

"As far as I can see, we have two options," Merlin said. "We follow Rourke or we go to what we think is the origin point for clues."

"We can't," Vane pointed out. "We agreed to help Rourke. Unless you're willing to let him die."

Merlin shrugged.

# 5

## ALL MY LIFE I'VE BEEN DEFINED BY EXCALIBUR

Merlin pinched the bridge of his nose. "But we also can't ignore another lead. We have two missions. One to find the Cup. One to find out why Excalibur has fallen now. Even if Rourke is right about the Cup, we don't know if Rourke can help us with Excalibur."

"We have two places to search," Vane said. "This is getting complicated."

"But isn't that a good thing? Before, we had zero leads. Now, we have—" I held up two fingers.

"It's not good," Merlin said. "Without my powers, I don't know what to do. And if we don't pick the right path, it's only the fate of the world hanging in the balance."

I let out a snort. "Only the fate of the world, you say. But, actually, we have no idea what is in the balance. Maybe the sword fell because we're supposed to make everything better, not because of whatever apocalypse you think is coming."

"The apocalypse is coming." Merlin snapped the book shut. "I saw that much before my visions got...stalled."

I flushed and dropped my gaze. "I made the right call."

"It doesn't make it any easier to live with."

Ryan watched us with interest. "The choice is easy—"

"You should divide up," Arthur said.

"I was going to say *split* up." She looked at him with an arched brow. "Grey and I should go to Boston. We know it well."

"I go where she goes," Vane said, pointing to Ryan. Ryan gave him a smug grin. Until he added, "She wields the god-killer."

Ryan stuck out her tongue.

He tipped an invisible hat.

Arthur had dubbed Excalibur the god-killer. Never mind I was the one who'd wielded the sword and did the actual killing. I rolled my eyes, but secretly I envied how easy they were with each other. Inevitably, my eyes sought Merlin.

He arched an eyebrow. "I suppose that means I'm going to Sri Lanka."

My lips curved up. "Then, I suppose I'm going to join you."

"So am I," Arthur said.

"You can't!" Merlin and Vane said at once.

"You can't stop me. I am tired of sitting around here. As you said, there is a reason I was woken. It's time I found out what the reason is."

I exchanged a glance with Merlin. It screamed, *can't you get us out of this?*

He shook his head. Instead, he leveled an unhappy look at Arthur. "Fine. You deserve to know as we do. Get ready."

Vane studied Merlin. He said, almost hesitantly, "It's settled then? You will let us go to Boston while you take Sri Lanka?"

Merlin tilted his head. "Isn't that what you wanted?"

"Yes," Vane sputtered. "But you barely put up a fight. You can't tell me you actually trust me with something this important—"

"Well, he does." Ryan grabbed Vane's arm. She said in a low

voice, "Don't look a gift horse in the mouth, Vivane." She turned to Merlin. "Grey will go with us."

Grey piped up, "I don't want—"

Ryan sent him a withering look, but he only glowered back. "I'm not going. I'm going with Merlin."

Vane put a hand on Ryan. "Let him go. He's not ready to be where Alexa was."

Ryan's eyes flickered in surprise.

Vane's chest puffed out. "I can feel things."

I let out a snort.

He turned and winked at me. "I rescued you, didn't I, little princess?"

I blushed. "You're never going to let me forget it."

Vane sobered. He walked to me and put his hands on my shoulders. "No. Take care of yourself and remember what I taught you." He leaned closer and said so only I could hear, "Take care of my brother. He's always a little too trusting."

Letting go, Vane walked off with Ryan.

"I'm going with them," Blake announced. "Maybe Gia will come."

"Gia?" I said. *Ryan's best friend agree to come with us? I don't think so.*

He turned red in the face. "Maybe." Turning on his heel, he left quickly.

Grey put a hand around Arthur's shoulder. "Let's get you packed. We'll need all the essentials. Power plugs and toilet paper."

With a serious nod, Arthur allowed Grey to lead him away.

Once everyone was gone, I whirled on Merlin. "What's going on? Why are you so easy about splitting up?"

"I didn't lie. We have two leads and we can't afford to ignore either one of them."

"I got that, but what's the other reason?"

"Why do you think I have another reason?"

Staring out over the stacks of books, I put my hands on the table and leaned forward. "You're Merlin. You always have another reason. Layers upon layers of reasons."

He walked up close to my side and leaned back against the table. He folded his arms. One arm grazed mine. "Once Arthur finds out Vane had an affair with Guinevere, in addition to the liaisons she had with Lancelot and half a dozen other members of the court, there is going to be war between them. I want Vane and Arthur apart."

My brow wrinkled. "I know you don't trust Vane, but don't you trust Arthur? I thought he was your favored king and your friend."

"I don't know him anymore. How did he come to be inside the stone? Has he lost his memories for a reason? I have a feeling all the answers will come to us once I restore my powers."

I rolled my eyes. "The success of everyone and everything should not be completely dependent on you."

"But it usually is."

While I sputtered internally at his arrogance, he said, "Maybe I can't get all the answers right now, but I would like to get one." He paused. "Speaking of answers, how long are you going to avoid me?"

Urges to giggle and run hit me at the same time. Not looking at him, I kept my eyes on the table though his arm against mine tingled as if it were a live current of electricity. "W-What do you mean?"

"You know what I mean," he said with a sigh. "Ever since the day at the palace when I—"

*Kissed you?*

"—asked you to do this with me."

"You know why. You left."

"Is it that the only reason you can barely look me in the face?"

*No. I remember your mouth on mine.* I said slowly, "We're not ready yet. *I'm* not ready yet."

"I see." His fingers tightened on the wood table. "Do you want to talk about it?"

"No."

He cursed. A stack of books on the other side of the table flew off in a whirlwind. They thudded to the floor.

My eyes widening, I said, "Good to know you have some power left."

He flexed them slowly with obvious effort. "And I should be conserving what little magic remains."

He stood, moving away.

My side suddenly bereft, I turned to face him. "Merlin."

He stopped.

"Look, I'm making a mess. With you. I haven't been with many..." I scuffed the floor with my feet. "I haven't been *in* any real relationships. It's just ...there are things you don't know." I swallowed. "Things I haven't told you."

Merlin sighed. "You *can* tell me."

*Blood splattered white-flowered sheets. The boy lay sprawled like a sacrifice to an ancient god. Sharp knife wounds drew jagged bloody lines across his chest. He'd been gutted. The knife, heavy in my hand, dropped to the bed.*

I shook my head. "I'm not ready."

He let out an unhappy laugh. "Wasn't it you who just railed at me for keeping secrets? For not asking others for help?"

"This is different. This is personal."

"What is more personal than you sacrificing me to a god? What is more personal than you almost dying to save the world?"

I winced. "Give it time."

His amber eyes shuttered.

I held my breath.

Finally, he said, "Two things."

"What?"

"All my life I've been defined by Excalibur, and now I've given over my power to save it." He lifted his eyes, his gaze locking onto mine. "But that is done and I'm not the same person anymore."

I blinked. "Then who are you?"

"Someone who is tired of waiting for things to happen to them. If you don't come to me, I'll come to you."

My eyes widened. "That's fair, I suppose."

He gave a small nod. "Good."

"What's the other thing?"

"The Regulars have taken an interest in us. Since Ryan's and Vane's declarations, the First Member of the Wizard Council—"

"You mean the Queen of England."

"The United Kingdom," he corrected. "She has been trying to keep the *Keltoi* world secret, but apparently, we were more exposed than we realized."

I frowned. "What are you saying?"

"It won't be just us in Sri Lanka. We're going to have company."

HE WAS PISSED. MY STOMACH ROILED AS THE PLANE DIPPED. Merlin gripped the armrest of the seat beside me. His face had turned a glowing sheen of green as the plane began its descent. At least the international flight had been on a giant airplane that minimized turbulence. But the artificial air blowing down from the overhead vents added to the stale stench of the metal flying death contraption.

"What is this pain?" Arthur moaned, clutching his hands to his ears. He sat beside Grey in the middle aisle of the airplane.

Sweat dripped from his forehead and his face scrunched in a constipated expression.

Poor guy. My hand gripped the armrest too. I had never gotten used to flying in a metal deathtrap.

"If you three are going to be sick, I'm not cleaning you up. Get a barf bag," Grey snarled from the other side of Arthur.

Directly in front of me, Marilynn leaned out from her seat. "Help him, Grey Ragnar. Unless you want to walk out of here smelling like vomit. We're not going to a hotel first, remember? We've got a van waiting."

The plane dipped again and so did my stomach. This time I didn't hesitate. I began rifling through a side compartment filled with useless magazines for the all-important barf bag. Merlin pushed open the plastic shutter of the window. Outside, the sky darkened as this part of the world turned away from the sun. A wide expanse of blue ocean showed directly below us. In the distance, the lights of the city rose from the horizon and the plane slowly approached land.

Merlin said, "We're close."

"Not close enough," Grey said. "Why did I get stuck with Team B?"

Marilynn twisted in her seat and shot him a nasty look. "Any team with Merlin is Team A."

Arthur said, "Eowlyn is team A."

I blushed. The plane landed with a thud. I took a sharp breath.

Merlin reached out to take my hand. "It's almost over."

As the plane rolled down the grey tarmac lined with lush trees, I put my palm against the cold glass of the airplane window. Drizzling rain streaked the glass in dreary warning. *It's just beginning.*

# 6

## DON'T OVERTHINK IT

My hand tingled at the touch of his skin on mine. It distracted me enough until the plane thudded down. We landed in the capital city of Colombo.

Arthur let out a happy sigh. "Thank all that is good and kind."

It took us an hour to reach our driver. After a quick exchange of immigration cards and previously completed forms, we got to baggage claim. With some magical inducement, the men in white customs uniforms inspected the questionable items in our bags. I wasn't keen to be detained in a country where a singular conviction of smuggling resulted in hanging.

Just outside the bag check area, a slim man, Raj, greeted us with shiny teeth and a big smile. He hugged Marilynn. "I finally get to put a face to the beautiful voice."

Marilynn blushed. "I've been wanting to meet the head of our South Asian school for a long time."

"You'll have to speak to my brother. He's the man in charge. I'm a humble second," Raj said, leading us out of baggage claim.

"Sometimes, it's us second-in-commands who get the work done," Marilynn said loudly. She glanced back at Merlin before walking ahead with Raj.

My eyes went to Merlin. He walked along without noticing Marilynn left. Typical male. A crowd of people, offering everything from food to car service, followed us. Most turned away disappointed, but Raj engaged a few to appease the crowd, clear our way, and help load our bags into the van. Outside the airport, gloomy clouds hovered over the horizon.

We passed a line of taxis and yellow-black, three-wheeled tuk-tuks, barely big enough for two. I eyed the three-wheeler. I'd always wanted to ride one. There were no doors on the tiny vehicle. The driver sat in the front on a seat that looked like a stool. The backseat bench had no sides. One hard swerve and the passenger would tumble onto the street.

Merlin caught my elbow and steered me clear of the tuk-tuk. Leaning close, he said, "You'll get your chance. Those death taxis are everywhere."

I let him lead me away with a sigh. "As if your Ducati is any less dangerous. You'd love the thrill. You know you want to try one."

"Maybe." Merlin hooked his thumb at Arthur. "But I don't think the king can handle any more thrills."

Arthur did look as if he still wanted to kiss the ground. I elbowed Merlin in the stomach. "You're enjoying his pain a little too much."

Merlin rubbed his front with a wounded look. "You can't blame me. His Majesty always rode on a high horse in Camelot."

I rolled my eyes. "So says His Majesty Merlin."

"I'm not so egotistical."

We reached Raj's van and I was saved from answering. Marilynn took the front seat, so I found myself in the middle between Arthur and Merlin. While Merlin studied a map of Sri

Lanka, Arthur gripped the door of the van and wore another pale and sweaty motion-sick expression.

We sped past white-sand beaches colored grey in the fading sun. A light sprinkle of salty rain peppered the van like minuscule bullets. Deep blue ocean, swaying palm trees, and beachfront hotels stretched as far as the eye could see on one side of the van as we drove along the outskirts of a huge island. On the other side, exhaust fumes and smog went hand in hand with the city's industrialization.

"There's a lot of construction," I commented as we passed another resort.

"The country's constantly rebuilding, it seems," Raj said. "Tsunamis are becoming more and more frequent in this region. We aren't far from the Pacific Ocean Ring of Fire, and all the volcanic and seismic activity means more water displacement in this part of the world."

"I like all the streamers and lights," Marilynn said lightly.

Raj chuckled. "You are right. We should enjoy the little things."

Marilynn pointed at a rainbow of brightly colored decorations that hung on the awnings of the small bazaars and hotels. Some had turned on their light strings, which twinkled merrily in the descending darkness.

"You just missed the grand Independence Day celebrations," Raj said, "but many places will keep up the lights for another week or so. We'll stop at a hotel tonight and head out tomorrow morning. It isn't all that safe to travel at night."

Grey spread out behind us in the van's third row. "This isn't the spring break I imagined."

"Trekking out to the jungles isn't your kind of fun? Don't worry, I've got plenty of gear lined up to make this trip enjoyable." Raj laughed. "Who knows? You might like it."

Grey closed his eyes. "Tell me when we get there."

"I would," Raj said, "but I'm afraid I don't know where I'm

going. My instructions were to get gear and head east out of the city."

Merlin looked up from a map. "We're going to a town called Ella."

The van slowed. Raj said, "That's where you think the Healing Cup is?"

Merlin's head jerked up. "How did you know what we seek?"

Raj pulled the van off the highway onto a small road. The road skirted many rowhouse buildings. The van turned into a narrow alley of an unmarked building.

Marilynn frowned. "This isn't a hotel."

"Did I say hotel? I meant a safe house." Raj slowed down. The van lumbered to a stop in the alley. "Don't worry—"

Two cars rushed up behind us.

"This isn't a stop," Arthur said. "This is an ambush."

Raj cut the engines. "More like being handed off."

Marilynn raised her hand. Raj blasted her with a quick sleep spell. Merlin reached in his coat pocket, but Raj sent another red wave at us.

My body froze where I sat. I tried to move but found I couldn't.

"A simple immobilization spell," Raj explained.

In front of us, Marilynn slumped.

Raj saved her from a nasty thump against the front dashboard. "I'm sorry, Marilynn. I wish we could have met under better circumstances."

Merlin said through gritted teeth, "I'll get free."

"I had to see it to believe it—the great Merlin incapacitated." Raj chuckled. "My friends will deal with you first. But do not worry, Merlin. I will let you know how Ella turns out. It's time to leave the mission to those of us who can actually carry it out."

"Why betray us? I'm trying to help." Merlin spoke to Raj,

but his eyes met mine.

His gaze traveled down to my neck. *The Dragon's Eye.*

Raj snorted and thumped the steering wheel. "You and Avalon Prep only want control. We're never consulted until you need something. Guess what? If your visions are true, this affects us all, and I'm not about to let you decide my fate."

The van door flew open. A crowd of heavily armed men with rifles surrounded the van.

"Not good," Grey murmured behind me.

I closed my eyes. Once again, I was plunged into never-ending dark water. Almost immediately, a wave rose. It went up high, as high as a building. Then, it came crashing down. Before it could hit, my eyes sprang open.

In a blur, Merlin's hand moved. He yanked off a glass vial from a necklace he wore and tossed it at Raj. "Don't breathe," he yelled.

A puff of red dust exploded in Raj's face. Raj screamed and clutched his throat. He collapsed in the front seat.

As my body unfroze, Merlin blew the red dust with a little bit of magic. It spread out past the van. An entire crowd of men dropped like sprayed flies.

Marilynn sprang up. Her eyes widened. "What happened?"

"We must go. We are under attack." Arthur jumped out of the van.

I followed. Merlin and Grey also bolted from the vehicle.

I bent down to one of the men and felt his neck for a pulse. Looking up at Merlin, I demanded, "What are you using? You killed them."

Merlin took off the rope necklace with a shattered glass vial. "Just because I have no magic, doesn't mean I'm no longer a wizard."

"He used a potion," Marilynn walked around to us from the passenger side.

"Deadly potion or nerve toxin. Which is it?" a mild voice

asked from behind us.

Slipping a knife from the fallen man's hand, I stood.

A slim man in a suit stepped out from behind a van wearing a black helmet. He stepped over the torso of another man lying on the ground wearing a leather motorcycle jacket and gloves. Slim-Suit tapped his borrowed headgear. "It's a good thing I had some protection." In his other hand, he held a handgun, which he casually pointed at Merlin. "You killed them all."

"They did have guns pointed at us. They assumed a certain amount of risk. And I didn't have a sleeping potion handy," Merlin said steadily. "Are you their leader?"

"I was." Slim-Suit eyed us. "I suppose it doesn't matter, at the end of the day, whether it was science or magic. Either way, it's deadly."

"Who are you?"

Slim-Suit smiled. "I've been assigned to watch you.

I pointed at the dead men. "This isn't watching. This is capturing."

"Assigned by who?" Marilynn interjected.

"SIS. Secret Intelligence Service."

"Regulars," Marilynn scoffed. "What do you know about us?"

"You have about half-a-million quid worth of magical amulets and potions in that bag." He pointed to the black duffel bag Merlin carried.

Grey's eyebrows went up. "Half a million. I knew selling magic was lucrative. We've stayed in business because of it, but I never knew how much."

Merlin nodded. "Sylvia procured this for me."

"You brought it this whole way without telling us," I said. "More secrets, Merlin?"

Merlin held up a red vial and took a menacing step toward Slim-Suit. "Sometimes discretion is necessary. We don't have time for distractions—"

"We don't have to be enemies." Slim-Suit held up his hands, loosening his grip on the gun. "I think introductions are in order. My name is Robin Chaucer. I work under the foreign secretary. Her Majesty has contacted the prime minister. The MP was called in to deal with the threat we now face."

Grey whispered, "It's James Bond."

"We should call the First Member," Marilynn said. "To confirm what he is saying."

"Even if he is real, consider Raj," I said, hooking a thumb at our dead driver. "He was *Keltoi,* a wizard, and James Bond corrupted him."

"Good point," Merlin said.

"You need help, Merlin," Robin said. "Don't be hasty."

"Not from you." Merlin threw a red vial in his face.

Robin shut the visor. The vial exploded against the plastic shield. Red powder puffed the air and all over his front. He laughed. "Not this time. I've got a few tricks myself—"

I tackled him, knife in hand. With one hand, I struck his hand with the gun. A shot went wild, whizzing past my ear. If he'd been expecting me, the bullet would have killed me. I didn't hesitate. I sliced his throat in one long swing. My body spun. I rotated and struck him again. He was already falling but the bloodied knife in my hand went for another slice.

Robin Chaucer dropped to the ground. I fell on top of him.

Merlin ran up. He grabbed my shoulders. "Eowlyn, stop."

My hand rose.

Merlin shook me.

As if waking from a haze, my grip on the knife eased.

"What. The. Hell?" Grey marched up. "You actually killed them. Not asleep. Dead."

"It's a sleeping potion," Merlin said, his arm still around me. "But I used too much. I didn't have time to adjust. There were too many of them."

Grey said, "So it was an accident?"

Merlin ground his teeth. "Tell me, would you rather get captured by ten men armed with weapons?"

"You did what you had to do." I took the knife and cleaned its bloodied blade on the dead assailant.

"And you?" Marilynn asked quietly.

Arthur walked up. He leaned down and helped me up off my knees. "She protects us. Those villains attacked. This is what happens in battle."

"Are we in a battle?" Grey asked.

"Most definitely." Merlin waved at the dead bodies surrounding us.

There were actually six, not including Slim-Suit and Raj. They all wore black clothes and carried machine guns.

Marilynn checked Raj's pulse. She sighed. "He's definitely gone."

Grey eyed me. "I hope I never get on your bad side."

My cheeks heated. *Don't overthink it*. Arthur's right—this is what happens in battle.

A car drove by the alley. It screeched to a stop, no doubt spotting the dead bodies.

"We need to get out of here." Marilynn walked to the van.

Arthur and Grey got inside.

More cars screeched up toward the alley. Merlin cursed. "Robin Chaucer must have sent for backup. Marilynn, meet me at the rendezvous." He ran to the fallen Robin and grabbed his helmet. "Go ahead. I'll throw them off and catch up."

The cars sped down the alley.

Marilynn nodded.

"Get in," Arthur yelled.

Shaking my head, I ran to the bike and jumped on behind Merlin. "Let's go."

In front of us, the van took off with a peal of its tires. Merlin turned the bike around. He aimed it at the approaching cars and sped straight at them.

# 7

# THE MOST INTERESTING PARTS

"Are you crazy?" I yelled.

"You should have gone in the van," he said.

The bike headed for a collision with the two cars. At the last minute, both cars careened sideways, narrowly avoiding the bike. One car hit a garbage container and went into the alley wall. The other car found a ramp in some broken stairs. It went up and flipped as it fell.

Not waiting to find out anything else from the wreckage, Merlin sped the bike away.

I sighed in relief. In his ear, I shouted over the noise of the bike, "Why would Raj attack you?"

"It could be Vane—"

"*No*," I said to the thread of insecurity in his tone. My arms tightened around him. "He's your brother. He's on his own mission."

"He convinced the wizards to follow him before," he said loudly, "You're seen his memories. You know what ruthlessness he's capable of. He wants the Healing Cup for himself."

"Vane's past may be gruesome but so was yours." I paused. "The Vane I know is the one who fought that day in Carthage.

The Romans who held him were cruel. He decided to rescue a little girl instead of kill her—"

"One good deed doesn't erase all the bad. He had a difficult past. It happens. So did I. Our current actions can't be excused because of it."

"I'm not excusing, I'm just telling you you're wrong. Vane isn't behind this and if you keep looking at him, you'll miss the real villain."

The bike veered, cutting off conversation. The soothing sounds of the ocean disappeared as we dove into the city center filled with diesel-induced smog and streets lined with billboards with squiggly writing. Renovated Colonial forts were interspersed with glass high-rise buildings. Lost in the cacophony of honking horns and fast-talking locals, we rode along for what seemed like a long time. The sky grew dark and I shivered.

The bike went along a long bridge that crossed a small lake. Men in paddleboats with lanterns rowed casually along it. I pressed into Merlin's back for warmth. "Where is the rendezvous?"

"At a hotel near Ella."

"We're not meeting them until we get to another city?" I said, shifting in the seat. We hadn't gone long but saddle soreness wasn't far behind. "How are we going to do that? The whole plan was to take a van there. We're not going to make it so far on a bike."

"I would argue we could." Merlin patted the bike like a baby. "But, it's too conspicuous. We'll take the train."

"Hallelujah. He sees reason."

"I didn't ask you to come with me. You could have gone in the very comfortable van."

"What a surprise you don't want to include me." We sped past another bridge with a huge Buddhist statue. It seemed to be a common motif. Silently, I asked the statute for some calm when dealing with *Sir Merlin Kiss-and-Flee.* "Do you have anything else you'd like to condescend to share with me?"

"Yes." The bike squeezed into a narrow street and down the heart of a bazaar. Shops and department stores advertised various clothing and crafts in rupee amounts. We headed directly for the most amazing smell of coconut, onion, and spice. Merlin pulled up to a food vendor. An industrial griddle offered up curried vegetables and saffron rice. He pulled the bike to the side and slid off. "I'm hungry."

He held out his hand.

Ignoring it, I stumbled off the bike on my own and then had to grab his hand when my legs threatened to fold.

His arm came around my waist and his palm rested flat on the small of my back. "You need more practice," he said in a husky voice.

*Boy, do I.* I leaned back onto his hand and looked up. His face was very close, his lips just a hair's breadth away. *Calm, remember?* Blood rushed through my body, speeding my heart. The musty metallic scent still lingering on my clothes. From the events at the van, from wanting too much, my body shook. As I hovered, debating whether I wanted to lean into him, a downpour decided it for me.

Rain pelted us.

Merlin took my hand and ran to some benches under a tent set out by the food vendor. "Save these seats. I'll get us food."

Before long, he came back with platefuls of food, most of which he attacked.

I picked at aroma-filled rice and vegetables.

Merlin glanced at my plate and dumped more onto it. "Eat up. The train is in the morning and we won't get anything more tonight."

I tapped a spoon against my plate. Forks were not a commonly used utensil. "I should get supplies for wherever we're going—"

"Raj got them. There were rucksacks in the van."

I raised a brow. "You want to trust Raj? Even if he wasn't a traitor, he's not necessarily going to have thought of the things I need. Do you really want to watch me wash my undies every day?"

"I don't mind." A gleam lit in his amber eyes.

*Was he flirting?*

He pointed up at the rain and the decorations around the bazaar. "You can't say I don't know how to set up a nice date."

My insides melted just a little, but I challenged, "Are we dating now?"

"I don't let just anyone take advantage of me," he said.

"A-advantage?" I sputtered. "H-how?"

Merlin chuckled. "That was a joke, Eowlyn."

I stared at him. Who was this, dare I say, *jovial* Merlin? I grabbed his drink and took a small sip. Nope. Not a potion. Just water.

Merlin took a bite of the curried rice on my plate and chewed slowly. "This is good."

*What game are you playing now?* But I lowered my spoon to the plate for another bite. "Have you figured out the train schedule?"

"There's one at first light. We can get your supplies and find a hotel for the night. I want to get cleaned up while we still can. We don't know if this hotel Marilynn found for us in the middle of nowhere is going to be any good."

"We're not meeting them tonight?"

Merlin shook his head. "The rendezvous is close to our final destination."

It sounded reasonable. So why did my heart suddenly start racing like it was gearing up for a marathon? Alone. In a hotel room. With Merlin. This sounded like an epically bad idea.

The next hour passed in a blur of shops with impressive fabrics and everyday conveniences. Luckily, my three-month pill put off my period another two months. We jumped back on the highway and Merlin drove until he spotted a swanky hotel along the beach. It was surprisingly easy to get a room. Apparently, wizards had credit cards.

"Vivane Northe?" the attendant confirmed.

Merlin smiled. "That's me."

The attendant handed back the card and Merlin walked off. I flashed the service desk attendant an extra bright smile—which he returned with a startled, shy one—and hurried after Merlin. "I can't believe you stole your brother's card."

Merlin pushed the button for the elevator. "Vivane's done well for himself. Better than I have. Being a good Roman works well in this age."

"And you're not at all still mad at him about telling the world he's Merlin."

He smirked. "What's good enough for him is good enough for me."

"I didn't think you had it in you." I said jokingly, but a hint of unease went down my spine. It wasn't like him to scheme so readily. First, "interrogating" the gargoyles from the pub and now, revenge? What happened to the Boy Scout Merlin?

We went up high in the hotel. When Merlin opened the door to the room, my mouth dropped. One wall was all glass and showed an amazing moonlit view of the ocean. Waves rushed back and forth, creating a soothing rhythm. I went straight to nearly invisible doors and onto a small balcony and took in a deep breath of ocean air. "It's amazing."

Merlin stepped out of the room and came up behind me. He pointed out to the twinkling beach skyline. "You can easily imagine it going on forever. In my day, we never imagined it wouldn't."

I glanced down. The beach lay a long way down. "If I jumped off right now, I could die happy."

Fingers tangled in my hair. He brushed the dark strands to

the side to expose one side of my neck. His warm breath blew against my skin as he leaned close to my ear. "Not yet. There's a lot left for you to do."

As if it heard him, a gust of wind blew hard at the balcony and pushed me backward. I fell against him. His arm curled around my waist. Despite the chill of the wind, a surge of heat engulfed me. On my neck, the Dragon's Eye stirred.

*Water. I dove into black water. Much like the beach on Colombo. But this one was murkier. Colder. No pretty skyline could be seen in the distance. There was only darkness, a pitch-black world that shrouded everything. I was drowning in the water. It wanted me.*

"Eowlyn." Merlin shook me. "Wake up."

My eyes flew open. We weren't on the balcony. I lay on a very large, very soft bed. Merlin sat on the bed, looming over me. The glass wall showing the ocean framed him.

I sat up. "What happened?"

He frowned. "You fainted."

I rubbed my head. "I had an odd dream."

Amber eyes hooded. He looked at my neck. "Yes."

I touched the Dragon's Eye. "You saw the dream?"

He shook his head. "I saw the necklace spark. That's more than anything since..."

Since the god-killer. Not wanting to think about that night, I glanced around the room. "You put me on the bed. The only bed."

His face reddened. "We got the room last minute. This is what they had available."

"Mmm." I leaned back against cushions.

He raked a shaky hand through his hair. "Are you going to tell me what you saw?"

With a sigh, I reached up and touched my neck. The damaged Dragon's Eye lay quiet. "You really didn't feel anything?"

He shook his head, letting his brown hair fall in waves around his face.

*No more secrets.* "I see water. Endless water. Then, I'm drowning in it. I can't get out. It's suffocating me and I'm sinking deeper and deeper. I make it out onto the surface sometimes. I see black all around me. The air. The world is black. I can't escape."

Merlin leaned back. "I see."

"I see," I huffed. "That's all you have is *I see*?"

He blinked. "I...have to think about this. I don't know what it means. It could be something. It could be nothing. Just a manifestation of the damaged charm."

"Nothing," I said loudly. Swinging my legs off the bed, I jumped up. "Well, when I'm drowning in water, it sure feels like something. How about instead of saying it could mean nothing, you figure it out first, Emrys."

"Emrys," he murmured. "You must be really upset."

I eyed a pillow and debated smothering him. "I would like for you to take me seriously."

He responded with a long stare.

"I'm going to take a shower and go to sleep. If you're not going to take the floor"—it was hard stone, so I doubted it—"stay on your side of the bed. Far away." Giving him my back, I stomped off to the bathroom. The bathroom turned out to be a dream of marble-laden heaven, with a shower that could fit five and a soaker tub with a fancy-looking bottle of bubble bath next to its silver tap. I was still furious, and my revenge to take forever in the bath worked.

By the time I got out, wearing only a robe, Merlin had fallen asleep. Not ready to forgive him, I shook his shoulder hard and barked, "Your turn."

He mumbled and got up with a groggy murmur of acquiescence. As he left, I climbed onto the bed. My eyes fluttered shut.

A wake-up call would be coming in at five in the morning. A clock beside the bed declared it to be eleven o'clock.

The wake-up call never got its chance. My eyes snapped open in the dark. I was being suffocated. For a moment, I panicked. But I wasn't underwater. I was on my stomach. A heavy weight pushed me into soft bedding. My robe had ridden up to fully expose my legs and higher. A hand gripped my exposed back. Merlin's hand.

The entire length of his chest lay heavy on my right shoulder and crushed my arm. Slowly, I tried to wiggle out from under him, but he was too close. His hand slid from my back and went down to land on a bare thigh. *This is worse.* I turned my head toward him, biting my lip.

What I saw made me take a breath. He slept naked. All right, not quite all naked. Lean muscles and perfect abs invited touching. He'd tied a white towel around his waist. His towel had also slid up to reveal very muscular legs.

To my disappointment, however, it covered the most inter-esting parts. Interesting parts that lay against my bent knee. I tried to slide my leg back toward myself to free it.

"Stop," he groaned, without opening his eyes. His hand on my skin tightened.

I stilled, sprawled on my belly with my leg hiked at an odd angle and my entire body tense.

One eye opened partially. "Why are you awake?"

"Do you think you can stop suffocating me?" I whispered.

Both eyes opened. Merlin looked down. His hand on the back of my thigh and close to cupping...other things. He met my gaze. For a moment, everything stood still.

He didn't move his hand. "Tell me what happened at the van."

"What?" I squeaked.

"It's been bothering me. You attacked the gargoyle at the pub. Then, I saw the same bloodlust at the van."

*And you want to talk about this now? Naked?* Knowing he wasn't going to let it go, I took a breath. "I did what I was trained to do. I protected us." Except I lost control. Just like before. *The boy lay sprawled like a sacrifice to an ancient god. I held the knife.* My head on the pillow, I whispered, "You killed more of them than I did. I didn't think you had that in you."

"I grew up in a different time. It wasn't my first battle."

"I was born there. I remember it too." I closed my eyes. The flash of steel in the dark, a knife and a carved-up boy ran jagged through my mind. "For a long time I thought I was broken. Then, Vane found me again."

"This is about what you didn't want to tell me." He moved. His towel opened partially.

I forced my eyes up instead of down at the very revealing towel.

He reached under my pillow. He drew out the knife I'd placed underneath the soft puff of feathers and put it between us. "Is that what this is about too?"

His hips shifted and more of his towel slipped.

In a strangled voice, I asked, "Can I move?" What would I be touching if I did move?

He cleared his throat and scooted back on his side.

I tucked my leg back underneath me. My eyes fluttered closed. "I'm tired. We'll talk later."

"Eowlyn," he said sharply. "Look at me."

I forced my eyes to open.

Amber eyes held mine. He sighed. His hand reached out and tucked loose strands of hair behind an ear. "It's all right. I can wait. Until you trust me."

The bottom fell out of my stomach. It would only take a small push to be next to him, on top of him, underneath him... I burst out, "Why don't you have any clothes on?"

He smiled. "You took the only robe."

"Don't smile," I said breathily.

His response was to lean closer.

My chin went up, my lips seeking his. I could almost taste him.

*Beep. Beep. Beep.*

"The train," I murmured.

With a groan, Merlin pulled back. He sat up and grabbed his phone from the nightstand. "We'll miss it if we don't go now."

I sat up, holding the front of my robe closed. "Matt—"

He twisted his torso around. "Did you just call me Matt?"

Heat filled my cheeks. "I didn't mean to. In my defense, though, I did know you as Matt first, you know."

"You haven't called me that since you first learned my true name." He gave me a searching look.

"Because I believe in calling you who you actually are. I'm not going to lie to you." I met his eyes. My lips curved up. "It would be easier if you were Matt, but I wouldn't be here with him. Merlin is more interesting."

"I wouldn't mind a bit of easier once in a while." His eyes raked over me.

I could picture what he saw from mussed hair to the robe playing peek-a-boo with my skin. "No?"

"But for Merlin, the mission always comes first." He got out of bed and held out his hand, a naked god-like being with bronzed skin and dark resigned eyes. "Ready?"

*A little too ready.* I put my hand in his.

He yanked me forward. I gave a shocked gasp as my robe gaped open at the front. But he didn't look. Merlin's eyes stayed locked on mine. Resting a knee on the bed, he pulled me against him. Warm skin slid against mine.

With my eyes all the way wide, I asked, "What are you doing?"

"You said you like interesting." He slipped his hands around my neck and his fingers closed around my nape. He pushed my face up. "This isn't the last time I intend to see you like this. Just so we understand."

Trying not to melt and beg pathetically, I arched a brow with more bravado than I felt. "When I'm ready."

His hands fell from my neck. They slid down the sides of the robe. After pulling the soft fabric closed, he leaned back. He picked up the knife from the bed and handed it to me. "You're in charge."

8
___

## ACTUALLY, I'M IMPRESSED

I was so not in charge. Half an hour later, I got my wish and we careened this way and that in a tiny tuk-tuk. The open-sided three-wheeler taxi sped through the city like a drunken ATV. Grey skies and industrial-tinged rain showered us all the way to the Colombo Fort train station.

We stopped with a sudden jerk. I grabbed a thin metal pole between me and Merlin to stop myself from toppling. I flew sideways on the worn pleather bench seat. Merlin caught me.

I scooted back from him. "I can see why cars have seat belts."

In a husky voice, he replied, "I can see why you might do without."

"Mmmm," I said, my brain becoming mush again.

He stepped out of the tuk-tuk and I had to take a hard breath before I followed. *Get a hold of yourself, Eowlyn Patience. You are never going to make it through this at this rate.*

Inside the main train station, vintage whitewashed wood railings and walkways crossed over concrete platforms below. Like the rest of the city, old Colonial architecture mixed with modern industrialized steel.

Khaki-uniformed guards heavily armed with long rifles patrolled the station. The country had recently ended a thirty-year civil war. A separatist liberation group in northeast Sri Lanka, the Tamil Tigers, continually used suicide bombers to gain attention. They'd been defeated by the government in 2009 but still weren't all gone. Luckily, we weren't heading north but toward the middle of the country.

A long metal diesel train with stripes of rusty red and blotchy white pulled up to the platform. Scratches and dents marred its sides, but the workhorse held like a sturdy pair of shoes. Merlin and I climbed up a metal ladder into the second-class railway car. This train didn't have first-class compartments—which meant no air conditioning. Inside, box-like sections lined the left side of the train, a walkway cut through the middle, and on the right a slim bench seat matched the length of each compartment. Inside each section, the bench seats faced each other and were long enough to sleep a mid-size person. Though he wasn't a giant, Merlin looked huge in the tiny space. Above the lower seat, another upper bench had been pulled up and tied to its respective wall to give enough room for a passenger to sit. Each section meant to sleep four—two up and two down. Between the seats, along the wall, a window showed the comings and goings of the busy platform.

Our seats weren't in a proper compartment, but to the right of the walkway. A bench seat ran parallel to the window. Here, an upper bench had also been pulled up so two passengers could sit with enough head room on the lower seat. We sat side by side with a window behind us.

As soon as the whistle blew, a crowd rushed into the empty stairs at the boxcar's entry. Boys and girls in similar short-sleeved cotton shirts and dark trousers crammed themselves at the exits, poised to jump out if the conductor asked for their tickets.

Another whistle and the train chugged out of the city.

Almost immediately, the sights turned rural. On-again, off-again rain made the countryside lush and fragrant. I put my foot up on the bench and peered out the window. The train broke sloping hillsides filled with bright flowers and the occasional waterfall. Unable to take in all the lush colors at once, I put my head against the metal window and sighed. "It's like riding along a beautiful tropical jungle."

"They called it the Garden of Eden," Merlin replied absently. He studied a guidebook he'd picked up at the bazaar. His nose completely buried in his book, he whispered in a fascinated tone, "This history predates mine. We'll see a mixture of ancient Dravidian architecture overlaid with Roman influence."

I put my hands on my chin, inhaling the wet lushness of ferns and sweet flowers. We passed farms upon hills with steps carved into them. Small villages held one lone platform and were marked mainly by a domed white temple at the center. Locals on the platform wore a mixture of western clothing, like shirts and khakis, and traditional garb, like sarongs and saris.

The train stopped at one platform, and merchants immediately began shouting and offering snacks. Some ran up to the window. A few boarded the train to offer hot chai or coffee. I stuck my hand into Merlin's pocket and flagged a girl hauling a thermos and small glass cups.

I put up my fingers. "Two, please."

The girl nodded, shaking her braids shyly at me. She stared with big eyes at Merlin. He did look a sight. Pale, with dark hair and his nose stuck in a book.

With a small smile, I took the chai.

After she'd left, I elbowed Merlin. "You're missing everything."

"I'm not here to enjoy the landscape," he replied without looking up from the guidebook.

I grabbed the book from his hands. "You might want to live

a little." I pointed to a passing white temple shrouded with green vines. "All the secrets of the universe are out there, not here." I shook the book.

Merlin shrugged. "I'm trying to make sure we're not all dead soon."

He ducked his head back down to stare at the guidebook.

We passed yet another towering waterfall nestled in the crevices of a hill. We chugged into the mountains and onto higher elevation. Outside, the foliage grew denser and the air purer and cleaner. We passed through a short tunnel made completely of rock. Beyond it, the countryside went from jungle to trim fields. Tidy rows of tea bushes layered hillside terraces.

I glimpsed a stately white plantation-style house on what looked like a large estate. I watched it all go by before putting my hand on his book to get his attention. "I understand you're under pressure, but think about it—if all you're concerned about is the mission, then you'll miss what it is it you're actually fighting for."

His nose stuck in a book, he said, "What I'm fighting for takes a lot of work to keep."

"Do you think the great Merlin can live in the moment?"

"Everyone's looking to me for answers. But I don't have any," he said in a grouchy way.

But when he shut the book, I smiled. "Not too egotistical to see it's right in front of your nose, after all?"

"It's not egotistical if I am the one everyone's counting on." He scowled, but his expression changed as he jerked forward. He put his head against the window.

"What?" I asked. "What do you see?"

"Look." He pointed out the window. The train was passing a small town. At its center stood a temple with a giant statue of a chubby-cheeked monkey. "That's Hanuman." Merlin grabbed his guidebook and flipped through its pages. "Remember the epic *Ramayana*? The monkey god helps rescue

Princess Seetha. King Rawana kidnapped her and took her to his home. Prince Rama sent the monkey god, Hanuman, after her."

"The creator god, Brahma, gave Rawana the nectar of immortality as a celestial gift. The Healing Cup—"

Merlin slapped a hand over my mouth. People continued to chatter on without paying any attention to us. I bit his palm lightly.

"Ow," he said, pulling it back. "What was that for?"

My eyebrow rose. "What do you think? It's not polite to slap a hand over someone's mouth."

He shook his hand with an injured scowl. "All right, crazy. You didn't have to bite so hard. We have to be careful of any Robin Chaucers."

*Crazy.* If it had been anyone but him, I would have let it go. But as soon as he said it, the memory rushed at me. *Get out. Get out. Get out,* the boy's mother screamed. *She gutted him like a piece of meat with a fraking steak knife... Just look at her. She's... crazy.*

Shaking, I thrust my full cup of chai at him and stood. "I need to get out of here."

"Eowlyn." He stood with a confused frown. "We're not there yet."

"I don't care. I need out." I bit out, "Don't come after me."

"Eowlyn!"

The other passengers watched us with avid eyes as I stalked off. I ducked my head, flushing under the heat of their scrutiny. But I couldn't do it, couldn't turn back to him. Tears burned in my eyes. I refused to shed them. He didn't understand. It's a trigger. Just a stupid trigger. He didn't mean it, but the word out of his mouth cut deep.

I found an empty spot at the narrow passageway next to the exit. Well, nearly empty, with only five other kids. One stood apart from the rest of them, the girl with braids and thermos.

One glance at my face and she shook her head. "He's not nice."

I stepped over to the wall opposite from her and leaned against it. "Sometimes. Not right now."

"I understand." She tilted her head at the four boys crowding steps down to the exit. Picking up her thermos, she asked, "One more?"

"Yes, sure." I felt for my wallet in my jacket and realized I'd left my money in the rucksack. I sighed. "Never mind."

She pointed to my wrist.

I glanced down at a small bracelet I'd bought at the bazaar. "You like this?"

She nodded and held out the steaming cup. "Yes?"

I'd paid a pretty penny for the bracelet in the capital city, a place the girl might not ever see. After slipping the bracelet off, I gave it to her and took the chai. "Thanks."

I sipped it, letting the sweet, hot liquid warm me.

"Eowlyn." Merlin came up. He held both rucksacks. "This isn't a game."

Putting the chai cup to my lips, I took a long, slow sip. "Are you this thickheaded generally or am I special? You could make a saint scream."

"Ryan and I get along."

My lips pursed together. My sainthood points at stake, I didn't point out Ryan had chosen Vane. "Ryan hasn't traveled with you."

The train pulled to a screeching stop. I wobbled. Merlin caught my elbow. Straightening away from him, I gave the chai cup to the girl. She took it and turned to leave with a wave. The bracelet showed on her wrist as she walked down the steps and out of the train. Those around us jumped up and began to grab bags from underneath the benches.

As the other passengers walked past us and down the steps

to leave, Merlin turned to me with a frown. "You traded your bracelet for a chai?"

A glance at the platform told me we were still about an hour from Ella. I took my rucksack from him. "We can go sit back down now."

"You paid four times for that bracelet than for what she asked for tea."

My eyebrows went up. "You were paying attention." At the bazaar and on the train.

"Why would you think I wouldn't be?" His voice lowered. "Tell me what's really got you upset."

"The mysteries of the male mind."

The train whistle sounded. Another stop. I began to walk back into the compartment.

Merlin put a hand on my shoulder. "Time to get off."

"What?" I didn't resist as he rushed me out of the train. A large green sign on the tiny platform declared the town as Nanu Oya.

Old-fashioned oil lanterns lined the platform's ceilings. Colorful hanging baskets of orchids swayed in the cool breeze of a grey sky. I blinked. "This isn't the stop for Ella."

"I realize that."

Realization hit me too. My eyes went wide. "You lied to Raj."

His lips curved up. "Don't tell me you're actually surprised?"

I laughed. "Actually, I'm impressed."

# 9

## YOU WANTED ME TO LIVE A LITTLE

An hour later, we hiked uphill. The main path into town showed Colonial-style bungalow houses with perfectly manicured lawns, a replica of any small village from England. However, the main path wasn't where Merlin directed us. We mucked through mud and tea leaves along the hillside.

The rucksack bounced along my back. I took in a deep breath of fragrant Ceylon tea and all its musty flavor. "This is amazing."

"Huh." Merlin trudged along behind me, glaring at his shoes every time he took a step.

I stifled a laugh. The hike had been his idea and he looked miserable. "Why did you choose dress socks and tennis shoes when you knew you wanted to go into the jungle?"

"The rendezvous place looked like it was somewhere in civilization. I didn't know I wanted to go into the jungle until I read the guidebook on the train." His eyes raked over my face. "You're not even sweating."

I stepped around another tea crop and sideways down a

muddy hill. "Vane and I traveled from Carthage to Britain. This is nothing."

Merlin slid, following my trail. "Vane would love this place." He dropped the guidebook and it tumbled down to me.

I bent and picked it up without stopping. "Nuwara Eliya. Nickname: Little England," I flipped the page. "In the central highlands of Ceylon, as Sri Lanka was called during its British occupation, the hill country retreat became a private sanctuary for colonists, civil servants, and tea planters, where they engaged in their favorite pastimes of hunting, polo, golf, and cricket—"

"Stop." Merlin plopped down in the mud, taking heavy breaths. He held out his hand. "I need to look at the book."

*It looks like you need a rest.* Wisely, I didn't say it. Instead, I backtracked and sat down next to him. I handed him the book. "Are you sure you know where you're going?"

"Yes," he said, rubbing his face with a muddy hand and streaking it with dirt. "I'm not sure how it's all connected, except our foundations go back to this region."

I took a small towel out of my coat pocket and handed it to him. "What foundations?"

"The council theorizes the *Keltoi*—"

"Wizards," I said.

"Yes, wizards first emerged in the civilizations of the Indus Valley roughly in 3000 BCE. Sects of the Indus people migrated across Mesopotamia, Greece, and up into Western Europe. Among them, us. If you follow the derivation of languages spoken in the region today, you can follow the migration of our people."

I raised a brow. "Am I your people?"

He wiped his face and raked a hand through brown shaggy hair. "Of course. You wouldn't possess the Dragon's Eye otherwise. I don't know why, but all these depictions of the stolen queen Seetha... I feel as if the Lady is guiding us somehow."

"And the map to the Lady's temple Ryan and the Scooby gang are trailing?"

"Maybe the map was drawn by followers of the Fisher King. In one version of his story, the head of the king came back and was buried, and its magic protected the Island of Britain from marauders thereafter."

"Is that where it got lost and ended up in gargoyle hands? The Vikings sacked Britain for a hundred or so years after Arthur."

Merlin scowled. "Because he lost at Mt. Camlann. Because of Vane."

"Don't start again. Vane is on your side."

"Vane is on Vane's side," Merlin said.

I glanced out over the long hill. "You really think one of Arthur's knights came all the way out here?"

"If Perceval found the Healing Cup, he would have taken it back to Britannia, but he never returned."

I winced.

"I'm sorry," Merlin said. "Do you remember much of your brother?"

I blinked hard. "Bits and pieces. So, Arthur sent Galahad and Perceval?"

"Actually, three set out after the Fisher King. Perceval, Galahad, and Bors."

I kicked at the dirt. "What do you remember of my brother?"

"Vane and Perceval were close. After you were lost, he brought Perceval to Camelot with him. As a noble, Perceval was allowed to be trained, even though he was an orphan. Vane trained him, and Perceval worshipped Vane." Merlin muttered, "Seems he has a thing for orphans."

*Ryan.* "I don't think she's just any orphan."

Merlin didn't answer. The valley below showed off a small waterfall. It streamed down between the crevices of a green-carpeted hill and watered manicured hedges of tea plant. I got up. "We should get going before it becomes dark."

"It's early afternoon."

I pointed up at the grey sky. "Let's not take chances."

He snapped the guidebook shut. "At least it's not raining."

A rumble of thunder answered on cue. Shaking my head, I held out a hand. "You had to say it."

Merlin took the proffered help. He yanked my hand down.

*Holy crap.* I went sprawling into wet mud. I came up sputtering, with goo all over my chest and face. "I was mostly dry."

A low rumble sounded from inside Merlin's chest. His lips twitched. He couldn't hold it in. A laugh burst out. "Now you're not."

"What was that for?"

With a wicked grin, he held out the towel I'd given him. "You wanted me to live a little."

As I grabbed the towel, a roll of thunder deafened me momentarily before rain poured down. I pulled my jacket hood up and eyed Merlin. "You are *not* nice."

"What can I say? You bring out the worst in me."

I threw mud in his face.

As he sputtered and spat it out, I wiped my face.

A shove to the back sent me sliding in the mud once again. This time I managed to grab Merlin's foot as I slipped downhill. We glided over the mud almost all the way down. I slowed to a stop first. Merlin landed against my back, his arms wrapping around me as he dug his heels into the mud to stop us from going down farther. We ended up on top of each as if we'd been sharing a sled down a snowbank. Except mud smeared us from head to toe.

The rain poured down even harder.

"At least it's making us cleaner." I wiped at my face, but my dirty hand only caked on more mud.

Merlin's arms tightened around me. "The hotel is close, I'm pretty sure."

"In a hurry?" I asked.

"No," came the heart-stopping reply.

"Merlin..." Marilynn's high-strung voice reached us before her form appeared out from a barrier of trees. She stormed up a short way from the bottom of the hill. "Well, I see you two are taking this seriously."

Merlin's arms dropped. He pushed up and out of the mud. He opened his rucksack and took out the guidebook. He shook it in front of me with a grin. It was perfectly dry.

I rolled my eyes and pushed myself up.

"You're here all right?" he asked Marilynn.

"We're all here." Her blonde hair damp from the rain, she added with a scowl, "I did my job."

Merlin frowned. "No trouble?"

"Not like with Raj," she bit out.

From her sour expression, I gleaned the van trip had not gone well. I began walking downhill. "Arthur giving you trouble?"

"He was fine. A gentleman." Marilynn's expression turned to one of disgust. "Grey drove us."

I suppressed a smile. So Grey Ragnar was the problem.

Merlin walked behind us. His nose stuck in the guidebook which he'd wrapped in clear plastic. Shaking my head, I let Marilynn lead me through the barrier of trees. I gasped at the sight on the other side. Soft rain kissed the slanted roof of a beautiful white plantation house with a wraparound porch. Painted railings framed small balconies on the second floor, and halogen bulbs spotlighted a garden with a quiet pond.

"If it had a few magnolia trees," I said, "We could be back home."

"St. Elizabeth's Hotel," Merlin said. "We're here."

"A bathtub," I said happily.

Marilynn eyed us. In her clipped accent, she said with feeling, "The two of you bloody need it. We have a suite on the third floor."

I tugged off my ruined shoes before entering the lobby. A clerk in a crisp white uniform and thin mustache eyed us with misgiving. "If *sir and memsahib* would like, we have a full-service laundry available."

I beamed at him. "That sounds wonderful. Also, some hot tea."

The clerk perked up. "Of course, *memsahib*. We also serve a high tea in the evenings with meat pies, local breads, and a scrumptious milk cake—"

"Eowlyn." Grey ran up with arms open wide. He stopped short at the sight our mud-soaked selves. His arms dropped. "I'm not hugging you."

"Eowlyn. Merlin." Arthur came up behind Grey. "It is a relief to see you safe."

Grey turned to the hotel clerk. "Do you have a dinner menu? We got here this afternoon. Marilynn"—he gave her a dirty look—"wouldn't let us stop at all."

"It was safer," Arthur murmured.

"Our restaurant has some wonderful local dishes the chef's prepared for dinner," the clerk said with a bright smile. "A blend of Indian and Colonial—"

"Good," Merlin said. "Send it to our room. We need to get to sleep early. We leave in the middle of the night."

He walked off. Marilynn and Grey argued with each other about eating before gathering more supplies as they headed off after Merlin.

Arthur held out his elbow. "Care to accompany me?"

I held out my dirty hand. "Are you sure?"

Without asking, Arthur tucked my hand into the crook of his arm. "I'm glad to see you."

A snort of laughter escaped me. "Was it that bad with them?"

"Like oil and water. All night long. It's easier keeping some of my warring knights in line," he said, raking a hand through golden hair. "I barely slept." Grey eyes fixed on me. "You and Merlin?"

A mostly naked Merlin flashed through my mind. I swallowed. "It was...fine."

Arthur gave a rueful smile. "You like him."

I gave a nod.

"So did Guinevere. At first," Arthur said. "He's a hard one to understand. His gaze never wavers from his duty. I always admired that about him."

It wasn't exactly what I wanted to hear. Ever since he'd gotten on the bike in Colombo, he'd been almost human. I had a feeling that was over. Arthur led me to an old, rickety elevator we rode to the third floor. The lift opened to another large open-air seating area. Rustic wooden tables and oil landscapes decorated the walls. We went to a suite, which had another sitting room with a private balcony. Colorful cushions and sofas had been placed inside the room and out on the open-air space. Gauzy white curtains, which I suspected also served as mosquito nets, swayed in the breeze of the darkening sky.

I didn't see Merlin. Grey sat on a vintage-style sofa, looking odd with a very modern TV remote in his hand. Marilynn had escaped to the balcony and was working away on a touchpad. She'd settled herself in a nest of fluffy tartan pillows befitting the Colonial décor. I looked up at Arthur. "She's settled in."

"A day can be a long time," he murmured.

"Yes," I said with feeling.

Arthur's keen eyes locked on me. "Be careful, Eowlyn. It's not easy to be second in someone's emotions, even if duty is their mistress. I should know." A bright sheen colored his eyes. "I trusted both Lancelot and Guinevere. I would have never imagined them... Your moving pictures have told me much about my future."

I winced. *It's your past.* But I didn't say it. "Are you upset Merlin didn't tell you?"

Arthur shook his head. "I'm not surprised. He would not have presumed. Not if he found out after they consummated. Nothing good can come from sentiment, he would say. It is a dangerous distraction." He paused. "But he's different here."

My head tilted. A large window in the open-air lobby showed lush hills and wet flowers. Merlin had said he felt different since the Dragon's Eye was damaged. "Different how?"

"More determined. Colder."

I would have agreed, before our little sojourn. But he didn't seem all that cold anymore.

"I should go get cleaned up," I told Arthur.

Arthur pointed to a doorway which showed two beds in a large room. "Marilynn took the bigger one."

Of course, she had. Suppressing a nod, I crossed to the room. Two canopied full-sized beds had white mosquito nets draped down their sides. In front of the beds, red cushions lay on a divan sofa. On one side of the room, green curtains hung around a large window showing swaying palm trees outside. My stomach rumbled. I yanked and sniffed at the muddied clothes. Ugh. They not only stuck to the skin but they smelled like dung. *Shower first.*

I marched to the bathroom for a much-needed shower and twisted the handle. It jiggled open. The door swung out and my eyes went straight to a very bare back, dripping-wet naked backside. *Oh, by all the gods.*

His eyes met mine in the mirror. Turning red, he yanked a towel off a rack on the wall and put it around him. "You're in the wrong place."

"No, you are."

He glanced around at the counter and spotted Marilynn's

toiletries. He turned and gave a devastatingly sheepish grin. "You have me."

*Not yet, but...* I stepped back. "I'll let you finish."

"Actually, I'm done." Raking a hand through wet hair, he padded closer. "I'll finish up in the other room." Before I could move, he pushed the door open and sidled by me, making sure to give my mud-laden self a proper berth. As he left, he tossed back in a husky voice, "The water isn't all that warm but enjoy the soap. I know I did."

The words turned out to be a trap. It was a good thing the shower was cold—apparently tropical resorts didn't believe in hot water—using the same bar of soap he used after catching yet another glimpse of his entirely bare body left me plenty warm.

The remainder of the evening went quickly. While everyone else ate and planned for our middle-of-the-night escapade—a hike up to a place called Adam's Peak—I stared out at the night sky. It had only been one day since I'd lost control with Robin Chaucer. I'd never even bothered to look at his face after I'd gutted him. He'd gone to his death wearing a helmet. No face. No condemnation. From anyone except Marilynn.

Yet it stayed in my mind as I climbed onto the bed next to an already sequestered Marilynn. I pulled the bed's net shut, blocking her light snores as well as any mosquitoes. I touched my throat and tugged at the neckline of tunic-style pajamas Marilynn had handed me. The Dragon's Eye sat quiet. I lay back on the pillows on one side of the large bed. I reached out to the pillow next to me and dug my fingers into the soft fluff. I'd spent one night with him, but it wasn't enough. I didn't dwell as exhaustion rode me. My eyes closed.

BLACK WATER SURROUNDED ME. I KICKED MY LEGS AND SWAM UP TO THE surface. My head broke through the cold, watery barrier, only to fall into more darkness. But this time, I didn't panic. I rotated in the water. The blackness transformed, going from complete dark to different shades of dark grey. In the distance, a jagged form took shape. Land.

Where am I? Why am I here? What brought me?

The dark watery world answered. *Merlin.*

# 10

# EVER THINK ABOUT WEARING GLASSES

Adam's Peak. Fifty-two hundred steps. Day three in Sri Lanka meant three hours of climbing to get to the top of the hill. It took our merry band a little over four. Mostly because one or another member of our party, She-Who-Shall-Not-Be-Named, kept stopping to enjoy one of the many bakeries and tea shops lining the trail. The steps were packed, even in the middle of the night. Tourists and pilgrims flocked the mountain staircase to the temple. At three bleary o'clock, electric lights illuminated our path and a rhythmic chanting blared from loudspeakers.

Heavy incense in the air made us all sneeze. Friendly dogs and statues of Buddha and Ganesha, the Hindu god of animals, greeted us along the trail. I spent all my cash trinkets sold by young children peddling cheap souvenirs. A steady drizzle kept us company, and as we approached the top, the rain worsened. We gripped the railings to keep our footing. I spent the time reading graffiti marked one the stone with names and countries of origin of the fellow visitors. The cargo pants I wore weren't completely waterproof, so my best hope was for them to dry quickly. Our group wore identical clothes, which made us easy to identify and also marked me, despite my Persian complexion, as definitely a tourist.

The higher we climbed, the more the island jungle atmosphere disappeared into a cloud fortress. Somewhere near the top, close to five thousand steps up, Merlin instructed Marilynn to buy lotus flowers from a street vendor. To my surprise, Grey bought two. He handed one to me and one to a startled Marilynn. I kissed him on the cheek, earning me a grimace from both Merlin and Arthur. But, to my satisfaction, I also got a glare from Marilynn.

Apparently, she didn't hate him.

We reached the very top of the mountain, where visitors crowded the last steps. From our vantage point, floodlights illuminated two buildings through a curtain of dark trees.

"There are two levels. Once we get up these steps, we'll be on the lower level. In those buildings, a limited number of guests can do overnight stays." Merlin pointed up. "You'll need to take off your shoes. You're on holy ground."

I followed his instructions and took off my hiking shoes. Piles and piles of shoes stacked the sides of the stairs. I decided to throw mine in the rucksack I carried. Just above the stairs stood a small belfry.

"A pilgrim can ring a tin bell once every time they come up the mountain."

"Five thousand two hundred steps," Grey said, making a beeline for the belfry. "I'm definitely ringing the bell. I need all the luck I can get."

"I'll join you." Arthur followed him.

I pushed my way through the crowd behind them at a slower pace. Every little bit of space had people lined up to gaze out at the dark landscape. They occupied the ledges and waited for sunrise. Merlin directed me to the center of the terrace. More floodlights lit up a huge rock that stood at the centermost highest point of the peak. The top of the rock was big enough to support a shrine and a small temple.

Merlin took out his lotus flower. "Here, put it there for luck."

Many other lotus flowers decorated the rock near the foot of the shrine. More raindrops fell from the dark sky. The sodden faces of the crowd showed despair. We'd climbed all the way, but the weather looked to be set on thwarting the sunrise.

I pointed at the greying sky. "I don't think our good luck is working."

"The tiny shrine encloses the sacred footprint, or Sri Pada. We need to get to it, preferably without anyone looking. The perfect time is when they are all otherwise preoccupied. Where is Marilynn?" Cursing under his breath, he slid back across the narrow space between drenched bodies until he reached one corner of the terrace. He waved down Marilynn and she began squeezing her way over to him.

When she reached him, Merlin pointed at the sky and helped her up on a ledge so she could get above the crowd.

Around me, the noise of disappointed pilgrims grew as many debated leaving.

Arthur touched my back. Over the noise, he asked, "What are those two doing?"

"*Kavas*," Marilynn yelled.

People turned to her curiously, but their attention diverted when the rain slowed. Above us, the dark rain clouds began to clear. The crowd first muttered, then cheered.

Merlin appeared out of the sea of bodies. "We have to hurry."

I began making my way to the shrine, only to be stopped by the onslaught of people.

"Allow me." Arthur stepped ahead of us. He plowed his way through, clearing a path.

We met Grey and Marilynn at the base of the stairs leading up to the small shrine.

Merlin mouthed, *Be ready.*

Two minutes later, the first tendrils of sunrise broke over the summit, dissipating any remaining rain clouds. An invisible Apollo rode his chariot across the heavens, ushering in the dawn. Yellow and gold lit up the sleeping island. On one side, mountains snaked with silvery waterfalls fell onto lush green fields. On the other side, blue and purple shimmered from the ocean.

A loud conch and thumping drums began the morning prayer procession. In a parade of saffron-orange-yellow robes, monks emerged from their temple on the lower level. People who'd been pilgriming inside the shrine came out. Musicians in white muslin banged on drums, some blew on trumpets, and others chanted. Many devotees held up platters of food and rice.

Using the distraction, Merlin snuck up the steps and into the emptied walkway leading to the tiny shrine the size of a small closet. Curtains kept out the rain, protecting the five-foot-wide space. The shrine opened on two sides, but a wall of people's backs closed off one. Merlin squeezed into the walled enclosure. We followed after him. Though the boys had to duck, there was enough room for all of us to fit inside the cramped shrine to the great footprint of Buddha.

The footprint lay within a casement of stone built around it. A window opened to the sky on the wall enclosing the top end of the footprint. This was the peak of the rock. I peered over Merlin at the engraving. "It's a hole."

Merlin pointed around the five-foot hole. "It's said to be the imprint of Buddha's right foot, the correct size for a thirty-five-foot-tall man."

"Or Shiva's foot as he stepped on Earth," I said.

"Or Adam's footprint after his exile from the Garden of Eden," Arthur said.

Merlin glanced at us.

"We were listening to your lecture last night, Professor." Grey peered at Merlin seriously. "Ever think about wearing glasses?"

"I don't need glasses," Merlin growled and turned back to the sacred footprint.

"Yet."

Merlin's head whipped back.

Marilynn pinkened. "I just meant glasses would look good on you."

Shaking his head, Merlin drew out a vial from his rucksack and threw it above us. A bubble of blue magic surrounded us briefly. "Marilynn," he barked. "Watch for another silence spell." He threw another vial at the rock. The rock blew apart, and with an ear-deafening bang, shrapnel flew at us.

"What are you doing?" Grey shouted. "They'll hear."

My gaze went to the people who stood just outside. They remained with their backs to us, unperturbed.

"No one can hear outside the bubble," Marilynn said calmly.

I eyed Merlin. "Please tell me why you destroyed a sacred relic."

"It is said the real relic is underneath. The top is only plaster." Merlin pushed aside the broken rock. Just beneath the top footprint lay another hidden one.

"I don't get it. Why are we here for a hidden foot?" I asked.

"We're not." He pointed at the window. "Actually, we're here for a hidden foot at a certain time."

Sunrise fully embraced the sky. Light burst in through the window in a wave. Outside, the music rose.

"They're finishing," Grey said. "You'd better hurry up before someone figures out we blew up their sacred foot and a mob forms to string us up."

"I don't understand." Merlin frowned at the silent footprint. "This is the spot. Adam's Peak is where all the different legends converge. The Buddhists say the Triple Gem, their holy trinity, manifests when the shadow falls over the mountain during sunrise. Alexander the Great thought the same when he came here." He paced in the small space and rubbed the back of his neck. "This place is marked by the legends." He looked up. "It's marked by the gods."

I grimaced. "Not them."

"Which gods?" Arthur repeated in confusion.

"The Lady of the Lake," Grey told him.

"Maybe," I said. We'd never figured out Golden-Hainey's true identity.

"Marilynn," Merlin said. "Try your magic."

She waved a hand in the air. Her mouth moved to utter something, but I didn't hear it as the music outside came to a triumphant finish. A blast of magic hit us.

Nothing changed.

Merlin marched to the blasted hole. He peered over it. "There has to be something."

A wave of nausea went over me as he leaned over the hole. I grabbed him and hauled him back.

"Eowlyn." He frowned. "What?"

"She felt something," Arthur said. "Danger."

I glanced at Arthur. How had he known?

He smiled slightly. "I recognized your expression."

*Gwenhwyfar.* He didn't say it, but I understood. I stepped closer to the exposed footprint and the rock started to hum. "Do you hear that?"

"What?" Merlin asked.

"I do," Arthur said.

Grey also stepped closer. "So do I."

Marilynn frowned. "I don't."

Grey put his hand over the footprint.

"Grey," I said in protest, taking a step toward him.

Merlin stopped me.

A shot of electricity from the rock zapped Grey's hand. "Ow." He pulled it back. "What is it?"

Arthur did the same.

I squawked, "Are you two crazy? When something bites you, you don't put your hand back into its mouth."

Grey grinned. "You want to try it, don't you?"

"I want to." Marilynn sniffed and walked to the hole. She held out her hand.

Nothing happened.

Scrunching my nose, I stepped up next to her. Electricity zapped my hand.

"It's the candidates. You're the key," Merlin said. He drew out another vial from the bag.

Something about the smell was familiar. I grabbed his wrist. "Is that blood?"

He smiled. "Ryan's blood."

"Why do you have Ryan's blood?" Grey demanded.

"After she became the sword bearer, the council recovered everything they could. Her mother cryo-froze her placenta from when she was born, did you know? This is a little bit of her cord blood. The purest bit of her we can get."

"Gross," Grey said. "That's just creepy."

He raised a brow. "Vane tracked them all down."

Marilynn added, "Really creepy."

The window darkened. Outside, dark clouds swarmed in the sky once again.

"Time's up." Merlin poured Ryan's blood onto the footprint.

Immediately, the rock rumbled. The ground underneath us trembled. Then, a groan from what seemed like deep within the mountain came.

Wind swirled over the footprint. Then, space itself seemed to part as a white glowing vortex formed. Inside it, a shape appeared.

"It's a portal." Merlin took a step toward it. "It looks as if it holds a cross."

On my neck, the Dragon's Eye thumped weakly. *In warning.*

I shoved past Merlin and reached into the vortex. My hand clamped around the cross. It solidified in my hand, which was on fire. The Dragon's Eye heated as a guttural scream tore from my mouth.

"Arthur, you're a candidate," Merlin said.

"I can help." Arthur stuck his hand into the vortex.

"Me too." Grey plunged his hand into the white light.

The world shook around us. I stumbled and felt Merlin's arms go around my waist to hold me up. Over the rumbling, he commanded, "Pull it out."

We yanked out a square metal cross. It was about a foot long with symbols engraved down its stem. A red gem sat at the center of the cross like an ancient eye.

The world kept shaking.

The walls of the shrine began to crack and the ground underneath us split. We hurried outside to find chaos as a thousand people ran to the steps in a panic to get off the summit.

The buildings on the summit shuddered as the mountain woke.

"Earthquake," someone cried out.

"Is it the Total Tremor?" another yelled.

Grey cursed. "I hate booby traps. The portal screwed us."

"We need to leave. *Now.*" Merlin pulled me down the steps off the shrine.

The others followed close behind. A loud clang sounded as the belfry tore apart and the pilgrim bell fell. The shrine crumbled. Rock and stone tumbled like cannons onto the summit terrace below. Shrapnel flew. Hysterical shrieks sounded and people screamed, some running to protect and all trying to flee.

I grabbed Merlin and stopped him, letting the river of humanity flow by us. My eyes fell on the monks and elderly pilgrims who'd huddled together, their mouths moving in silent prayer. I pointed to them. "The whole summit will collapse. Not everyone will make it. There has to be something we can do."

He shook his head. "I don't have any power, remember?"

I looked to Marilynn.

"This is beyond my level." She shook her head. "We can't do anything about this."

I refused to give up. "After the trial, with Golden-Hainey, you were able to channel power from Excalibur."

"We don't have the god-killer," Grey said.

"If we are the conduits, then we can take power from anywhere," Arthur said. "Maybe we should call to Arriane DuLac?"

I bent down and touched the trembling ground. "Or maybe we should take it from the mountain." I looked to Merlin. "Can you?"

"I don't have anything—"

"We know this does." I touched the Dragon's Eye. The dark world held power.

He sat down and crossed his legs yogi-style.

"She asked you to do magic," Grey said. "Not drink tea, Emrys."

Merlin closed his eyes in response. The entire length of the summit shook violently.

Marilynn yelped as a crack in the earth opened next to us.

Arthur met my gaze, shrugged, then crossed to Merlin. He sat down next to him. Marilynn did the same. She tugged Grey down to the ground. He sat with a we're-going-to-die look on his face. I moved to sit down but never got the chance.

Merlin's eyes snapped open. "The portal. We've displaced energy by taking out the cross. We need to put something in its place." He glanced around at the others curiously. "What are you doing sitting? I just needed to think."

Grey jumped up. "I knew it!"

"We were supporting you." An unfazed Arthur rose. "How do we do this task? Do we give up the cross?"

"Not the cross." I turned on my heel and ran back toward the footprint. I went up the shuddering steps. Dodging falling rock, I stepped around the hazard the shrine had become. In seconds, I reached the portal.

The vortex formed as soon as I neared it. I took off the Dragon's Eye.

"No," Merlin yelled. "Eowlyn, stop."

I stuck the necklace into the portal. A white light pulled me in. The portal expanded and my body flew into the vortex.

"*Help her, Merlin,*" a voice yelled.

A hand caught me before I submerged completely.

An onslaught of power went through me. Unfiltered, raw, angry magic threatened to tear me apart. I held together by sheer will.

In that moment, half of me remained in the shrine and the other half stood on a rocky cliff inside the dark world. The world inside the Dragon's Eye.

~

THE SEA SPLASHED BELOW THE CLIFF. BLACK WATER MOVED IN tumultuous waves. It beckoned, a throbbing began at the apex of my being, deep inside my core. I yearned to jump in the water.

A figure swam out of the water. He stood on the beach. A proud dark god with wet rippling muscles and golden eyes.

"Eowlyn," the gold-eyed god beckoned. "All you have to do is let go."

# 11

# I WOKE UP ON A TRAIN WITH A SPLITTING HEADACHE

I wanted him. I took a step toward the cliff. I would jump off. For him.

"Eowlyn," Merlin's voice yelled from behind me. From somewhere far away. But when I glanced down, his hand appeared to be clamped around my wrist.

*Leave me be*, I asked silently.

"Never," his voice promised.

"Pull her," another distant voice, Arthur's, called.

Merlin yanked me out.

Above us, clouds thundered. Lightning flashed. A heavy rain poured down on the shrine.

Merlin's arms wrapped around me.

The Dragon's Eye glowed on my neck. I screamed as he yanked me halfway out of the vortex. Merlin's mouth clamped on mine.

He took control. Blue fire surged through me like electricity through a wire. Pain infused every atom of my body. Pain clamped around my heart, choking it. Blue fire streamed out of me into Merlin. It leaked from the vortex to me to Merlin to the world in a chain. Seconds passed like excruciating hours. Finally, the mountain calmed.

Merlin's arms dropped.

He crumpled.

I went with him.

Arthur caught us. He lowered Merlin to the ground. He helped me stumble off the unconscious man.

On my knees, I stood shaking. I didn't dare move. My body ached to crawl back into the womb of the vortex.

Arthur knelt. His palms cupped my elbows. Steel-grey gaze fixing on me, he declared, "It's done. The portal is closed. You are safe."

I turned in his arms and sobbed.

~

EOWLYN – SIXTEEN HUNDRED YEARS AGO

I shivered in the cold. My brother pulled his blanket around me and snuggled close to feed me his warmth.

"The Vandal king was her father?" Vane asked.

My brother yawned. "I don't know much about it. From the gossip, I know the incident surprised them all. My father chose to ignore my mother's dalliance. What else could he do?"

"How did he treat your sister?"

"He didn't. He mostly ignored her."

"And the bow? She's exceptionally skilled."

My brother said in a sleepy tone, "She always has been. My mother had the bow made. She said she had a dream she should."

"A dream?"

"She said my sister's father spoke to her in it."

"The Vandal king?"

"I don't know. It was a dream."

"A dream." Vane sighed. Flames crackled on the fire Vane had taught us to build. Abruptly, he said, "Perceval."

My brother yawned again. "Hmm?"

"Your new name."

My brother held still. I could tell from the steady beat of pulse where he held my hand.

"Perceval," Vane repeated. "Do you like it?"

My brother's hand around me tightened. But not in a death grip. In happiness. After all, this man had saved our lives. My brother said, "It seems a good name."

"Then it shall be." Rustling came from the fire as Vane threw another stick on it. "Perceval, one query, where have you hidden the apple you took from the vault?"

I woke up on a train with a splitting headache. We never returned to the hotel.

"Is he dead?" Grey asked.

"Shhhh," Marilynn hissed. "What he did wasn't easy. Let him recover."

"What Eowlyn did wasn't easy either," Arthur said.

Merlin let out a groan and straightened from where he'd passed out on one side of the compartment. He sat up and hunched over, holding his head in his hands. Brown wavy hair spilled between his fingertips. A green weatherproof shirt and brown cargos cemented his young-professor look.

Grey sighed. "Where are you leading us to now, oh-so-wise Merlin?"

Merlin's tired face looked up to meet my gaze, his expression turning sheepish. "Ella."

I didn't say anything about the looming possibility of a Robin Chaucer waiting to ambush us. My eyes fixed on rolling hills and colorful foliage from Nuwara Eliya on the way farther into the island nation to Ella.

Grey slumped and pulled the top of a hoodie over his head. "I'm ready for this trip to be over."

Marilynn gave the scarf she wore a tug. Taking it off, she stared at its colorful pattern. She'd picked it up on Adam's Peak. It brightened up her drab grey shirt and cargos. She slid out a slim black phone from one of the cargo pockets.

Arthur sat as alertly as ever. His blond hair didn't look even a bit mussed and his athletic black shirt and pants held their crisp look. He smiled, catching my eye. "Merlin can't do this by himself. If anything, I have come to understand this much. I am bound to Excalibur as are you candidates. We are all in its service too."

I returned a weak smile of my own. My own weatherproof shirt and cargos stuck to me uncomfortably.

"Adam's Peak." Merlin asked, "Was the summit all right?"

Arthur nodded. "You and Eowlyn saved it. They will need to rebuild, but it is still intact."

"Mostly," Grey said.

I rubbed my head and looked at Merlin. "I'm still not sure why that worked."

"You helped me pull the energy out of the portal and calm the mountain. You were able to power the Dragon's Eye, and because you're a conduit yourself, I could channel it through you into the mountain."

"Conduit," Arthur murmured. "What an odd word."

"A connection point," Merlin clarified.

Marilynn, who'd been sitting to the side talking on a phone, turned it off. "That was Vivane. They've found an artifact and they're leaving Boston and heading to Greece." Her gaze went to Merlin. "They were attacked. By a man called Robin Chaucer."

My eyes widened.

Everyone glanced at me and then glanced away.

Grey cleared his throat. "I'm pretty sure Eowlyn took care of him."

"I have a feeling there are multiple Robin Chaucers," Merlin said. "If the one Eowlyn killed was assigned to watch us, it wouldn't surprise me if that was a code name."

Grey said, "James Bond is a better code name."

To my surprise, Merlin added, "I like 007 myself."

"I rather think you would make a better Q," Arthur said. When I looked at him with surprised eyes, the king shrugged. "Blake Emerson recommended I watch it. 'Tis a favorite of his. One of his folk heroes, I believe."

"Folk hero," Merlin exclaimed. "Bond is a legend."

I met Marilynn's gaze. She rolled her eyes, but her lips curved up at the male bonding.

Grey elbowed her. "Fancy yourself as M?"

She tossed her hair. "Isn't it obvious?"

"I think that leaves me as the double agent," I said.

Grey gave a wide grin. "The hot double agent."

Marilynn cleared her throat. "Shouldn't we get to Vane? He's obviously on the trail of something big with this artifact."

"No," Merlin said. "We can't get distracted. We haven't gotten what we came for. I don't know how the cross fits into all this, but it wasn't what I expected to find."

I looked up. "Did you expect to find a tear in the universe? How can such a thing like the vortex exist?"

His lips curved up. "You are dealing with gods. We saw a doorway to another dimension."

"That's impossible," Grey said. "You can't just have doorways to another universe randomly floating around."

Merlin stretched. "I have a feeling the entire mountain came to be because of the doorway."

"The shrine marks the forgotten," Arthur added. "It explain why Alexander of Macedon sought it out."

Merlin smiled. It was the first time since he'd woken they seemed to be in sync.

"How many other doorways do you think there are?" Grey demanded. "Because I never want to see another one again."

"You already have," I said. "Remember, the trial? We were in limbo for hours."

Grey cursed. "You mean that place where, once you get caught, it's nearly impossible to get back out?"

"That's the one." Turning to Merlin, I said, "If you don't tell us what your plan is, you're getting off at the platform without me, and I'm turning back to Colombo and the nearest airport. I'm not going in unprepared again."

Merlin glanced around the train. Satisfied no one was paying attention to us, he said in a lowered voice, "Al-sikandar or Sikander or Iskander conquered every piece of land from Macedonia down to the Gaza Strip. He found the sanctuary of the oracle of Amun-Ra, the sun god. The Greeks believed the Egyptian Amun-Ra was the god Zeus. All the kings of Macedonia maintained they were descended from Hercules, the mortal son of Zeus. Iskander's mother believed Alexander to be conceived by the god disguised in her husband's mortal form. Alexander gained confirmation of this demigod status by the oracle and declared it to his kingdom."

I shifted in my seat. It sounded oddly similar to the dream where my brother stated my father hadn't been my father.

Merlin met my gaze. "Alexander conquered the Middle East and India. His horse, Bucephalus, his most prized possession, was said to be a gift from Poseidon. The oracles at Delphi declared whoever should ride the beast would rule the world. Then, the horse was killed in the battle. After losing Bucephalus and suffering his own brush with death, Alexander went through India, down to old Lanka, in search of one thing."

Grey asked, "What one thing?"

Merlin nodded. "A mountain that holds the water of life."

"Water of life," I said. "Or as we know it, the Healing Cup."

"Chasing immortality." Arthur leaned back in his seat. "It seems shortsighted. Immortality is hardly a blessing."

I studied him. "You're not happy that you were asleep?"

"Entombed," Marilynn corrected. "But you grew younger, which sounds pretty great."

"It is hardly great to lose all your memories. I don't know who I am." A glitter of anger sparked in his eyes. "Or what."

A steel steak knife. The boy bloodied and gutted on the bed. Images flashed through my mind. I said softly, "I understand."

Arthur tilted his head.

"But you're in the right place at the right time because you are needed." My gaze flickered out at the green jungle vegetation. "As am I."

The train screeched to a stop. Someone shouted out, "Ella."

We scrambled off the train and stepped down onto a long, Victorian-era building with a tiny platform.

"As soon as we reach our destination, I need you to be on alert," Merlin said. "We don't know how many Robin Chaucers exist."

Marilynn paid for two tuk-tuks. She squeezed in with Merlin.

Yanking me into the three-wheeler with them, he barked, "Ella Caves."

The tuk-tuk ambled off. No Robin Chaucer or the like stopped us. We passed a row of street vendors.

Marilynn sighed. "We haven't eaten in a while."

"Forget it." Merlin handed her a cereal bar from the rucksack he carried. "We have to move fast. If Vane is on his way to Greece, we need to get there as soon as possible."

The tuk-tuk flew past the one-street town and up the steep hill country. We drove a brisk eighteen to twenty-four miles per hour, while Marilynn clutched the edges of the doorless three-wheeler with a sheen of sweat beading on her forehead. The fresh air helped my nausea. I took in the fragrant blossoms and moist air. Sitting in the middle, Merlin stared out of the tuk-tuk, looking surprisingly alert and not motion sick. The three-wheeler dangerously swerved toward the open ravine. I careened out of the side of the tuk-tuk.

Merlin caught me, his arm curling around my waist. "Be careful, this mountain may take a liking to you too."

"I'm a one-mountain kind of girl."

"Good to know," he said in a husky tone that didn't have anything to do with mountains.

Warmth filled me.

Marilynn dry heaved, sounding on the verge of vomiting. She hung her head out the door. Merlin caught her and patted her back.

I smiled at the sweet gesture.

The tuk-tuk stopped before a sign. Written both in a native language I couldn't decipher and in English, it stated, "Rawanaella Ancient Temple and Cave."

A small square temple with a wraparound veranda stood to the right of the sign. But Merlin headed to a picture showing steps leading up into a vine-laden jungle cave. A group of skinny kids mobbed us, offering to be guides. Marilynn handed two some money and they ran off.

"I think you're supposed to pay them after," I said.

She shrugged. "Either way, we've helped the local economy."

The second tuk-tuk with Grey and Arthur pulled up.

Grey came up and flicked her hair. "Softie."

Her spine straightening, she smiled pointedly at Arthur before walking off and leaving Grey behind.

"Smooth, Ragnar," I commented.

"She'll come around." He grinned. "They always do."

I shook my head. "Tell me, how has your home managed to contain all of your ego these years?"

"Because, neighbor, my home is a mansion."

A pang of homesickness went through me. My foster family, the Gladwells, lived next to the Ragnar estate in Boston. Not that the Gladwells' cottage ever competed with the Ragnars' mammoth mansion.

The five of us trekked up steep stone steps carved into the side of the mountain. We navigated up the gravel path and avoided encroaching vines and vegetation. No railing had been erected to stop a sharp tumble off the side if one got too close to the edge. Only one or two tourists walked the path and they headed downhill. By the time we got close to the top, we were all panting hard.

Marilynn sat down in the dirt. "I'm not taking another step until you tell me what's in these caves."

"Walk." Merlin pointed up the trail. "And I'll tell you."

"If it's not too far, I might be able to carry you," Arthur said. He looked her over as if he were imagining himself bouncing her like a small child in his arms, testing her weight.

Her entire face turning beet red, Marilynn stood with effort. "I'm all right. I can do this."

Arthur's brow furrowed in confusion. "It would be rude to burden a lady unnecessarily."

Marilynn gave him a look that clearly said, *You can burden me anytime.* "Um, well, yes. That's all right, though. I'm used to walking."

Arthur bowed politely. "If that is your wish, so it shall be."

I eyed the big blond king and elbowed Merlin's side. "Where's your chivalry?"

"I lost it along with my powers," he returned, sticking the verbal blade in deep.

My nose wrinkled. "Sounds like it was lost along with your fun."

"I promise you I will show you fun." His amber eyes flashing, he leaned close to my hair. "Later. Maybe after another mud bath?"

**12**

---

## CONTROLLING THIS IS GETTING
## HARDER FOR YOU

*He is a tease.* I wasn't sure if he meant when mud soaked him head to toe, making his clothes cling to his muscular body like a second skin, or when I'd actually seen his skin completely unadorned. A rush of heat blasted me in the cold air.

Leaving me with that epic bait laid out, Merlin rummaged around in his rucksack and drew out the dog-eared guidebook.

I groaned. "What did you figure out?"

He resumed the climb. "In the *Ramayana*, King Rawana's ten heads signified his knowledge of the Vedas as well as magic and celestial events. Because of this, he was given the nectar of immortality by the creator god, Brahma. By the time Hanuman, the monkey god and agent of Rama, discovered Seetha at Rawana's grand palace at Ashok Vatika, near our hotel in Nuwara Eliya, the king had to escape with the princess. He flew Seetha on a winged chariot to secret caves and a tunnel system under the island. The tunnels are said to hold many secrets, including Rawana's tomb."

I ran to keep up with him. "The water of life is in Rawana's tomb?"

"Mmmph." Merlin walked faster uphill. "But where is the tomb?"

Running up to his side, I grabbed the guidebook out of his hands. "Rawana hid the kidnapped Princess Seetha in the mountain gardens of Ashok Vatika, but when the monkey god, Hanuman, discovered her, Rawana took her in a flying chariot to these caves. The Rawana Caves are built inside Rawana Ella Rock. On the other side of it lies a pool, where the princess bathed under a wondrous waterfall."

I flipped to a picture of the Rawana Ella Falls. I stopped and squinted at the grainy picture.

Merlin walked ahead toward the entrance of the cave at the top of the path.

Grey caught up to him. Marilynn and Arthur hurried in front me.

"Did you know Lord Shiva, the god of destruction, gave Rawana a divine sword? The sword could have been Excalibur," Marilynn said. "You see, at the trial, we found out a divine sword can kill—"

"A god." Arthur shook his head. "How could I not have any idea what my sword was truly capable of doing?"

"We never needed it in such a manner," Merlin said. "Until now."

Finally, we reached the top. The entrance opened like a beast's mouth in front of us. Almost no light shone from inside. I walked slowly, trailing the others. Ahead of me, the trio lined up beside Merlin. All four peered into the large cave but didn't make a move to step into its dark mouth.

"I wouldn't mind having the god-killer with me now," Grey said.

"God-killer," a clipped voice cut through the air from inside the cave.

Robin Chaucer walked out into the light. Several men in

camouflage carrying heavy artillery walked out with him. They aimed the guns at us.

Robin smiled. "Now, that sounds promising."

SUDDENLY I UNDERSTOOD WHY THE TRAIL HAD BEEN SO EMPTY.

Not bothering to talk to the eerie-zombie Robin, Merlin chucked a vial at him. "Marilynn!"

Marilynn extended her hands. A yellow-colored wave spread out from her fingers.

"Muzzle her," Robin yelled. He held up a charm and a red wave exploded the vial Merlin threw before it got close to Robin.

One of the camouflaged men threw a vial at Marilynn. The ground before her exploded as if he'd set off an invisible bomb. She flew backwards with a scream.

Grey ran to get in front of her. "Marilynn!"

I edged closer to Robin. The camouflaged men took aim, the barrel of their guns set straight at me. Their fingers poised on the trigger for release.

"Do you really think guns will stop us?" Merlin sneered.

I took another step closer. "How are you still alive?"

Robin's blue eyes fixed on me. "Oh, he is not. You gutted him well. I am the new Robin." He smirked. "You'll find out, Regulars have a bit of magic too."

My brow wrinkled. "So you're a science experiment?"

He shrugged. "Magic. Science. Labels aren't important. What is important is our common enemy. We don't want an apocalypse."

"That is what we're trying to prevent." I strode forward. "Maybe you would kindly get out of our way?"

Robin shook a finger in my face. "Tsk, tsk. Not so hasty. We have a common goal but not a common plan. You see, we don't want Merlin digging in and creating the very apocalypse he claims to be trying to stop."

Merlin huffed in disbelief. "I *am* trying to stop it."

"Sometimes one cannot see what is in front of their own face. For example, my friends here thought you would probably to go the falls like all the other tourists. But no, I rather thought Merlin would like the idea of a musty old cave. You see, he is so used to being the wise one, he hasn't considered the other possibility."

Merlin scowled. "You make no sense. What else could I possibly want?"

"Power," Robin said. "Many men acquire power by creating the problem. War. Famine. Terror. It doesn't matter what it is, as long as their actions make them look like heroes—"

I took the last step.

"Now," Merlin yelled.

Grey and Arthur clamped on to Merlin. Grey put his hand on Marilynn. Her power flowed and a charm Grey wore around his neck lit up. He put out a hand. It blasted a wave through the camouflaged men.

Arthur pulled a small sword from his rucksack. He ran at the closest camouflaged man and disarmed him. As he moved to the next one, Grey and Marilynn charged the remaining two.

Taking the blade out of my pocket, I leaped at Robin Chaucer's clone. My blade did the rest. He fought back. We sparred. I sliced him. As he reeled, Merlin hit him with another vial he'd conjured from the pockets of his cargo pants.

Robin fell facedown onto the ground. Merlin caught my arm before I could do anything else to the unconscious man.

"It's over," he said. As I took panting breaths, he used a boot to turn the man over and kneeled. "He's out."

"For how long?" I gripped my blade tight. It hadn't tasted enough blood.

Merlin pulled me in close. "Easy."

Inexplicably, the Dragon's Eye twitched. It warmed as it drained excess energy off me. Still, I had to make an effort to lower my blade.

"Controlling this is getting harder for you," Merlin said quietly.

Bloodlust. I put a hand on the arm with the blade and held it tight to stop the trembling.

Grey, Arthur, and Marilynn hurried to us. Behind them, the camouflaged men lay in a broken mess across the dirt.

"Get into the caves before someone sees all this," Merlin said.

"No," I said. "Robin is right. We're not looking at all the other possibilities."

Merlin frowned. "What do you mean?"

"The picture of the falls. The shape of it, I've seen it before."

Merlin stood. "Where?"

"When I was in the portal at Adam's Peak. The picture in the guidebook. I saw the same waterfall. It *is* Rawana Ella Falls. Robin must have figured it out. That's why he said sometimes we fail to see what's in front of us."

Marilynn scoffed, "How can you know it's the same?"

"The portal gave me a glimpse and I have no reason not to trust it," I said, turning. "We can split up if you want, but I'm going down."

Merlin caught my arm. "You are not going alone."

"Should we split up?" Grey asked.

Merlin glanced down at the unconscious Robin. "No, we're stronger together. We will all go back down."

An hour later, we stood on a road in front of the falls. Clouds shaded the afternoon sky.

Merlin read from his guidebook, "The waterfall lies nestled in a V-shaped crevice in the hill. It cascades from a rocky outcrop above and falls about a hundred feet down over tiered boulders. Trees line the perimeter of a limestone bedrock. The legendary Seetha bathed at the base of the pool. Here, the water is blessed."

*Which is probably why people are standing knee-deep in questionable water.* I leaned on a railing before the falls. A few women in wet sarongs carried water in tin buckets. The soft twitter of monkeys on the grassy area of the waterfall called my attention. They roamed tiered boulders stacked uphill like stepping-stones, waiting for the giant monkey god who'd once stood there and scoured Rawana's realm for a lost princess.

Grey pointed to metal pipes installed above the pool to facilitate the flow of water and make a nice shower for bathing. "Looks like the blessed need a modern hand." He turned to me. "What now?"

"Now, we climb." Merlin came up carrying rope they'd bought from local vendors.

Arthur carried some too.

Merlin pointed up at the boulders. "That way."

We tied ropes around our middle and each other. The boulders turned out to be surprisingly rough. The climb went easily, but several minutes later, Marilynn and Merlin sat down on a damp boulder and huffed for breath. Slowly, we made it to the second tier near the top of the waterfall. Arthur led the group. He moved with relentless energy. I climbed just behind him. Since the encounter with Robin, I burned with excess energy too. Grey, Marilynn, and Merlin trailed behind.

I caught up to Arthur and signaled him to wait. Turning towards the others, I cast a worried look at Merlin. "He's spent a lot of himself the past few days."

"He's always pushed himself too far," Arthur said. "Ever since I've known him."

"How old was he when you met?"

Arthur smiled. "I was older. He was ten and two years, I think. Though he never seemed young."

*An old soul.* "I can see that."

Marilynn reached the top with Grey's help.

Merlin came up after.

"Ready?" Arthur walked onto a thin ledge that led us behind the waterfall.

A few steps in, a gush of water surged from the top of the falls and drenched us all with buckets of bitter cold liquid. We sprinted to the end of the ledge.

Merlin held up a hand for us to stop when we reached the other end. Water kept drenching the small alcove.

He pointed to an engraving on a wall of solid rock. "A horned deer. Rawana used a deer to lure the princess to him." He stepped back from the engraving. "I wonder if there's a cave behind this—"

Marilynn blasted the wall with a fireball.

# 13

## NINE WATER NYMPHS

"Marilynn," I said in protest as rock cracked and the wall fractured.

She shrugged. "I got tired of waiting—"

The rock crumbled. Another giant whoosh of water slammed down on us. Arthur yanked me into the darkness. I stopped at the entrance and the others piled on. I got squished in between Merlin and Arthur.

Hard thighs pressed against mine from behind and in front. I put my palm flat against a wet, lean back. Woodsy, aquatic scents mingled within the warm humidity of the cave. Cold drops tapped my head and a hiss sounded from somewhere down below us. Hard pellets of water shot up in a scattered burst as if we stood next to a sprinkler. Hands gripped my hips. I couldn't tell whose.

"Don't move." Merlin's voice cut through the noisy dark.

I asked, "Do we have a light?"

Fabric rustled as Merlin fished around in his cargos. His hand brushed my thigh. I dug my fingers and I gripped a masculine side. More sounds resulted. Then, light shone. Merlin held a glowing orb in this hand.

"Whoa," Grey said. "Don't look down."

I looked down. Just past our feet, a sheer drop-off showed a deep, dark canyon.

"Look," Arthur said from behind me. His breath blew against my ear. On the other side, to our left, liquid ran from the walls and out of the hole that had been our entrance.

Grey edged closer to the group. "Is this a good idea?"

Marilynn nodded. "Are we going to be able to leave?"

"We've come this far. We're not giving up now." Merlin let go of the orb and it floated in front of us.

It led us like a cheerful robot in the narrow path down a dark chamber. We walked carefully, making sure not to get too close to the cliff. A solid crunch made us all turn.

Grey lifted a foot and shook it. He pointed at the floor and exclaimed, "This is a skull. The creepy cave has human skulls."

"Ugh," I said. The orb floated higher to show a maze of stalagmites. Strewn along the path, several skeletons and scattered bones lay piled throughout the chamber.

"Look at this." Merlin pointed to a wall. Ten human-sized heads had been placed into the rock. On the fifth head, at the center of the grisly wall hanging, two upright stone slabs made the sides of a rectangle. It was topped with a horizontal slab to create a doorway. The doorway had closed red doors.

"Rawana's ten heads," Merlin murmured. "Ten heads for the four Vedas and the six Upanishads, which make up all knowledge of magic and celestial events."

"Wasn't he called the demon king?" Arthur asked.

We all looked at him in surprise.

His cheeks reddened. "I *can* read. It's just hard to get used to a new language. Your way of speaking is quite different."

Merlin walked closer to the door. "The winning side called Rawana the demon king, but in Lanka, he was a great king before he succumbed to his lust for a married princess."

Marilynn tilted her head. "Would you have kidnapped her?"

"No," Merlin said. "Vane would."

"Probably," I murmured, wondering if Vane had stolen Ryan. Before the trial, I would have thought so, but after sacrificing his power, I rather thought Merlin's greatest love was duty.

Merlin took out the golden cross. "There is a lotus flower shape on this door that matches the ridges on the cross." He put the cross against the circle.

Nothing happened.

Arthur and I stepped forward at the same time.

He said, "You need a candidate—"

"A candidate might be needed—"

We spoke at the same time.

Merlin grabbed my hand and pulled me close. He reached into my jacket and pulled out the blade I had strapped to my hip. Without warning, he sliced my hand.

I hissed.

"What are you doing?" Arthur stepped forward with a growl.

"Need candidate blood." He stuck my hand on the cross and held the golden metal to the door.

A whoosh sounded like a sucking vacuum.

The chamber shook and a doorway opened. On the other side, first darkness showed.

Then a roaring blue blaze lit.

Air whooshed again and a strong wind urged us forward. We all grabbed the closest stalagmite and held on as our bodies tried to go flying into the mouth of the fire.

Closest to the door, Merlin hissed, "It burns."

"Blue fire burns hottest," I murmured.

The fire completely blocked our way.

"What shall we do now?" Arthur asked.

"Besides trying not to die," Grey shouted. He clutched the same stalagmite as Marilynn.

"Hold me," she told him. "I need to get close."

Grey grabbed her hand. She stretched out the other one toward the door. "*Zamaka.*"

The fire protested. It winked in and out.

Grey pulled Marilynn back to him.

"No." She stretched out her hand to the door. "*Zamaka.*"

With a scream, the fire died. As the wind lessened, we let go of the stalagmites. Merlin drew another orb out of his jacket.

"Prepared, aren't you?" I said.

"Always." With a grin, he let the orb fly.

The glowing bit of light floated up high. It showed a tunnel past the quiet, and no longer blazing, doorway.

Arthur crossed to it. "Shall we see what we've found?"

He stepped into the darkness.

I followed him into what shaped into a narrow tunnel, but as soon as I took a few steps inside, my body began sweating. A rush of excitement and hunger filled me. I stopped and grabbed Merlin's arm. "There's something odd here."

Ahead of me, Arthur also stumbled. He leaned against a jagged wall of rock.

"I'm dizzy," Grey moaned.

Marilynn caught him. "I don't feel anything."

My grip on Merlin's arm tightened painfully. I shut my eyes. My heart strummed. I could only think of hunger and blood. The rush of the bloodied blade and... My eyes snapped open, wide and delirious. Need filled me and I shivered from a disturbing rush of desire. *Merlin.*

My nostrils flared at the musk-scented air.

"Grey, what?" Marilynn made a muffled sound.

He smashed his mouth against hers. It lasted a second. She blasted him with a glowing light. He fell backwards. She caught him before he cracked his skull on a jagged rock.

"Sorry," he mumbled before slumping.

"It must be a trial," Arthur said, keeping one hand on the wall. He stumbled back toward Grey.

Another wave of hunger rippled through me. I choked out, "What trial?"

The Dragon's Eye tingled in a weak burst of power. It was enough. My skin electrified where I touched him. In my mind's eye, all I could picture was pushing him against the wall and ripping off his shirt...and everything else.

Beside me, Merlin let out a hiss as if he could see every detail in my mind. His arm muscles tensed under my touch. Every muscle clenched.

*He wants.* I swayed closer and put my hand on his face.

He sucked in a breath.

Heat spread through me. *His and mine. One.*

My body throbbed.

A hand shook my shoulder.

"Eowlyn. Merlin." Arthur's sharp voice cut past the fog.

Like a cold shower, his voice sent a calm through me. I blinked. Arthur stood in front of me.

Arthur held Grey, with the help of Marilynn, who held up Grey's left shoulder. "It's a test of chivalry. We need to get out of this tunnel before we lose our minds."

Shaking my head to clear it, I squinted into the dark tunnel. I took a step forward, away from Merlin, but I couldn't let go of his arm.

Merlin lifted his arm. His hand touched my hair at my nape. He squeezed the strands like a reflex as if he couldn't squeeze the bit he really wanted. He said roughly, "C'mon."

Yes. I would have said 'yes' to anything. Shivers of pleasure shooting down my spine at even the smallest touch, I put one foot in front of another. Finally, we made it to the end and stepped out of the tunnel.

"What. In. The. Creepy. Hellfires?" Grey groaned, rubbing

his temple. He put his hands on his knees and dry heaved. "Is this what it feels like to be mind-altered?"

Beside me, Merlin took a long slow breath. "It's possible the tunnels are laced with some kind of chemical." He glanced my way but didn't meet my eyes, muttering instead, "At least we know the Dragon's Eye still works a little."

My body flushed cold and hot. *Dammit.* Did I admit I had a near overwhelming urge to run back into the tunnel?

As if he could read my mind, Merlin straightened. This time his eyes locked on mine and enigmatic brown pupils lit up with a certain smugness.

I jerked my gaze away to fall on Arthur. "You weren't affected."

His cheeks darkened in the dim light. But he said dryly, "I have some training. We spent entire years out on a campaign. One masters self-control."

*In the bedroom, he means, unlike you.* Eighteen meant something different in the Dark Ages.

"Yes, well, I suppose my *Keltoi* blood gave me immunity." Marilynn glanced at Merlin. "But—"

"My magic is diminished," Merlin said. "Or it was the Dragon's Eye."

I squirmed in place. Stupid tunnel. How much of my wants had he felt? My evil side snickered. *All of it.*

I glanced around at our surroundings. We'd come out into a closed cavern. Merlin's floating orb showed a small pool rippling at one end.

Marilynn stared into the darkness hidden past the orb. "What now?"

The orb shot into the water. Small waves glowed blue as the orb sank deeper and deeper.

Arthur pointed to it. "We go that way."

I peered into the pool. The orb bounced this way and that. "I don't think so. It looks like it's searching for something."

The orb shot out of the water. It moved deeper into the darkness, past the pond. We followed. Eventually the orb slowed as we came to another edge. The darkness lifted to show we stood at the edge of a cliff. It showed off an enormous cavern, big enough to house a small town except there was only one structure. From where I stood, we had a good view of a ceiling packed with stalactites pointing down like sharp fangs. At our feet, past the cliff, a large canyon showed more rock and a large pond. An island lay in the middle of the pond.

The island had monoliths erected, giant stones standing in a circle like Stonehenge.

"We found it," Marilynn breathed.

"We found something," Merlin said.

The island looked like a miniature replica from our vantage point. I pointed at it. "But how do we get down there? I don't see stairs."

"Or a path," Arthur said, going to the very edge. He peered down. "It has to be another test."

"Virtue," Merlin said. "The first test was for virtue. The second test is—"

I peered over the towering cliff. "Faith."

Arthur asked, coming up beside me. "How does one prove that?"

Merlin came up on my other side. "You jump." He shoved me off the cliff.

Then, he jumped.

I screamed. I free fell into dark nothing. Cold air blasted me. I shivered but the wind slowed my fall. Another gust of air slammed me with the force of a sledgehammer. I went down the canyon like a bouncing rubber ball carried by invisible force. Until it finally plopped me into water.

Inside the pond, I flailed. But regaining my bearings, I swam to the island.

Merlin fell in beside me. Recovering faster than I had, he

began swimming. Arthur managed to tuck and roll and landed on his feet on a rock outcropping that protruded from one part of the island. Grey and Marilynn both ended up in the water too.

At the edge of the island, spaced evenly around its circumference, nine stone columns rose out from the water. A stone roof lay on top of the columns. The entire structure resembled a rough temple. We waded through the waist-high water and crossed past the giant stones.

Arthur walked up. He knelt down to touch the rock. "Merlin, is it me or is this stone the same as the one I held Excalibur—"

"Ow." I cursed as a rock scraped my ankle. My skin tore at a vulnerable spot between my boots and cargoes. The sock at my ankle ripped. Blood dripped out onto the rock.

A rumble shook the island.

"What is that?" Marilynn exclaimed.

She pointed to white mist rising out of the moat at the nine stones. It surrounded us. The way the mist folded around the stones made an outline of a woman.

Grey groaned. "Is this another booby trap?"

The chamber shook as if to confirm his deduction.

"The stones are all women." Merlin glanced around at the nine monoliths. "In ancient Greek, the nine water nymphs, the Muses, the daughters of Hesperides, guarded the isle of immortality. During Camelot, nine stood for the nine Morgans."

I walked up beside him. "Nine Morgans?"

"Morgan Le Fay and her sisters guard the entrance to Avalon," Arthur said. "They are supposedly the ones who entombed me."

"Arthur was entombed inside the rock that held Excalibur." My eyes flew to Merlin. "If this stone *is* what Excalibur was forged with, then—"

"This is the same rock that fell in London?" Marilynn ran up in a panic. "Then does that mean this is another—"

"Trial," I said grimly.

"There's a casket." Grey pointed to the middle of the dark enclosure, where the orb floated. A white stone tomb sat on a rock pedestal at the center of the island.

"Rawana's tomb," I breathed. "We found it."

Another rumble shook. The mist thickened.

Merlin muttered, "Rawana held the nectar of immortality *inside* his navel."

"The casket." I ran up toward it. "We have to open it."

The island trembled. As we hurried to the center of the monoliths, the columns moved around us. Not in a good way. They started sinking into the water. The roof began to lower.

"If we don't get out," Arthur said, "this place will crush us."

Merlin came to a stop at the foot of the casket. "First, we get what we came for. That's how we get out." He put his hand on the stone slab. It hummed. "There's a portal in here."

"Like the vortex? What are you waiting for? Open it." Arthur pushed at the top of the casket. It didn't budge.

"Marilynn," Merlin said. "Open it."

"*Gati.*" She uttered one word. The top slab flew off like a lid. The roof rumbled and the ceiling started coming down. Marilynn muttered another spell and aimed it at the ceiling. The falling roof halted in its tracks before it could flatten us.

Arthur peered into the casket. "It's empty."

We stared into a wide stone box, which held nothing.

"We are still in a trial," Merlin said. "We haven't proven our worth yet."

"What do we do?" Marilynn asked, her face strained as she kept up the roof.

I stared at the dark space. "Just like the cliff, we jump in."

Merlin directed Marilynn. "Let go."

Marilynn's magic cut off in a whoosh. Wind surrounded us

and a soulful aria filled the space as the Morgans sang. Above us, the roof came hurtling down.

A sharp rock fell from the roof and sliced my shoulder. I let out a sharp hiss. Strong arms lifted me up. Arthur threw me into the casket.

# 14

# RAWANA SENT ME FLYING BACKWARDS

I fell, plunging straight down into dark water. Just like I'd seen within the Dragon's Eye, the skies had gone dark. I swam in the stream, swallowing some of the water.

Finally, I made it to the darkened riverbank and stepped onto sand. I sat down and took hard, panting breaths. Above me, a quiet sky showed a fading sun. The moon had begun to emerge alongside a few stars. I didn't know where I was, but it seemed like I was alone.

"One cannot enter Elysium so easily, little one."

I was not alone.

I turned away from the water and looked up to find a giant, an actual giant almost three times the size of a normal man. He sat on a large boulder and wore a mustache and a pair of poufy, billowing, Arabian-style trousers. Two gold armlets decorated beefy arms. Tattoos of heads, five on each arm, had been drawn above the bracelets. A tanned naked chest rippled with killer pectorals and a strong neck. From a handsome face, in the middle of a wide forehead, his third eye winked at me.

I swallowed. "Rawana."

"You know my name." He tilted his head. Long dark hair

spilled over his shoulders. "Who are you? How did you come to be here, little girl? I await the sword-bearer."

*Ryan.* "I am the sword-bearer."

All his three eyes scrutinized me. "I would say you look too delicate, scrawny, but there is something about you." The third eye stared. "You have taken lives. Blood surrounds you." He smiled. "Maybe you are the one."

"Or I am," a male voice said. A splash came from behind me.

My head jerked back. Arthur rose out of the waters. His clothes clung to him, emphasizing hard muscles and tree-trunk legs.

"Or I am." Grey swam up. He, too, rose out of the water. He walked up and stopped beside Arthur. His dark hair contrasted with Arthur's, but the resemblance in their athletic physique was undeniable.

Rawana jumped off the boulders. He landed and stood as tall as an evergreen tree. The giant clapped his hands. "Oh, this is an auspicious day. Three champions."

I asked quietly, "How are you still alive?"

"One must pay penance for their misdeeds. You have found a piece of my spirit, left to guard this place."

"Guard? Who set you to protect this space?"

"The Lady, of course," he said. "She is the great mother."

A growl came from behind Rawana.

A big black lion jumped onto the boulder. Though a magnificent beast, the lion's ribs stuck out from malnutrition and scars covered his hide from body to leg. When I met his gaze, solemn and all-knowing, the Dragon's Eye sighed.

I squinted at the lion. Deep inside, I knew him. A gasp escaped my mouth. "Merlin."

The lion leaped off the boulder and bounded over to me. I put my hand on his mane and he rubbed against my palm.

My head whipped to confront Rawana. "What have you done to him?"

Arthur and Grey came up to stand beside me, forming a line.

"Tread carefully, *warriors*." Rawana drew out a scythe from behind his back. "I am not one who suffers slights. You will show me the respect I deserve."

He'd kidnapped Seetha in retaliation for an insult to his sister. My hand tightened on the scrawny Merlin. "Of course," I said lightly. "You will have to excuse me. I did not mean to cause offense. I would like to know why Merlin is in this form."

With a mollified nod, he lowered the scythe.

Another smaller growl came from the boulders. A yellow lion leapt off the boulder. A female with a shorter mane, she landed next to Grey.

Grey put his hand on the big cat head. "Marilynn."

She purred.

Sharp teeth flashed. Rawana smiled. "Their magic has changed them to reveal their true form."

My stomach churned. The black lion looked barely alive. I stroked Merlin's matted mane. I had to find a way to fix him. "The water of life can fix him. Do you have it?"

Rawana laughed. "The River Lethe, the stream of oblivion and mortal life."

I stared out at the gushing river. "This is it? It's so big."

"If you bathe in the river, you will be cleansed. This is the place that heals." Rawana pointed to my torn shirt. The cut on my shoulder before Arthur had tossed me into the casket didn't hurt. I touched the spot. Nothing marred the skin.

"I will take him into the water," Arthur said, stepping up to Merlin.

The black lion growled.

Arthur backed up. "Mayhap, you should take him."

A hungry wind dove down from the cliffs past the rock and attacked giant boulders lining the beach.

"What is up there?" Grey took a step, staring up at an outline of trees at the top of the cliffs.

"This is the final resting place of heroes," Rawana said. "If you go into the forest, you may not come back."

"It calls to me." Grey moved toward the trees as if he were in a trance.

I hurried to Grey, fearing what he might do. Merlin trotted along with me.

Rawana stepped in front of us and thrust out a hand, making a stopping gesture. "You cannot enter. Neither can he." Rawana grabbed the black lion's mane. "This one is marked. He has taken a soul from Elysium without permission."

The lion froze at the touch.

Rawana pulled the lion's head up to expose its jugular and thrust the scythe against the vulnerable spot. "It is time to give another soul in return."

"No." I got in between the lion's mouth and Rawana. "You will take me, demon king."

Arthur strode up. "And me."

Marilynn, the yellow lion, bounded up.

Grey broke out of the trance and walked to the yellow lion. "You will have to take us all."

The tattooed faces on Rawana's arms went this way and that. He let go of the black lion and scratched his third eye. "We could make an exchange—"

The black lion leapt at Rawana and grabbed his wrist.

*Eowlyn*, Merlin's voice screamed in my head. *The navel.*

Not questioning the voice, I leapt at Rawana. Using momentum to grab his wrist, I stepped on his knee. He swatted at me, but I ducked and swung up the giant, holding the blade from my side in my free hand. As if taking an ancient jewel from a wall of rock, I carved out a gold ball from Rawana's exposed navel.

The golden ball fell to the ground.

I dropped off Rawana. I reached for it.

Rawana sent me flying backwards. He straightened. All three eyes glowed gold.

Marilynn attacked Rawana as Grey went for the golden ball. Rawana threw Marilynn at Grey, knocking them both down. Arthur ran forward and punched Rawana. The giant fell back a step but quickly recovered. He grabbed Arthur and tossed him. Arthur's head grazed a boulder, making a sick scraping sound. Arthur fell facedown on the ground. He didn't get up.

The black lion growled and leaped.

Rawana laughed. His eyes glowed with gold. He caught the black lion by the neck.

My breath caught. *Gold eyes. It can't be.*

"The golden apple does not belong to you," Rawana said in a different, deeper voice. "I didn't get a chance to crush you before, but now, you have wandered so willingly into my lair."

A chill froze me completely. The voice, deep and resonant, was the same one as Golden-Hainey. *How is it possible?*

Golden-Rawana lifted the black lion high, as if he were a scraggly pet cat. All four of the lion's legs dangled in the air as Golden-Rawana choked the life out of him.

"Eowlyn," Arthur said weakly. He rose up on his knees, clutching his bleeding head. He pointed to Rawana's feet. To the giant's scythe.

I darted to Rawana, who didn't notice me as he strangled the black lion. The scythe fit easily in my hand. I swung it at Rawana's knee, cutting deep into the tendons.

Rawana screamed and dropped the black lion.

Merlin fell back onto the ground with a dull thud. He landed with his belly up. He lay limp.

With a cry, I sliced at Rawana's other knee. His legs buckled.

He fell backwards onto the rocky beach. I moved swiftly. Stradling him, I stabbed at his heart.

Golden-Rawana's eyes burned bright just before they closed.

Above us, the sky let out a scream and rain began to pour. I got up and stalked to the giant's head to cut it off. Reaching his face, I stabbed down on the third eye. His huge hand stopped me before I connected.

Another hand wrapped around my waist. For a second, I expected to be ripped apart. The giant gripped me. Three golden eyes opened to lock on me. "Surprised? I am not dead yet, Gwenhwyfar." Golden-Hainey's familiar voice rippled down my spine.

A cold sweat broke out on my body.

"Always so quick to rise to the occasion." The god smiled with approval. "Though you are proving to be quite troublesome. I wonder how distraught Merlin would be if I crushed you."

My fingers gripped the scythe. "He will not care."

"You underestimate yourself, my champion. The Eye knows all."

I whispered to the Golden-Hainey, now inside Rawana, "Who are you? How are you here?"

"You are in the crossroads, a bridge between worlds." Golden-Rawana let go of my waist and pushed up on the freed hand. Three golden eyes locked on me. "As for who I am—you will know soon enough. It won't be long now. We are coming."

One hand still holding the scythe at bay, his other hand went around my chest. The giant crushed my ribs as he squeezed me tight. Stars ran in front of my eyes as I began to black out.

The river called. *Come, Gwenhwyfar.*

Golden-Rawana crooned, "Your time for a swim, my sweet—"

"No," Arthur yelled.

*No, Eowlyn. Fight*, Merlin's voice shouted in my head.

My eyes snapped open. I blinked to keep them so.

The black lion and Arthur charged the giant. Merlin broke out ahead and his massive jaws clamped onto the arm holding me. He shook the giant's limb, tearing at it like a dog with a bone.

Arthur leaped at Golden-Rawana. He hacked at the arm, severing it.

Golden-Rawana roared.

I stumbled off him. The severed arm's grip loosened and I thrust it away, gasping for breath.

Golden-Rawana rose. Arthur grabbed the scythe I'd dropped from the ground. He stabbed a raging Golden-Rawana, who clutched his severed stump. Arthur leaped up and swung the scythe. He got the giant in his third eye. The giant screamed. He stumbled and then fell, landing hard on his back on the ground.

The black lion continued to mangle the bloodied arm with its fangs.

Unconsciously, I touched the *Dragon's Eye.*

*Merlin.*

The black lion dropped his chew toy and bounded up to me.

Arthur came up and crouched down beside me. He lightly touched my hair. "Are you all right?"

I nodded.

He smiled, a golden glow emanating from him as if he had an orb inside him. I would have shrunk back, but it wasn't in his eyes. This glow came from love.

*Love? For Gwenhwyfar.* The black lion nudged its way between me and Arthur. A toothy mouth grabbed my arm and pulled me.

Arthur looked up at the beach. "I think he wants us to take him into the water."

"Marilynn?" I croaked.

My entire body had been squeezed and it hurt to even speak.

The black lion growled. *Me first.*

I rolled my eyes and put my head to his snout. "Even as a lion, you're bossy."

"I'll help them," Arthur said, getting up.

Feeling as if I'd taken a tumble off a mountain, I grabbed the black lion's mane and hauled myself up into a sitting position. I eyed the black lion. Would he let me ride him?

Arthur grabbed my waist and lifted me up. He set me astride the black lion's shoulders. He slapped the black lion's side. "Go fix him, Eowlyn."

Merlin grumbled at the treatment before trotting forward. I held on to his mane. About halfway to the water, I folded over and laid my face in the thick dark hair. We reached the end of the beach and Merlin hesitated at the edge of the water.

"I know cats don't like to swim, but you'll be fine," I whispered in his ear.

He put one paw in the water. He took it out of the water. He licked it.

*Take water to Rawana.*

I balked. "You want me heal him?"

The black lion shook its mane. *Yes.* The black lion turned. Merlin sprinted back to Rawana's body.

Arthur, Grey, and the yellow lion all looked up in surprise. They sat, resting on the beach.

I pointed down at Merlin's big cat head. "He wants us to haul Rawana's body to the water."

Grey groaned. "I'm too tired to be surprised."

Marilynn bounded over to a foot and clamped her huge jaws around it. Grey took the other foot. Arthur went to the shoulders and picked them up. I got off Merlin with effort and grabbed the giant's remaining arm.

Huffing and puffing, we managed to drag Rawana across the beach and into shallow water. Waves lapped at the big king. Arthur paced over him, holding the scythe ready. My entire body still hovered close to collapse, but I waited on the sand. The black lion paced with its hackles up close to me.

Finally, three eyes blinked. Rawana woke. Clear, non-golden eyes fixed on us. He asked, "Why have you brought me back?"

I stepped up. "We need information."

"My spirit is linked to the apple. Now that you have severed it from me, I will not last long."

It took me a second to realize he referred to the golden ball we'd taken from his navel. I went up to Arthur, who held it, and slid it from his hands. I walked back to Rawana. "We will return it to you."

He gave me a weak smile of surprise. "You defeated me. The apple is rightfully yours."

"What does it do?"

"I do not know. I was denied its vision. However"—Rawana tapped his third eye—"all the knowledge of the stars rests here. A young knight, Perceval, brought it to me."

I blanched. "My brother?"

Rawana blinked. "He was asked to keep it safe."

"By who?"

"The Lady came here later." Rawana grunted. "She also wished to see. To cheat fate, but the time was not right. The event was too far away. Now, you have come. The time is right. You must cut out the eye."

Arthur strode forward with the scythe and a dangerous gleam.

I stepped in front of him. "No, this task has to be mine."

## 15

## THE BLACK LION CAME UP TO MY SIDE

rthur gave me a long look, but handed me the weapon.

I went up to Rawana.

The giant put a hand to my face. His third eye fixed on me. "One to save it. One to destroy it. One who can change the fate of all. Which will you be?"

I kneeled down next to the giant.

"What about the lions?"

"The golden one will be fixed. The black one has defiled Elysium. He will not be forgiven so quickly." Rawana's hand fell away. "But I may use the last bit of my strength to make amends. I can restore the lion's soul or I can share the Eye. It will be your choice."

*The Eye.* I hesitated, glancing back at Merlin. *I'm sorry.*

He gazed back steadily. *I'm not.*

Rawana's three eyes teared. He rasped, "Hurry, warrior. You must cut it while I live. The water cannot keep me long. My strength fades." Rawana coughed. "Take the apple. You hold the heart of a star in your hand. It will be your guide. Take the eye, dip it in the River Lethe, and then, take it into your mouth."

I balked. "What?"

"Eat it." Rawana's body shuddered. "Now, warrior."

I grabbed the scythe. With furious slices, I pried out the eye. It came stubbornly but I had the skill to hack and cut at flesh cleanly. Rawana held still, though his remaining eyes bled. Tears of blood streaked down his face. Long moments later, I held the slimy organ in my hand.

He caught my hand and held it. "Knowledge does not come without a price. Our paths are not mapped, they're made." His hand fell. "The father, he will know—"

"Wait," I cried. "Who will know? Who is the father?"

It was too late. Rawana's eyes shut. On his arms, the tattooed heads disappeared.

He was gone.

The black lion came up to my side. He nudged me with his mane. I climbed onto his back. His ears flicking backwards, he charged at the water. The cold took us. The black lion's legs moved as he swam, keeping us afloat. Wind blew, causing rough waves to take us. Above us, the sky dimmed.

I held the golden ball. Then, I plunked Rawana's Eye into my mouth.

Another wave swelled.

Rawana's Eye slid down my throat and my esophagus. The eye hit my stomach and hardened. Darkness engulfed me.

## Inside Rawana's Eye

My body had no weight. This was not the dark world.

This was the trial. I was everywhere, nowhere, and in a single place.

In the stars. I floated in space. The cold darkness marked by white burning stars that dotted the universe. Shiny balls of gas and dust spun around powerful stars. Then, a bright spot with its glowing yellow sun heated a small blue planet.

Home.

The solar system spun with a quiet serenity that soothed the restless soul. For once, peace reined in my body. I sat in a place far away, high up on the branches of a celestial tree. My planet stayed safe.

Then, a sharp light drew my attention. Against the canvas of space, bright pinpoints of light outlined a shape of stars—the hunter with a bow and arrow. He seemed to stretch, reach back to pull the arrow. On his shoulder, a red star dimmed as it died. Then, in fury, it exploded as the hunter pulled back on the string and released the arrow.

Fire and brimstone unleashed and a wave spread out from the dead star. A supernova shook the branches of the celestial tree. The tree rooted the galaxy with its tremendous power, but the dark wave caught me and sent me hurtling toward the yellow sun.

The celestial arrow flew deep into the heart of the yellow sun, charging it. Tentacles of fire flared out as the sun tried to absorb the impact of the supernova. Solar flares struck out with unintentional wrath. One tentacle, simple and clean like a whip, lashed at its fragile child. The flare penetrated the blue planet's thin barriers.

As I floated outside in the painting of space, the blue planet burned.

Collateral damage.

If I had form, it would have recoiled in horror. As it was, all I could do was to watch in the cold empty as the apocalypse engulfed my home. Flames burned land and evaporated the oceans. In seconds, all civilization melted. The slate wiped clean.

It was the end of existence. An extinction-level event.

Then, I spotted him. The black lion. As if we were still wading through the dark river, he swam to the burning planet.

I hurtled into the dark empty of space after him.

I landed on black rock, which I'd known as Earth. A scorched world once blue, now stank with sulfur and death. Nine stones circled the spot where I'd landed. The Nine Morgans. This was a passageway back to the crossroads. I could return to Avalon.

Out of the night, the black lion galloped through the air like a winged horse. It landed at my feet. Then, it opened its mouth to let out a roar.

An aria filled the air. The nine stones pulled together. Two vertical slabs and one horizontal one melded together to make a trilithon. The nine stones made three trilithons.

The black lion walked to the middle trilithon as if he knew where he was going. He shook his head at me, ordering me onto his back.

I ran and climbed up on him.

The golden ball was still clutched in my hand.

The golden ball glowed.

I rode bareback on the black lion, as it charged into the trilithon.

A white shimmer glowed inside the slabs of stone. A portal. We ran into the doorway.

I TUMBLED OUT, LANDING FACE DOWN ON A RED BEACH. SOFT sand kissed my lips. I lifted my head. In the distance, a familiar bridge came into focus. A brilliant sunset painted the sky in blood and anger. Darkness shimmered just at the horizon. Surrounded by red dirt on an abandoned beach, I stood at the bottom of a great cliff. On top of the cliff, a hilltop city showed. Rows upon rows of white stucco houses lined the hillside. In the evening, they glowed like orbs with dark blue roofs.

"This is new." Merlin's voice washed over me.

He climbed out of the water.

The Dragon's Eye heated on my neck.

He rose, completely dripping naked.

"Um." I turned my head away.

Merlin chuckled. "Don't tell me the bold Eowlyn is shy."

"I liked you better as a lion," I growled and lifted my shirt over my head. Thankfully, I wore a full-coverage bra.

"What are you doing?" came a slightly high voice.

I held out the shirt. "Helping you."

He took it. Fabric rustled for a few seconds.

"Where are the others?"

"I don't know. We'll figure it out."

A cold hand touched my shoulder. *His hand.* I didn't want him to touch more. But I needed it.

Merlin's rough palm slid down my spine. "Eowlyn, look at me."

"Are you decent?" *Say no.*

"No," he said softly.

I turned slowly. He wore my shirt around his waist. It covered him somewhat. *You look good.*

In the dim light, his cheeks darkened. He said in a husky tone, "You look good too."

My eyes widened. My hand flew to my neck. *The Dragon's Eye.* "You can hear me."

"Rawana wasn't completely right. The water of life healed after all." He reached out and picked up the ruby necklace nestled against my skin. "But it's still black."

His finger drew a circle on the gemstone.

I shivered. He could have been touching me. "Maybe it takes time for your magic to come back."

"Hmmm." His hand dropped from the necklace.

Trying not to feel bereft, I glanced back at the distant cliffs. "We should try to figure out how to get there. This place looks abandoned."

"One thing first." Hands went around my backside. Merlin hoisted me up.

In reflex, I wrapped my legs around his barely clothed waist. To keep from falling, my arms went around his nape and my front pressed into his naked one.

I whispered, "What's the one thing?"

"I'm done waiting." His mouth closed the gap between us.

Hot and cold shot through me. An uncomfortably hard pit in my stomach became forgotten as I plundered his mouth. His lips, warm and smooth, dueled back furiously. His hands on my backside squeezed and I moaned against his mouth.

The grind of tires driving over sand came to a screeching stop just behind me.

A dry voice interrupted us. "Welcome to Greece, kids. The home of the gods. I see you're already partaking in its pleasures."

My arms tightening around Merlin, I pulled away with stinging lips. I looked over Merlin's bare shoulder. I groaned. "Vane?"

From inside a big-wheel ATV, Vane wagged a finger. "Are you taking advantage of my little brother?"

At his side, Ryan's eyes were wide with vivid curiosity. "Did you find anything?"

Vane snorted. "I'd say they did."

Without dropping me, Merlin turned. He met his brother's gaze. "We found Fury. The end of the world."

Vane frowned. "What—"

The hardness in my stomach spasmed. My legs unfolded. I slipped out of Merlin's hold, dropped to the ground, and landed on my knees in the sand. My stomach twisted, eating itself from the inside out. I clutched at it and moaned.

"Eowlyn," Merlin cried. "What's wrong?"

"Rawana's Eye," I choked out. "It's still in me."

Then, I threw up.

# 16

## IT WASN'T A BAD WAY TO GO

"What the hell did you do to her?" Vane demanded.

Merlin knelt down beside me and put a hand on my back. "We found something left by the Lady. It's called the Eye. An ancient demigod gave it to Eowlyn...to eat."

My stomach seized and I heaved again. More vomit came out, though I didn't know how that was possible. My stomach felt empty, except for the hard ball inside, which refused to get out.

Ryan got out of the ATV. The sky darkened quickly as the sunset ended. Soon, night would be upon us. Another squeal of tires sprayed sand as an ATV sped to a stop near the first ATV. Grey jumped out of it. The headlights of the ATVs shone brightly on the darkening beach.

Merlin gave Grey a look of disbelief. "How are you here?"

"We're all here—Marilynn, Arthur, and I. Long story." He hurried closer. "What's wrong with Eowlyn?"

"Oh, gross." Ryan stopped at a distance. She switched on a flashlight. Its beam hit my face directly.

"Ah," I raised a hand to shield my eyes.

She quickly switched off the light. "Sorry."

I forgot about the light as my stomach clenched. I heaved again, only to emit a small bit of vomit. My throat burned with the effort.

Vane kneeled down. "This has blood in it."

"How do you know?" Merlin asked.

"I can smell it."

Ryan switched on the flashlight. She pointed down at the vomit on the sand. "He's right."

Streaks of dark liquid colored the mucus and mingled with light sand. I touched my stomach tenderly. A hard lump pressed against the skin from the inside, like a parasitic alien. "The Eye wants out."

Merlin's palm pressed on my back. "We have to get her to a healer."

"A doctor," Ryan said. "There has to be a doctor on the island."

"There is a hospital," Grey said.

I heaved again. This time the burn increased tenfold. Liquid flooded out of my mouth. My entire body shook.

Merlin held my hips, trying to steady me. "She's not going to make it to a hospital." He looked to Vane. "I still don't have any magic. You have to do this."

I coughed, throwing up more blood.

"H-How?" Vane said. "I can't just yank it out. It will tear her apart. Without enough magic to heal her, she'll die."

Another shudder went through me, my fingers digging into the sand. My knees sank in deep. My stomach burned and so did everything else. I coughed and more blood came out. I heaved more and more blood came out.

"She'll die anyway," Merlin said harshly. He waved a hand. "Ryan, bring Excalibur."

She marched up, holding the sword tight in her hands. "What do you want me to do?"

"Cut her stomach open," he said.

Her voice shook as she balked. "W-What?"

Merlin hesitated.

Through a mouthful of metallic blood, I tried to speak, but only a choking sound came out. *Just do it.*

"Vane has enough magic to keep her together until we get her help." Merlin squeezed my hip before turning me over. He helped me fall onto my back.

I landed with a soft swish onto the hard-packed sand. A cough burned up my throat, liquid like fire searing my throat. Blood came out of the sides of my mouth and I turned my head to let it spill off my cheeks onto the ground.

"Now, Ryan," Merlin said harshly.

"Can't we numb her somehow?" Grey asked anxiously.

Vane put a hand on my shoulder. "*Zanta.*"

My body shook hard, but red fire spread from his hand over me in a wave of power. Everything eased, and while I wasn't floating on a cloud, pain didn't consume me. It ached as if the pain belonged to someone else.

"Now." Merlin slid his hand over my bare stomach.

When had my shirt been pulled up?

Excalibur sliced through my skin.

I screamed.

"I thought you numbed her," Ryan cried.

"It's the most powerful sword in the world," Vane gritted out. "Made for cutting down a god, remember?"

My body shuddered.

Merlin held me tight. "Grey, get her other side. Hold her down."

Grey grabbed my shoulder and pinned me to the sand.

"Get the Eye, Vane," Merlin said.

"I don't know if I can hold both." Vane cursed. Letting go of my shoulder, he put his hand over my stomach. "*Uprari.*"

I screamed from the sensation of being skinned alive.

The hard lump in my stomach pushed and pulled before it popped out.

"I have it," Vane yelled. "Your turn, Merlin."

The world blurred. The sky, a dark river of stars, distorted.

Merlin cupped my face in his hands. "Just keep your eyes on me."

My lashes fluttered. I blinked, struggling to stay awake. My stomach was a box of pain too big to define. *I can't.*

*Yes, you will.*

On the cold beach, surrounded by the soft hiss of the ocean, wrapped in the smell of sea, it wasn't a bad way to go.

*You are not going,* Merlin's voice buzzed in my head like an annoying fly.

I tried to swat him away, but the fly held on with teeth. *Teeth which ate your stomach.*

"Stay awake," he commanded.

The engine roar of an ATV sounded. Though I couldn't see it, I could tell when it sprayed sand everywhere.

"Finally," Vane said. "Ease her into the buggy. The hospital..."

His words faded as my body suddenly seized. I choked.

"Merlin," Grey yelled. "Help her—"

"No." Merlin put his hand on my forehead. "It's all right, Eowlyn. Sleep."

My eyes closed.

I SAT ON THE DARK BEACH. WATER RUSHED UP. FOAM AND SEAWEED tangled my toes. A wave slid up to my thighs. Oddly enough, I couldn't tell if the water was warm or cold. I wore clothes, but they stuck to my skin much like the seaweed on my feet. Their heavy weight sunk my body into the sand.

Very little light shone in the world. The outline of a towering cliff showed in dark grey. I was alone.

Then something shifted in the water. Slowly a figure emerged.

He walked out of the water.

Of course, I knew who he was. Even though I couldn't see his face, I could barely make out his body, even if I'd had my eyes closed, I would know who he was—I would always know.

Water moved, the waves getting sharper as he walked closer. They fought him. But he waded through the current, knowing when and where to step, without wavering. He stopped just in front of me.

"You're here," I said. "You shouldn't be here."

Behind him, the water slapped the beach harder as if to agree.

He kneeled down. "Why didn't you tell me about this place?"

I blinked. "Because it's in my mind."

Reaching out a hand, he put it against my cheek.

I flinched at the unexpected touch. At least I could tell its temperature. "Your hand is ice."

"You did say I shouldn't be here." He smiled. "Do you mind?"

No. Part of me wanted to jump him. The only problem—I couldn't move. An inertia held me in place on the sand. I wanted to curl my toes into its softness. But I couldn't. My legs refused to move. I whispered, "What is wrong with me?"

His smile faded. "Don't think about it. Just look at me—"

No. My legs. My body. I gasped as searing pain racked my body. Overhead, a loud crack of lightning streaked in the black sky. Water all around me churned as a storm brewed. Waves rose high, as unrest and chaos invaded the black world.

"Eowlyn." His other hand came up and he cupped my face. "This is your world. You get to choose here. Choose me."

Wind picked up and swirled around us. My hair flew like a fan, hitting him in the face. It wrapped around me like a sickness, suffocating and without mercy. Pain centered around my middle. I put a hand to my stomach, only to meet with sticky wetness. The wetness wasn't water. My heart began to race. Panic seared through my veins.

My eyes fluttered closed.

Cold hands shook my face. "No, you don't get to give up now."

Trying to shut out the racking pain in my lower extremities, I took a shaky breath. "I can't—"

He didn't let me finish. His lips slid over mine. Cold lips seeking invasion.

*No, you can trust him.* My lips parted.

His tongue slipped inside, warm and wet.

Fiery hurt consumed everything else, but the little bit of him shut the storm out. Pressing myself closer, taking him in deeper, I reached up to hold on to his shoulders. My fingers found only bare skin. I swallowed on a gasp. *Are you naked?*

He smiled against my mouth. *Yes.*

# 17

# HIS EYES GLOWED WITH GOLD

I woke slowly. Cold met my bare skin. I lay inside some kind of loose material. No underwear. No bra. No pants. I was naked. *What the hell?* My eyes snapped open, only to tear up under the glare of stark white lights. I blinked hard.

"You're in a hospital," a deep voice said, coming from the side.

I turned my head.

Arthur sat in a chair by the bed. "You've been asleep for two days."

I was a mess...and basically a floating head. *But, oh...that dream.* "Why can't I feel anything below my neck?"

"You almost died," Arthur said in an unhappy tone. He pointed to my wrist. "The healers have you on all kinds of bags."

An IV had been stuck into a bulging vein just below my elbow. I twisted my head to the IV stand hung with different bags of clear liquids. It stood over calmly beeping monitors. One displayed a steady heartbeat. *Mine.* I tried to sit up, but my body was nowhere to be found. I eyed the IV on my arm.

"Don't," Arthur said.

I slanted him a look. "How did you get here?"

"The same way you did—a doorway appeared in the other-world of crossroads." He raked a hand through blond hair and rubbed a tired face. "In Avalon."

"You think that place was Avalon? Isn't Avalon where you were taken after...you died?"

"I don't remember." He leaned back, his muscled body filling the spindly hospital chair and making it bulge. "However, 'tis said to be an island of great power and restoration." He pointed to my stomach. "And you are somewhat restored."

I glanced down, only to spot the Dragon's Eye against my chest. "I'm surprised the doctors let me have this. You usually have to take everything off."

"It was Vane. Some sort of spell has made it invisible to them. He didn't think it would be a good idea to take it off you." Arthur stared at the gemstone necklace. "Guinevere never would take it off either. But then I knew why she wore it. She always worried about her safety. Even in Camelot, there was much intrigue."

"They were uncertain times."

"Like now." He leaned over and put his hand on my arm. "But I don't think that's the only reason for you. You want the connection to him."

*Merlin. Where is he?*

Arthur shook his head. "It is not good. You are in here because of him. I fear you do not understand that is how it always happens with him. It is his destiny to be at war. Trouble follows him, because he is one of the few who can do something about it. But you don't understand you are a soldier, a tool, and a weapon for him to use. Like me. Like Ryan."

I blinked. "What are you trying to say?"

"Look at where you are." The king gave me a raking glance from head to foot. "This is what happens if you trust him."

Though I couldn't feel much, I tried to squeeze my hands. A

tingling went up my arm as my body struggled to do the small action. "Where is he? We don't have time to argue with each other with what's coming."

Arthur shook his head. "Merlin was close to collapse. Vane made him sleep."

"Vane spelled Merlin?" I shook my head. "He's not going to like that."

"I didn't give him a choice," a cheerful voice declared. Vane strode into the white room, with slicked black hair and the confidence of a rampaging rhino. He marched close and picked up my hand. "I'm glad you are awake. Maybe you can enlighten us."

"Give her a minute to breathe." Ryan came into the room.

"We might not have a minute." Vane sighed. "Rourke is only getting sicker, gargoyles are following us, and now you are here. This isn't good."

"Where are we?" I asked.

"Santorini," Ryan said, "or in classical Greek, Thira. We are on an island in the southern Aegean Sea. About a hundred and twenty miles off the mainland. The place where one of the biggest volcanic eruptions in history happened during the ancient world. The eruption was thought to have inspired the story of Atlantis."

My head throbbed. I blinked—unable to do anything else over the complete numbness of my body. "We're on Atlantis?"

"The locals call it Thira." Merlin's voice sounded from the doorway. He wore a sweatshirt over regular trousers. I'd never seen him in something so casual as a sweatshirt. Merlin had always struck me as the sweater sort of guy.

Grey held his shoulder. Merlin leaned against him and Grey helped him walk with obvious effort. His face pale, he walked unsteadily to the bed.

I asked, "What happened?"

"I depleted myself holding you together," Merlin said.

"I'm fine," Vane grunted. "I did most of the work. He only distracted you."

Blake and Gia came into the room. Blake gave a goofy smile behind black glasses. Gia smiled determinedly under long red bangs, which were nearly the same length as her short hair.

Gia rushed up to my side and gave me a loose hug. "I'm so glad you're all right."

Blake adjusted his glasses. "You're just in time for the real treasure hunt."

I winced. Everything below my neck lay in a limbo of nothingness. "I don't think I can take more treasure hunting."

Gia patted my back. "You're not going to want to miss this."

*I seriously doubt that.* Rawana's Eye sat heavily in my mind.

"Oliver is after the Healing Cup." Merlin met my gaze. "Our old friend wants it so his father doesn't get it. We can't let him go there. We're going to need to restore me to full strength if we want to defeat what is coming at us."

Vane's boot heels clacked against the stone floor as he paced short steps in the tiny room. "Would you, almighty one, care to tell everyone what is coming at us?"

My head jerked to Merlin.

His head hung as if he didn't want to face it.

"The end of the world," I said quietly. "An extinction-level event."

Merlin reached into the front pouch of his sweatshirt. He drew out a small, hard ball. Rawana's Eye had hardened into a gross golf-sized ball covered with red solidified veins around its surface.

"Gross," Ryan said. "What is that?"

"It shows the future," I said quietly.

Merlin handed it to Vane. "Spell it to open."

"*Vivrnothi.*" Red light rose from Vane's palm and surrounded the shriveled eye.

Nothing happened.

Merlin blinked. "Maybe you have to swallow it again." He took the eye back from Vane. "What happened when Eowlyn took it into herself—it was incredible."

I shuddered. "Incredibly terrifying."

"Let's avoid the whole almost dying thing," Vane said. "We've had enough scrapes."

Ryan stepped close to him. "What caused this extinction-level event?"

"A massive solar flare," Merlin said.

"A superflare," Vane said. "I researched it after you told me. It's scientifically impossible."

"A whole day's research?" Merlin asked in a dry tone. "Anyway, do you really trust a Regular's predictions against—"

"Against a shriveled lump of something's eye?" Grey said. "Can't imagine why Vane's skeptical. Isn't it more likely that the Eye made you hallucinate?"

"It isn't a drug!" Merlin scowled.

Vane raised a brow. "You ate it and saw things. Sounds like a drug…"

"We both saw it. We both *experienced* it." I shuddered. "Like a virtual reality simulation that showed you the end of the world. The flare lashed out. Within seconds it evaporated the ozone and pretty much melted the whole surface of the planet."

Merlin waved a hand in my direction. "Exactly what I told you before she even woke up. If it was a drug, how could we have seen the same thing?"

Vane grinned. "It's a magical eye, isn't it? That's the magical part."

"You are impossible," Merlin bit out.

Ryan shook her head and glared at Vane. "This is how he is when he worries."

Merlin stilled, considering her words.

Despite the heavy conversation, I almost smiled. Merlin could also be super-grouchy when he was worried. I met Ryan's tawny eyes. "There is a reason why Excalibur returned to us. Which puts you at the center of all this."

"Which puts her in danger," Vane said.

Merlin sighed. "We are all in danger."

Arthur stood up. "I don't know what your 'scientifically' means. But I think we can all agree there are many things we couldn't have possibly imagined that have come true." He clasped and unclasped his hands. With a faraway look, he murmured, "Things of the past never really let us go, and the things of the future we never really see coming."

My head turned to him. The stark white hospital should have saturated his golden hair. Instead, it made it stand out more. Suddenly, I could see him as the king he couldn't remember he'd been. "You're right. We are lucky to have seen this before it's too late." My gaze flitted back to Merlin. "What do you think?"

"The Eye's prediction is real," he said flatly. "I don't need a crystal ball or a deep examination of the past to know we went to a place outside the mortal realm. I didn't imagine Rawana's sacrifice to give the Eye to us. I may not have my predictions, but I know people." He held up the hardened organ. "There was a reason why this was worth safeguarding by a demigod."

*Demigod.* The word sent a measure of feeling wandering down my body, an ache that forewarned of upcoming pain. "Do you think Golden-Hainey is still out there?"

"We need to find out," Merlin said.

In my head, I faced the cliff and water below. Taking a shaky breath, I brought myself back. "How?"

"The mission hasn't changed." Vane backed up to the wall and leaned against it. His hooded eyes fixed on Ryan. "We need to get Merlin healed up or he's useless in a fight. I am strong but he's Merlin. Eowlyn couldn't have wielded the god-killer without him."

Merlin's shoulders turned inward. "I hope we never have to do that again."

"She did what she had to do." Ryan faced Merlin. "She did what you would do."

He inclined his head in acknowledgement.

"Are you strong enough to go to the excavation?" Vane asked.

I blinked. "What's this?"

"Rourke's quest led us to the House of the Seven Gables in Boston," Ryan said. "And a trident."

"A trident?" I asked. "Like the sea god's all powerful weapon?"

"The magical trident showed us a woo-woo magical-type map," Blake piped. "It said to go to the Lost City of Thera. Or as they now call it, Thira."

"We landed in Athens," Gia said.

Ryan shot Vane a dark look, to which he shrugged. She said, "*Things* happened in Athens and the trident led us to—"

"The Parthenon flooded and nearly killed us," Blake interjected. "You should have been there."

"—a metal snake we still need to find a way to open," Ryan finished, giving Blake an amused look.

"Rourke can't wait," Vane said. "The poison weakens him more and more. We have vehicles booked to get into the excavation today."

Which meant I wasn't going. I nodded.

"You don't need me," Arthur said, "I will stay with Eowlyn."

Vane shook his head. "It's best if we stick together. We don't know what we're about to step into. Oliver tracked us to the trident in Boston pretty easily. Ryan is the sword-bearer, but you are too. She might need you."

"No. If these gargoyles are on the hunt," Arthur said, "Eowlyn can't be left alone and defenseless."

I wanted to contradict him, but at the moment, the only thing I could move was my mouth.

"I will stay," Merlin said. "You can go."

"You are the only one who truly understands all this. You need to go." I glanced to my side at the towering king. "I'll be all right."

Merlin's brown eyes fixed on me. "Can I get the room?"

Everyone filed out.

Merlin caught Vane's gaze as his older brother headed out the door. "Get the vehicles ready. I'll be down shortly."

Arthur left last, giving a reluctant look as he went.

Only Merlin remained. He walked to the chair Arthur had been sitting in and collapsed. "I don't want to do this without you."

"Because of the Dragon's Eye?"

"No." He leaned forward and took my hand. "Because of Eowlyn."

The floating ache that was my body heated at his words. "I didn't realize you considered me of any help."

He snorted. "You took down Golden-Hainey. You could have taken Excalibur and you didn't. You are the person I need in this fight."

In this fight. I should have been elated but instead it was exactly the opposite. I took a steadying breath. "I promise to get better for the next fight."

He squeezed my hand. "There is one other thing."

I inclined my head. *What?*

"We've been working to figure out what is coming at us and we have," he said. "But now I need you to figure out why Golden-Hainey woke Arthur."

"How?"

"Guinevere was always Arthur's—how do you say— Achilles' heel." Merlin let go of my hand. He placed Rawana's Eye on my palm and closed my hand around it. "I have an inkling that Arthur and this shriveled little organ are connected. Let him play with it. Use the Dragon's Eye to open it. Try Vane's spell."

My eyes narrowed. "What exactly do you think is going to happen if it works?"

"I have no idea, but his guard needs to be down. It won't be with us around."

"Why can't I just tell him?"

"To bring his guard down, sometimes surprise works best." Merlin reached up and cupped my face with one hand. "We need to find out. This is for the greater good."

I sighed. "For the record, I don't like this."

"Neither do I, but you've seen what's coming. If the end of the world wasn't enough, we need to figure out how Golden-Hainey fits in to all this."

I studied him. "What do you think is in that metal snake?"

"They found it in a temple at the Parthenon, said to be built by the king of Athens. He was the grandson of Erichthonius, who was half serpent, half human. Poseidon had sex with Medusa, one of Athena's priestesses, in the goddess' temple. But instead of punishing Poseidon, Athena cursed Medusa for the affront. She turned her into a monster—her hair became snakes, and she sprouted bronze metal wings too heavy to fly. Her eyes would turn anyone to stone. When Perseus killed her, her blood fell to the earth. Athena kept the blood and gave it to Erichthonius."

"The metal snake has blood?" My brow wrinkled. "How does that help you?"

"If we open it, maybe we find the next step toward getting to the Lady. Either way, it's worth a try. The end is coming, and we don't have a lot of information to stop it."

"Either way—don't die."

Lifting my chin, he kissed my forehead. His lips grazed my

skin until they reached my ear. "It's not my first plan. Because I really, really want to live."

It was a good thing my body couldn't feel anything, because I would have melted.

"Ahem," a throat cleared loudly. Arthur stood in the doorway. "They're ready for you, Merlin."

Giving my hand a squeeze, he left.

Arthur walked closer. "You and he have gotten...close."

I tried not to blush. *Maybe a little close, but not close enough.*

A nurse bustled in, and for the next twenty minutes, she fussed over me, fixing pillows and giving me more medicine. I began drifting off.

"Sleep," she ordered.

I fought the order. I had a job to do.

*Zap.* A spark went through me like a lightning bolt. My eyes snapped open. My body shuddered. The Dragon's Eye glowed red. Something was happening somewhere.

"Eowlyn." Arthur grabbed my wrist. "What is happening?"

While my body shook and quivered, I whispered, "*Vivrnothi.*"

Red spilled from the Dragon's Eye to the hard lump. Suddenly, the lump's mass increased a thousand fold. It threatened to crush my hand.

I blinked.

THE WORLD CHANGED. STARS FLOATED BENEATH ME AS I SWAM THROUGH cold, dark space like a giant god. I'd gotten back inside Rawana's Eye. But this time it didn't replay the origin of the superflare. This time, I drifted close to the little blue planet that looked like an overcooked marshmallow at a campfire. Not a soul in the universe seemed to remain. I held out my hand and tried to wrap it around the beach-ball-sized black planet that had once been full of life.

Instead, I fell. My body hurtled down from space onto the surface of the once-blue land. I set down on my feet without any sort of reentry burn. Returned to normal size, I walked a black land with the occasional stream of lava and glowing hot rocks. It was hell on Earth.

For a long time, it seemed, I wandered the wasteland. Until I reached a dune. The rounded hill wasn't empty. A man sat on top with his back to me.

The blond hair gave it away.

As he heard me approach, Arthur turned to face me.

His eyes glowed with gold. *Gods.*

18
———

# STOP FIGHTING, GWENHWYFAR

I gasped.

Arthur held out a hand. "You've come."

I reached for it and used it to climb up the black sand dune. "You can speak."

Apparently so could I.

"Of course," he said. His voice deepened. "You opened the doorway. I came through."

I stilled, his hand suddenly unfamiliar. "Who are you?"

"Arthur, of course." He smiled easily. "I would never lie to you, Eowlyn. You are one of mine. He"—Arthur tapped his forehead—"is very impressed with you. But that is no surprise for me." He wagged a finger in my face. "But this would have all been much easier if you'd just accept me."

The gesture sent a shot of fear down my spine. He'd used it before. *Golden-Hainey.* Everything inside me tightened, my breathing labored. "What do you want?"

"Welcome to Tarturus." He waved his hand around him. "I must say, I quite like my handiwork." He glanced around the barren wasteland. "Though I do think I should decorate. Some curtains, maybe?" He laughed.

"This is funny to you?" I gritted out.

"Of course not," he said in a silky tone. "This is plan B." He jerked my hand and yanked me toward him.

I avoided stumbling onto his lap and instead landed on my knees in front of his sitting form.

He pulled my face closer. "Because you wouldn't join me, I've got to work a little harder. But I'm never not around. This is a war, dear girl. One I intend to win." His free hand came up. His fingers tangling in my hair, he gripped my scalp. "But unlike your name, my patience is not infinite. You've cast your lot in with Merlin. Someone who will never truly care. You might want to rethink that—"

He waved his hand. The world changed again.

This time we stood below a cliff, much like the dark world of the Dragon's Eye. However, this place wasn't dark. On the contrary, this beach teemed with crystal-blue water. A wave built behind me. I stood in shallow waves.

Merlin walked the beach, but he hadn't spotted me.

I lifted my hand to wave, only to realize I didn't have a stitch on. Stark. Naked. Frolicking in the water.

But the Dragon's Eye and its dark jewel hung on my neck.

As if sensing the Dragon's Eye, Merlin's gaze turned out toward the water. He spotted me, but his brow wrinkled as if he couldn't quite make me out. He stared into the waves with intensity. He took a step forward to enter, but before he could, a girl ran out the dark mouth of a cave from the cliffs behind him.

"Matt," Ryan cried.

She wore a diaphanous toga-like gown that flowed like a wispy cloud around her.

Merlin hesitated.

The wind shifted. It came from behind me. I turned my head. A gigantic wave of water built as the sky swirled with a gathering storm. Darkness shadowed the world and closed in with overbearing malice. Turning back to the beach, I ran forward fighting the current of the receding water. Merlin.

On the beach, Ryan grabbed Merlin's shoulder.

His gaze remained on the water.

Around us, the wind picked up. The storm turned darker.

Ryan whirled Merlin around. "Wake up!"

He turned to her, his hand going to her face. Her hands reached up to tangle in his hair. His head bent. His mouth took hers.

In the water, the Dragon's Eye went red hot.

I stumbled and fell into the shallow water.

A sharp rock underneath pierced my knee. I gasped, tearing up.

A quiet hiss made me turn.

Behind me, the mammoth wave the size of a building built higher. I sat in its direct path, just before its watery mouth.

Slowly, I stood. I looked to the beach. I caught a glimpse of Merlin and Ryan, standing close together, before water hit me from behind.

I expected to drown. But the wave didn't bury me. Instead it sprayed over me in a light sprinkle. My gaze dropped. Water rose to my waist. Two hands settled on my hips under the water. Arthur stood behind me.

He leaned forward and grazed his lips along my shoulder, the completely bare skin of my naked shoulder. I tried not to react, but my body tightened anyway.

"Still think your loyalty is in the right place?" He bit my skin lightly. "Don't discount what I can give you."

The bite seared through me. A golden haze filled my vision.

I blinked to clear it.

But the golden haze grew instead, putting life in every cell and every molecule of my body. It hungered. Pain mingled with pleasure. The more I resisted, the more it consumed me.

"Stop fighting, Gwenhwyfar," a voice whispered. "Consider this a gift."

I let go.

My eyes opened to the white fluorescent lights of a hospital room.

Arthur stood holding my hand, his face ashen. Slowly, he laid it on the bed and stepped back with a shaky breath. He sat down in the hospital chair as if his legs could no longer hold him.

Energy flowed through my body. Every nerve hummed. Every cell. Every molecule. Life infused me. I sat up and swung my legs over the side of the bed. I wriggled my toes. The rough fabric of my hospital gown bit into my thighs and back. *I felt.* I stretched my arm up high and neither stomach or spine protested.

My eyes fixed on Arthur, who sat like a blond god fully occupying a tiny plastic chair. I let out a breath. "You healed me."

"Yes. I saw it. I saw you." Confusion lit his gaze, partially afraid and partially something... *other.* Arthur splayed his hands out in front of him and stared at them as if they were not his. "I healed you. But I don't know how."

The hospital lay only ten minutes from the capital city of Fira, on the western part of the island of Santorini. The city of Fira sat in the middle of the crescent-shaped island, along the edge of the ancient caldera of a submerged volcano.

When the volcano on ancient Thera erupted over thirty-five hundred years ago, it blew the island into pieces. On the modern island of Santorini, the city sat on a rocky cliff that rose high above crystal-blue water. The caldera could be seen rising out of the sea in a mix of green, red, and brown.

Curved white stucco houses crowded the hills and peacock-blue rooftops sparkled in the sun. A church with a blue-domed top clanged an old metal bell. The car turned into the private drive of a multi-level house.

Arthur got out of the sedan first. He held open the door and I climbed out a little unsteadily. He caught my elbow. "Are you sure you should be away from the healers?"

I squinted at the long, skinny house. It had to be a mansion, but it didn't look as if it could hold more than a handful of guests.

After going inside the house gates, the car stopped next to an open-air courtyard.

Merlin stepped out of glass doors that led to the infinity pool. He skirted the edge of the pool and crossed past cherry-wood patio sets to the car.

He stopped before me and raked a hand through his hair. "Eowlyn, let me explain—"

"I don't want to hear it," I gritted out. My hand trembled. Part of me wanted to take a sword and drive it into him. Another part wanted to throw him into the pool. My fingers curled into fists. I stalked past him before I decided the latter was better.

Had I just jinxed myself? I'd known about Ryan. I had truly believed him when he'd declared he was over her. Just past the glass doors, I ran into Ryan. She didn't look happy. And for once, Vane wasn't tied to her hip.

"I'm sorry, Eowlyn," Ryan said, turning red in the face. "We were at Akrotiri excavation. The snake opened and Merlin drank the blood inside. He desperately wants a cure, and then either Excalibur or this minotaur pulled me into his dream state. The minotaur chased me through this cave until I found Merlin. When he saw you in the water with Arthur, I had to get his attention." She took a hitched breath. "I thought we would all drown. I'm sorry. *So sorry.* I had to get his attention."

"You said the last part twice," I whispered.

*"I'm sorry."*

"That's three times," I said, but my shoulders eased. The steam had gone out of me. "You saw the dream? Arthur?"

"Yeah," she said with a half sigh. Her face colored. "And you."

Naked, she meant. My cheeks heated. "Where's Vane?"

"Apparently we acted out what was in the dream state in real life. Vane watched Matt kiss me." She winced. "Everyone did. V-Vane left."

"Oh." It couldn't have been pleasant. Vane had the same hang-ups where Ryan and Merlin were concerned.

Ryan's eyes dropped to the floor. "I honestly never... I don't know what I was thinking."

"Merlin kissed you." My hand reached up to touch the Dragon's Eye. The connection between us had conveyed desire and desperation. "I think the Dragon's Eye pulled me into the dream state."

"And Arthur?" Merlin asked.

He walked inside the doors with Arthur behind him.

"He was holding my hand when the Dragon's Eye woke." I glanced between the two of them, one with light shining down on him, one who remained in the shadows. I'd always liked the shadow myself. It was more comfortable, but I wondered if I secretly longed for the light.

Arthur looked at Ryan. "I need to see it."

Her brow wrinkled. "Excalibur?"

He nodded. "Please."

"This way." She led him off down the hallway.

"What was that about?" Merlin walked closer. "What happened with Arthur in there?"

I punched him in the stomach.

He doubled over with an *ompf* sound.

"I wish you hadn't done that." Vane walked in through the glass doors. "I wanted to do it. And worse."

"Dammit." Merlin straightened. "I kissed Ryan to get out of

the dream state before we all died in there. I needed to wake up and I couldn't reach you." His gaze met mine without flinching. "I wanted it to be you."

"I don't know if that makes it better or worse," Vane said in disgust.

My eye twitched. "Why exactly was kissing the only solution?"

Merlin colored. "I didn't have a lot of time to think. I had to activate the Dragon's Eye."

"Kissing Ryan activated the Dragon's Eye?" I said slowly. "How?"

He gave a sheepish look. "I had to create a strong reaction between us somehow. I did."

He'd been counting on my jealously. My nostrils flared. "*Ugh.*"

Vane crossed his arms in front of himself. "Is there nothing you won't stoop to?"

"I took it from your playbook." Merlin's expression turned stubborn. "It did save all of us."

"Which is why you're not dead right now," I said.

"Stop taking my lines." Vane scowled. He turned to Merlin. "Tell me you actually figured out something."

Merlin's face turned serious. "The dream state has the clue. I think it's an actual place. We need to figure out where. Examine the land masses and figure out where we should go next." His gaze fixed on Vane. "You're the best at tech. I need your help."

"Lead the way," Vane said.

He shook his head. "I'll meet you in Rourke's study in a few minutes."

Vane tilted his head at me. "Is that what you want?"

"I'll be okay," I said.

Vane squeezed my shoulder before he strode off. As soon as he left, I wanted him to return. My words were hollow. Being alone with Merlin was too much. I moved to leave. "We don't have to do this now."

He stepped in front of me, blocking my way. "Are we all right? Do you understand?"

"Those are two different questions." My lips pursed. I strove for restraint. "I do understand."

His lips tightened as he waited for me to say more.

But I couldn't give him more.

His brown eyes hooded. "What happened with Arthur?"

Immediately, my body tightened. I wanted to tell him, but it had been so...intimate. "I don't want to talk about it." *Not with you.*

Merlin closed the distance between us. A hand lifted up my chin. "You're angry at me, but I can sense your guilt. The conflict in you. You liked what he did. In there."

I jerked out of his hold and put my hand over the warm jewel of the Dragon's Eye. *Stupid necklace.*

"It saved us," Merlin said quietly. "My connection to you is strong enough for it to work, even when I'm not with you. That's good to know."

"Great," I snapped. "Glad we figured it out."

He sighed. "Eowlyn—"

"No." My entire body shook. "You used me. Like you used him. Like you used Ryan. Vane is right. Do you have any morals?"

"I don't have time." His hand went to the Dragon's Eye. He touched the surface of the jewel. "I'm sorry."

My fingers curled, biting into my skin. My breath hitched. "You can't be sorry. I'm not ready to forgive you."

Merlin's eyes lightened. "As you wish."

I ground my teeth. *Stop being nice.*

*As you wish.*

I rubbed my temple. He could be so infuriating. I sighed. "The healing was like..." I didn't want to say it.

His expression tightened angrily. "Mating—"

"No." I shook my head. "Submission."

Merlin let out a sharp breath. "What do you mean?"

"He had gold eyes in the dream state," I whispered. Not daring to say the word, I emphasized, "Golden eyes."

*Gods.* Merlin's voice burst into my head. Merlin stilled. His face paled. "Hainey's alive?"

"I don't know," I said. "He said he could reach me because of the crossroads."

Merlin blanched. "He knows about the crossroads?"

"Whatever it is we are here to do, we should hurry."

Merlin nodded. "We'll work all night if we have to. I have the landforms in my head, but Vane needs to write a search algorithm to find them."

My lips twitched as I suppressed a smile. I would *not* smile for him. "Search algorithm? Did the great hater Merlin just tech-speak?"

"Just because I don't like it doesn't mean I haven't learned things," he growled. "I'm not a complete caveman."

"Could have fooled me—"

He grabbed my elbows and his mouth swooped down. Lean lips pressed against mine and took advantage of the surprised parting of my mouth to slip in his tongue. Pleasure exploded where he touched. This time it wasn't some drunken dream but real. *Good.*

"It is good," he repeated, lifting his head. He took a step back and said quickly, "Before you hit me again, I just wanted to remind you...that it has been good since the first time. That hasn't changed. Not for me."

I bit my lip. I would not melt. I would. Not. *Bastard.*

# 19

## DO I HAVE TO GO?

"You bet it was good for him," Gia snickered. She and Blake came inside the house wearing swimsuits. She elbowed Blake. "See all the stuff you miss when you sit at the pool? First, Ryan. Now, Eowlyn. Merlin's a total degenerate."

Red rising up his cheeks, Merlin ducked his head. He strode off—or rather ran off—mumbling, "Have to get to work."

Gia grinned.

I sighed. "Feeding off our pain?"

Sobering, she turned to me. "Sorry, Eowlyn. But he deserves it. I can't believe I'm going to say this—but Vane is better for her."

Blake looked at Merlin's escaping back with a moony expression. "He is amazing."

Gia glanced around. "Where is Ryan anyway?"

The sound of hands clapping cut through the small alcove where we stood.

I glanced around. The alcove opened to a much bigger room where two women sat on a sofa. Grey's mother, Sylvia, sat with another older woman sporting a chic silver bun.

"That was quite a show," Sylvia said.

Grey came down the hallway. "You *would* enjoy a show. It seems you've been keeping in a lot of drama yourself."

Sylvia rose. "I know you're a little upset—"

"I am more than a little upset." Grey said. "When were you going to tell me I'm a gargoyle?"

My mouth dropped open. *A gargoyle?*

"Not just any gargoyle," the older woman on the sofa said. "He is heir after Oliver."

I gaped at Grey.

He shook his head. "Apparently, my father had some secrets."

"Dierdre." Sylvia turned to her. "Please, let's not assume the worst. We will find a cure for Rourke."

The older woman stood. "You are right. Rourke is my son, and if we have anything in common, it is we are stubborn beasts." Dierdre looked at me. "Welcome to our house party, Miss Patience. If you'd like to get refreshed, a room has been set up for you upstairs."

I gave the woman a considering look. "Actually, I am hungry."

Grey glared at his mother and crooked a finger at me. "C'mon, I'll show you the kitchen."

With a nod to the others, I followed him. Every line of his body held tense as he stalked down the narrow corridor of the house. I hurried on the stone floor, caught up to him, and put my hand on his shoulder. "What happened in Akrotiri?"

"I found out my father was Rourke's older brother and a half wizard. He was a gargoyle who never got *activated*." The last word he gestured in double quotes.

My eyes widened. "But you can become a gargoyle?"

"I am already becoming one." Grey ducked his head. "Something about acute sense of smell and sensing them even when they look human. I am transitioning."

He led us to a white room with a long counter stacked with various food. Grey handed me a gyro sandwich while he described the visit to Akrotiri, the buried ancient Minoan city which was currently undergoing excavation. Somewhere around 1500 BC, the huge volcano Thera erupted and blew apart Santorini and covered it in two hundred feet of ash and debris. After the group found a secret chamber, Grey told me Colin turned on them. Rourke's enforcer had signaled for Oliver. Rourke's son, who had been lurking on the island, nearly killed them.

"We beat Oliver by blowing up the roof and burying him in the buried city," Grey said with flourish. He took a huge bite of his sandwich dripping with white tzatziki sauce.

I chewed on a bit of bread and hummus. I'd been miraculously fixed, but my stomach still remained tender. "Kind of ironic, isn't it?"

"He's still alive," Grey grumbled. "That's more ironic."

We walked into Rourke's study. Vane and Merlin and Ryan peered at a large touchscreen computer. Colin, another gargoyle, sat on a comfy-looking sofa at one end of the room.

"What is the traitor doing here?" Grey thundered.

"Colin betrayed us, but he saved you," Rourke said. He sat behind a huge desk surrounded by large bookcases. Books went all around the grand study, placed neatly on floor-to-ceiling bookshelves with ornate woodworking. He tapped a large touchscreen on his desk. "This spot has to be it."

"No, something about it doesn't feel right," Vane said.

Merlin stared at the screen of serene blue water and landscapes in the distance. "It doesn't feel right to me either."

Ryan shook her head. "I agree."

Vane turned to me. He crooked a finger and motioned me forward. "Take a look at the following images side by side and tell me which formations seem correct from the vision." He tapped the computer screen. Two images, one marked A and the other marked B, sprang up.

"A," Ryan and I both said at once.

Vane touched the screen again. Two more images popped up, also marked A and B respectively.

"B," Ryan and I said.

"A," Merlin said.

We did about twelve more. Then Vane went back to playing with the computer. "Here…" He looked at Rourke and pointed to the touchscreen. "Is this correct?"

Vane turned the touchscreen to Rourke.

Rourke played the new sequences. "This is at least twenty nautical miles off where I thought." He leaned heavily on his cane to get up. "I'll contact the boat captain right away—"

*Thwack.* Rourke's cane smacked the stone floor. His body began to follow.

Colin woke with a start. He jumped up off the sofa. "Sire!" He ran to Rourke.

Merlin got to the gargoyle king first. Ryan ran forward too. The three hauled Rourke back in the chair.

"I can't feel my legs," Rourke gasped, his face pale and in pain. He clutched his arm and started to jerk in the chair.

"He's having a seizure," Ryan said.

Merlin stepped back. "Vane—"

"I'm here." Vane strode forward. He put a hand to Rourke's chest. A red sheen of light flowed from Vane to Rourke. Rourke stopped shaking. The gargoyle king slumped in the chair with his eyes closed.

"What did you do?" I asked.

Vane swiped a hand across his sweating forehead. "He's healed for the moment. But the poison must be getting worse. I don't know how long he'll last."

"Grey," Ryan said. "Get your mother and Dierdre. He's had some kind of stroke."

Grey hurried out. In a little more than a minute, he, Deirdre, and Sylvia were in the living room.

Dierdre crossed to her son and touched his face. "What happened?"

Merlin told her about Rourke's seizure, finishing with, "He needs bed rest."

Deirdre asked, "You've figured out where to go?"

"Rourke can't go," Vane said. "He won't survive it."

"You will take one of my men as our representative," Deirdre said. "If his uncle passes, rule will fall to Grey."

Sylvia nodded. "Grey needs to stay."

"I am going," Grey declared. "I'll get the cure for Rourke. I am not taking the throne."

"No," Sylvia cried. "I'm not losing any more children."

"I will go," Colin said. "I will protect him."

Vane snorted. "We are not taking a traitor."

Colin blushed a deep red. "I regret my actions wholly. I have always protected this family, and only acted as I did because I thought it was in the best interest for all gargoyles. I bear no love for Oliver."

"Nice speech," Vane said. "You're still not going."

Colin hung his head. "You have a right to mistrust me." He drew out a knife from his side. It elongated into a sword. "Allow me to prove my worth."

Vane put up a hand to blast a fireball at him.

However, Colin didn't try to move. He turned the sword over so the blade pointed at him and knelt. He offered the sword's hilt to Grey. "Run me through if you cannot trust me. I offer myself to prove my fealty."

Grey stiffened. He threw Ryan a *help me* look.

Ryan crossed the room. She took the sword from Grey. She examined the blade. Then, without warning, she arched the blade in the air and drove it with force at Colin's neck.

"Ryan!" Merlin cried in surprise.

The sword sliced a single blade of hair. His pupils dilated, but Colin didn't move.

Merlin cursed. "What are you doing—"

"Getting to the truth." I took a step and caught Merlin's arm to stop him from interfering.

Ryan held the blade against the back of Colin's neck. Colin stood still with a resigned expression, expecting a final blow. Ryan drew the sword back. The blade broke through soft tissue as she drew it back, leaving behind a thin red line of blood at the base of Colin's neck.

"He isn't lying. He *is* ready to die," Ryan said. She held the sword out to Grey. "Now you know."

Grey took the sword from her with an angry jerk. "You've been hanging around Vane too long."

A clap sounded from the door. Arthur leaned against the doorframe with a small smile. Gia and Blake hovered beside him with uncertain expressions.

"She is becoming a sword-bearer," Arthur said. "Wielding Excalibur is more than just hacking away at your enemy."

"And what exactly is more?" Vane ground out.

"More," I said, "is deciding who lives and who dies."

Arthur smiled. "You've always understood, Eowlyn."

My skin prickled. I could feel Merlin's eyes on me, but I refused to return the look.

"I don't know if I want to become *more*," Ryan murmured.

Grey lowered the sword and leaned on it. "You can get up, Colin."

"I may go with you?" Colin asked without moving.

Grey looked at Merlin. "Emrys?"

He gave a slight nod.

Colin stood, vowing, "I will not betray your trust a second time."

"Good," Dierdre said. She took a loud, shaky breath as she

looked down at her son. "Colin, please help me carry Rourke upstairs."

"I will come as well," Sylvia said.

Dierdre nodded.

Grey stepped in front of Sylvia with a frown. "Mom, are you sure? You could go to a hotel—"

"We're family. This is where I should be," she said. "I have not told you, but this is why I couldn't believe gargoyles would harm Alexa. Rourke helped us a great deal when your father passed away. I believe him when he says he did not know of Marla's and Oliver's actions." She reached for his hand and gave it a squeeze. "Leave the past in the past, my son. It's time to look ahead. I don't want you to go, but if you insist, then, help him if you can."

Dierdre gave Sylvia a grateful look.

Colin hauled Rourke into his arms. Dierdre led the way out with Sylvia and Colin following.

Vane leaned back against Rourke's desk. His eyes held an odd glimmer as his gaze fixed on Ryan. "When do we leave?"

"First light," Merlin answered. "Rourke arranged the boat for six."

"I'm going to eat," Ryan said. "Anyone want to join me?"

Though she didn't look at Vane, her voice held hope.

He didn't return it.

After an awkward pause, Gia and Blake said at the same time, "We'll come."

They headed to the door.

Grey moved to go with them. "I'll come too."

My eyebrows rose. "We just ate."

He grunted and thumped his chest. "I'm always hungry."

After they'd left, Vane straightened from the heavy desk. "I'm going to research what we might find in this mystery spot we're traipsing off to."

"Don't hold your breath," Merlin said. "Whatever we're on the trail of has been hidden for a long time."

Vane rubbed his neck. "There is something about it though. Something familiar." For a second, uncertainty flitted across his expression. "Something...not right."

"Danger is part of treasure hunting," I said lightly. "We are trying to save ourselves from an apocalypse."

"And we're going up against gods to do it." Masking his expression, Vane turned to his brother. "I hope you're up to it."

Merlin scowled. "What do you mean up to it?"

"You never want to get your hands dirty, little brother," Vane said. "Something about this place screams...dirty."

Arthur laughed. "You worry too much. You've got Excalibur, two sword-bearers"—his eyes found mine—"and a god-killer. We are well-armed."

"You always were cocky, Arthur," Vane said. "That didn't turn out so well at Camlann."

Arthur's expression darkened. "You know I don't remember anything of all that, but I've been given a second chance for a reason, Vivane." His eyes found mine. "I will not fail you."

Vane let out a snort. "You might not want to, but we all do things we don't want. You are here for a reason. I just hope that reason isn't against us. It might be best if you stay here." He glanced at Merlin before his gaze flitted over to me. He said in a curt voice, "I'll see you two in the morning." He walked out.

That left Arthur, Merlin, and me in the room.

Arthur took an uncertain step toward Merlin. "I am coming."

He said it as a statement but knew it was a question.

Merlin hesitated. Then, he gave a nod. "You are tied to this somehow and it's better if we all stay together."

"So you can keep an eye on him?" I asked.

Merlin shrugged. "Does it matter?"

"The reason doesn't matter, as long as I get to go," Arthur said.

I put my hand up to the Dragon's Eye. I mind-spoke, *Do I have to go?*

Merlin met my gaze. *I'm not giving you a choice.*

THE NEXT MORNING, WE WALKED ABOUT A THOUSAND STEPS FROM the top of the cliff down to a boardwalk area called the Old Port, a place filled with different boats and small cruise ships. I took in the grand landscape of the crystal water of the Aegean inside the red and green caldera, which lay a short distance from Fira. I could imagine at one time there had been no white city on a cliff. Instead the island would have stretched all the way past the water to the caldera.

Merlin grunted as he hurried down the last few steps. "Five hundred eighty-seven," he huffed.

"You sure you didn't miss one?" I teased, following him to the bottom. A tail whipped at me and I swerved to avoid the back end of a donkey.

"Why did the cable car have to be broken today?" Gia huffed, coming down next. "It smells."

"Fresh sea air with a hint of donkey dung," Blake said cheerfully, catching up to her. He tugged a strand of her short hair.

She swatted him away.

"Clarence." Merlin waved at the older wizard, who'd come down with three other wizards from Avalon Academy. Our eager head of the Wizard Council, Claudine, sent reinforcements. Clarence and the other wizards showed up in the middle of the night.

Vane, Ryan, and Arthur already stood on the deck, waiting for the boat Rourke arranged. Ahead of the trio, Colin and Grey spoke with another gargoyle, a girl named McKenna, who sported a straight bob and was dressed head to toe in black. Faced away from Grey, a small group of gargoyles watched the pier and stood in protective formation around the heir apparent.

I looked up at the long length of the white yacht. "The little boat Rourke arranged is not so little." With a grimace, I put my hand to my stomach. "I'm not sure I'm going to like this. The only time I've been on a boat before, I threw up."

Merlin stepped up behind me. His lips twitched as he suppressed a smile. "Want me to carry you?"

*I'd rather throw you down.* I tensed, still unable to get the picture of him kissing Ryan out of my head. I said primly, "I'm not sure how that will solve seasickness."

"At the very least, it will distract you."

"If you don't want him, I'm happy to do the task," Arthur said from below.

Heat crawled up my cheeks. I blushed.

# 20

# GUESS WHO'S THE MASTER WIZARD

Merlin scowled, though he hovered behind me as if he would actually carry me aboard. Part of me wanted him, but part of me was still upset. With a shake of my head, I walked up to the yacht and began climbing the ladder.

Arthur followed.

The yacht maneuvered out of the port fairly quickly and soon we left the crystal-blue waters of the Aegean Sea and headed out into the Mediterranean. I stood at the railing, half-hidden under a bulkhead to shade myself from the sun. Colin informed us the boat was a ninety-foot yacht that looked big enough to hold fifty, not just the fourteen of us. Colin explained it actually housed only twelve people.

Not that I would have time to enjoy the staterooms. It would take us six hours to get to our destination. Nor did I have the inclination. As the others ducked below deck to meet with the captain, Colin ordered the other gargoyles to stay with Grey on the upper deck.

Even in the quiet waters, only the fresh air of the sea kept my nausea down.

Then the yacht dipped. Acid in my stomach burst up. I grabbed the railing in panic, intending to throw up over the side.

*Easy. I can hear you panicking from in here. Is a little bit of water defeating the mighty Eowlyn Patience?*

*Shut up, Merlin.* Putting my hand to my mouth, I tried to control my roiling stomach. *This is worse than a plane. Also, why aren't you out here with me? You get motion sick.*

*But not seasick. I've been on plenty of ships in my lifetime.*

My grip on the railing tightened. *Well, good for you.*

*Close your eyes. You need to center yourself.*

*Why?*

In my head, he sighed. *Just do it.*

*Why don't you come out here and make me?*

A sharp image invaded my mind. It was on a beach in dark water. The same beach the Dragon's Eye had taken us to before.

A HAND TOUCHED MY BARE SHOULDER. THIS TIME, THE HAND WAS different. I turned and faced Merlin. This time, he was in the water. His face angled to show off sharp cheekbones and soft brown eyes. His chest was naked above the water, and like me, he probably didn't have a stitch on.

"Why am I here?" I asked him.

Merlin put a hand on my cheek.

I tensed, though the touch was warm.

He smiled. "You can feel that?"

I gave a slow nod.

MY EYES SNAPPED OPENED. *HOW? WHAT?* I BLINKED, UNABLE TO believe it. I'd just been in a waking dream. *Did Merlin just*

*conjure the dark world?* The dark world only came to me when it wanted and he had called it at will.

*Guess who's the master wizard?* His smug voice sounded in my head.

Caught up in my own mind, a swell caught me off-guard. I fell against the railing as the yacht bobbed in the water. Above me, the sky had turned dark and the waves turned choppy. Acid shot up my throat like a volcano, but nothing came out. My motion sickness returning, I dry heaved against the railing.

"Does the sea call you?" Vane's voice carried across the deck.

But he wasn't speaking to me. My head turned to the nose of the deck. Through bleary eyes, I spotted him at the top of the deck with Ryan.

"No," Ryan said.

They stood several meters away, and as tucked into the corner as I was, I doubted they saw me. I opened my mouth to alert them.

"Do you know how easy it would be to toss you overboard? To give you to the sea? A creature such as you would be a bountiful sacrifice." Vane stepped close to Ryan, who faced out toward the water.

I squirmed in place. This was going to be a private conversation, and they were so focused on each other they hadn't seen me. I eyed the glass doors that led inside to an escape, but then the wind blew hard and the boat rocked like a giant seesaw. So did my stomach. My grip on the railing tightened and I tried to breathe.

"What are you doing, Vane?" Ryan asked.

"I am done," Vane exploded. "I'm done waiting. I've tried to understand you and my brother, but I'm done being—"

"Easy?" Ryan said dryly.

"Patient," he said sharply. "He always gets what he wants. Not this time."

Ryan put a hand on his chest.

Vane made a sharp sound and grabbed her hand, pulling it away from his chest. "No touching unless you're offering a lot more."

*Crap.* The boat rocked hard in the corner where I stood. *Get out.*

"I'm not," Ryan challenged him.

"I stopped in the club," he said. "I won't next time. I don't care who might be watching. I won't care if it displeases you."

"You can't displease me."

Vane stepped back from her, making a furious sound. "Are you trying to be *nice*?"

A wave rose high and the boat dipped where I stood. It went down fast and deep. My grip on the railing slipped. A hurricane force of wind and rain sent me reeling into the railing. My hand slid along a drenched railing.

"Ahhh." I flipped over the side. My hand held on tightly to the railing. My feet dangled in the air. "Help."

"Eowlyn?"

Vane's shout distorted over the noise of the sea. The boat rose up while the other side dipped. I struggled to hold on. A hand grabbed my hand and my shirt before I could slip. But before I could be pulled up, the boat dipped on my side again.

"Hold onto me," Arthur shouted into my ear as he held my shirt tight.

"*Uprari*," Vane yelled.

Water rose as the boat seesawed the other way.

I began to float a little.

Arthur hauled me up and over the railing easily. We both landed hard on the deck floor.

I pushed myself up on all fours. I moaned, "I'm going to be sick."

Vane and Ryan ran up.

Ryan knelt on the floor and put a hand over my shoulder. "I didn't think you had any vomit left in you after the last time."

I forced myself upright on my knees. "I didn't think so either."

Another swell made the boat rock. I let out a shaky breath.

"We should get inside." Arthur stood and pulled me up.

We hurried in through heavy glass doors. Vane shut them with a wave of his hand. Arthur sat me down on a long sofa in the boat's main salon.

Ryan stared at the storm. "What is going on?"

"Certain powerful forces are against us, I think," Merlin said, coming up an inside staircase. "The captain's having trouble navigating."

"You almost drowned," Vane scolded me. "How long were you out there?"

My cheeks turned red. "Long enough."

Vane's cheeks turned a ruddy red.

"It doesn't matter," Ryan said quickly. "The point is we can't go out on our own."

Merlin cleared his throat. "She wasn't. I knew she went up top. Then the storm started. It distracted me."

Arthur scowled. "You forgot about her."

Merlin said tightly. "Eowlyn is more than capable of looking after herself."

Vane snorted. "She almost drowned."

"*She* can speak for myself," I said. "Merlin's right. I don't need to be babysat."

Arthur said softly, "No, *lune*, this isn't about what you can handle, but how much more you can do together. That is what brotherhood means. That is the Round Table. That is who we are."

"Team Merlin," Ryan murmured.

Vane glanced at her and then turned to glower at his

brother. "Unfortunately, the one member of Team Merlin who isn't on it is Merlin."

Merlin exploded, "I'm not—"

The yacht pitched back and forth. A loose can on a table dropped. Vane shot a stream of magic at it and the can landed softly on the floor. "What you're not is being useful right now."

Ryan frowned. "Vane, you're being unfair."

"How?" Vane snapped. "His powers are gone but we are still doing his bidding."

"His power isn't all in magic," Ryan said evenly. "It's his guidance we're relying upon."

"You're blinded by his name. You always were," Vane snarled and gave her a heated look. "And I've had enough of it." He stalked past Merlin, deliberately hitting his shoulder as he brushed by him to the stairs.

Ryan move to follow.

Merlin stopped her. "Let him be. You're not going to be able to reason with him when he's in a rage. He'll only hurt you in his state."

Ryan whispered, "He won't hurt me."

"I wouldn't be too sure," I said.

Ryan whirled to face me. Hurt made her eyes huge. "Why would you say that? He adores you."

I fiddled with a sofa cushion. "Because we are alike, he and I. Always riding the edge and hoping it doesn't overtake us." I glanced around the luxurious room, at its soft leather sofa and gaming table. A grand piano stood bolted to the floor. I lay my head on a sofa pillow. "But it so often does."

"No one escapes the darkness completely." Arthur put a hand over mine. "We cannot bicker. If we do, we will all fail."

Merlin strode up. Putting an arm under my knees, he plucked me off the sofa.

I squeaked. "What are you doing?"

"I'm taking you downstairs," he said. "You look terrible. You were just released from the hospital. You need rest. We have two hours."

I would have protested, but when the boat teeter-tottered and my stomach roiled again, I clenched my teeth tight.

*Eowlyn*, Merlin mind-spoke. *Stop fighting me. Sleep.*

I woke up in a dark stateroom, nestled in bed and wrapped up in a very soft comforter.

"Sleeping Beauty awakens," Merlin said.

I sat up with a groggy yawn and stretched.

Merlin sucked in a breath. I glanced down. I had a sheet on and not much else. I squawked and pulled up the sheet to my neck. "How did I manage to wind up naked again?"

"Your clothes were completely soaked. I didn't want you to catch a chill."

I groaned. "Please tell me you got one of the girls or used magic."

He smirked. "I don't have magic and it's not as if I've never—"

"Ugh." I held up a hand. "Stop. I don't want to know about former exploits."

"Exploits? Is that what such things are called?" His lips twitching in amusement, he held out a rubbery suit. "Here, to go underwater. We'll need to dive below. Better hurry. It might take you awhile to put on. We're only half an hour away now."

He held out the suit, and when I reached to take it, he sat down on the bed. This time he didn't try anything, only looked at me seriously. I told myself I wasn't disappointed.

"Eowlyn," he said. "You can trust me."

With a shaky hand, I picked up the suit. "I am trying."

"I don't know what we'll find down there, but I don't want it to be like it was during the trial with Excalibur. You hid what you were going through then and it cost us. I don't want surprises again."

"You know what I know," I said.

"Have you not realized the golden-eyed man only appears to you? He has connected himself to you for some reason."

"*You are my Gwenhwyfar*," I murmured. "That is what he said. Whatever that means."

Merlin raked a hand through his hair. "Which is exactly how Arthur sees you."

A cold tingle went down my spine and I shuddered. "He is not the golden man. Believe me, I would know."

"He was when we were in the dreamworld," Merlin said. "Arthur is tied to this god. We can't ignore that either."

A giggle came from outside in a narrow hallway.

"Stop distracting me," Gia said as she walked past the open door. "We need to get our gear."

Blake followed her. "Just one more cat meme. You wouldn't believe this one I found..." His voice was drowned out under his heavy footsteps as he hurried upstairs.

"He likes her," I commented.

"Grey's already—how do you say—*blown her off*." Merlin stood up and stretched. "Blake is a better fit."

"Hmm." My eyes lingered on his shirt which stretched nicely across firm muscles. "I could say the same about you."

His eyes following the direction of my gaze, he grinned, "If you're trying to distract me, it's working." He stood. "I'll let you get dressed. But one thing first—" In a blink, he put a knee on the bed and pulled me forward. A hot, no-tongue kiss pressed against my lips before he stepped back. He eyed the sheet I held bunched at the top in my hand. With a disappointed sigh, he turned around. As he walked off, he called over his shoulder, "Be up in five."

I touched the warm Dragon's Eye on my neck. *Tease.*

*I'm just glad you didn't punch me.*

*I should have.*

My mind echoed with his chuckle.

It took me seven minutes to get the sticky, no-shape,

skintight diving suit on. I still didn't have all the buttons done when I ran out of the stateroom. I slammed straight into Arthur.

Catching my elbows, he steadied me. "Eowlyn, I am sorry."

I took a breath. "We're here, aren't we?"

"Yes," Arthur stepped back. He smoothed a hand down an identical diving suit. "This is surprisingly warm."

"I haven't gotten there yet." I put a hand to the neckline of my wetsuit that threatened to fall off my shoulder.

"Here." Arthur turned me around. He deftly did the zipper and tiny buttons.

When he was done, I stared at him in surprise. "You've worn something like this before?"

"Pulling on one's armor in my time took a great deal of patience." Arthur grinned, revealing a dimple and dancing blue eyes. "Also, I am not wholly inexperienced in the boudoir."

Boudoir meaning *bedroom*. Heat rose up in my cheeks. I did not want to picture the naked Thor of a man lounging in the... boudoir. I muttered, "You and everyone else, it seems."

Arthur smiled. "It's not what you think."

My cheeks heating, I said quickly, "Um, well, thanks. We'd better hurry." Turning around, I ran upstairs and away from the super-embarrassing conversation. Apparently, I was the only one with no *exploits* what-so-sadly-ever. I emerged from the lower deck to find Ryan and Vane glaring at each other.

"Your colossal ego is so frustrating, but I'm not getting into it," Ryan said. "I'm going to get my gear."

He frowned. "What gear?"

"*Diving* gear, because we're going *underwater*."

A small, harsh laugh burst from Vane.

"What is so funny?"

"You do realize you're traveling with wizards? Besides, do you really think where we're going any diving equipment will work?"

Ryan put her hands on her hips. "Seasoned divers can only go a mile. The depth of the Calypso Deep is somewhere around three miles—"

"You are being naïve."

Ryan bit out, "Why don't you explain it to me?"

"In the whole Mediterranean, maximum depths have been measured here. It's not a coincidence. Triton's Island has gone undetected because they know how to keep it hidden. I would wager they are more like five miles down."

"Five miles down in the cold dark," Ryan murmured.

An endless open sea stretched from the boat. We'd left the Aegean Sea and crossed into the blue-green waters of the Mediterranean. I glanced around at the landforms and they eerily matched the dreamworld. My eyes went up to the thunderous sky. Even that had been the same.

Merlin walked forward. He held something in his hand. "We should hurry. I don't like the looks of this storm. It's unnatural." He handed me a ring. Going to Arthur, he handed him another one.

"What are these?"

"They're spelled with magic." Clarence came up. He also handed out rings to everyone who didn't have one. "They'll allow you to breathe underwater."

"We'll pair each wizard with a gargoyle—"

"And one Regular," Vane said, going to Ryan.

I slipped on the ring and immediately started coughing. Suddenly every bruise I had on me, not to mention the line on my stomach where I'd been cut, burned as if I'd baked myself under the direct glare of an unfriendly. My epidermis flared and blistered. I fell to my knees and clutched my throat. My throat had closed and so had my nose. I couldn't breathe.

Ryan cried, "What is this?"

Merlin kneeled down beside me. "Eowlyn, relax. Just take a

breath—in and out. Breathe deeply. You'll need to get used to the gills."

I tugged at the neck of my wetsuit.

Merlin slid down the zipper that closed the suit up to my neck. Finally, my lungs expanded and contracted, and I took a breath.

Ryan turned on Vane. "You could have warned us."

"Don't look at me," Vane said. "Merlin got the rings."

Merlin gave her a sheepish look. "I've never used a mermaid charm before."

With a low growl, Ryan slid hers on.

"What happened to the easy life of a wizard?" Gia demanded.

"The charmed life," Blake chortled.

Gia socked him in the shoulder before slipping on her ring. Blake followed.

One by one, everyone went through the transformation.

"This is beyond words." Arthur pointed down at his feet. They had grown to almost twice their size and flared out just like fins.

I looked down. "I'm a fish."

"A mermaid," Merlin said.

Grey and the gargoyles slid on their rings. When Grey rose, his skin had turned blue.

"My turn," Merlin murmured. He slid his on.

Vane changed without any drama. Gills formed and his feet flared out. He didn't make a sound. His body didn't jolt under the strain as ours did. His reacted eerily, as if it had been waiting for the change.

"That is so unfair," Ryan said, staring at him.

However, his skin didn't turn blue, but an odd blue-green.

Ryan continued to frown. "But your skin."

He smirked. "I am the most powerful wizard in the world."

"At the moment." Merlin got up shakily from the floor.

I gulped at sight of a blue Merlin. I'd never loved the Smurfs, but suddenly I saw the appeal.

Grey pointed to Ryan. "What happened to your ears?" His eyes went to me. Then, to Gia. "All three of you."

Immediately my hand went up my lobes. They felt normal until I reached the top. They pointed in a tip.

Ryan had rushed to a nearby window. She screamed, "I'm a blue Vulcan!"

"Eowlyn's more of a green Romulan," Blake snarked.

I shot him an evil look.

"So is Vane," he added quickly.

I held up my hand and had to admit my skin, like Vane's, did look more green than blue.

Gia crowded next to Ryan. "I have them too."

Blake's snark turned to mush. "You look...brilliant."

Gia blushed. Her cheeks turned an odd purple, a mix of red and blue.

Blake's ears were completely normal. Ryan demanded, "Why don't you have it?"

"It must only happen to females," Merlin said. His skin had gone nearly blue. It oddly went with his dark hair and the color of his eyes had changed from brown to a purple-black.

I sighed.

Mckenna, the lone gargoyle female, put a hand to her ears. "I don't have tips."

Grey eyed her and blushed when she caught him staring. He cleared his throat. "It must be because you're a gargoyle."

McKenna nodded shyly. "I suppose, sire."

Arthur touched his ears. They were pointed. "I agree. The ears cannot be because they are female. I am not one, yet I possess them."

Merlin raised a brow and exchanged a glance with Vane.

An odd, amused light gleamed in Vane's green eyes.

"Does this really matter?" A blue-skinned Colin came

forward, carrying a sword. "Get your weapons. Let's get this done."

Clarence shrunk Excalibur for Ryan and gave it to her. She slid it into a hidden pocket in the wetsuit. Vane carried the trident they had found in Boston.

Merlin tucked the snake into his backpack, along with some bulky equipment. "A paging system for the boat to come get us when we're ready."

I patted a small pouch stuffed with emergency provisions on my wetsuit.

We all crossed to the railing. I took a breath. "We're really just jumping in?"

"Straight down," Vane said cheerfully, coming up beside me. An odd light shone in his green, catlike gaze—hungry.

It made me pause. "Vane, everything all right?"

He hooked a small light onto a clip I hadn't seen on my wetsuit. "I'm not entirely sure. It's all a bit hazy." He put a hand on my back and murmured, "But I think I've been here. Before I met you."

Vane shoved me into the choppy water.

# 21

# THE GOD ZEUS HAD A BULL

I managed to get into some semblance of a diving form and hit the water cleanly. Darkness surrounded me, reminding me eerily of the dark world inside the Dragon's Eye. The gem lay nestled against my chest inside the wetsuit.

A watery laugh came from my right side. I blinked but despite being immersed in the murky water, animals and plant life stood in clear view. The sensation of weightlessness hit me. It slid away all worry and fear, until only peace remained. The deeper we dove, the colder the water, the more my mood softened.

Ryan, Gia, and Blake laughed and did flips in the water. The deeper we went, the darker it became, but our eyes kept adjusting to accommodate it. Grey flicked bubbles at his sister. Grey, Gia, Blake, and Ryan began doing races, twisting and turning through the water. Some of the others had to be reeled in by Merlin as they tried to swim away with the brilliant swarms of sea creatures. However, no one seemed as easy as Vane. He swam farther and faster than anyone, including the muscled gargoyles.

We kept going down. I did another flip, but this time, a certain darkness in the water caught my eye. Vane had already seen it. He headed straight to the darkness.

An unexpected chill broke the easy revelry I'd been enjoying. I swam after Vane. He went up to an arch made of black rock and covered by drapes of seaweed. He pushed aside the curtain with a wave of magic. Through the opening, I peered out into a deep valley. A mountain extended up from ocean floor. Below us, two pillars, giant stone men holding a shield and trident, had been chiseled into black rock.

Merlin swam up beside me and pushed aside more of the seaweed to look through. He hissed, releasing bubbles in the water. *It reminds me of the pillars of Hercules,* he mind-spoke.

*Is it Aegae?* I asked.

*It's not made by sea creatures.*

*That we know of,* I pointed out.

*Let's find out.*

The rest of the group came up behind us. They also stopped to gaze out at the pillars.

Vane was already halfway there. He swam to the pillars without hesitation, stronger and faster than all of us. His words came back to me. *I've been here before.* I pushed out into the water past the seaweed curtain.

Instantly, the Dragon's Eye responded.

It quivered. *In fear.*

Beside me, Merlin tensed as he tuned in to the Dragon's Eye. *Is this a trap?*

*Possibly.* I grabbed his arm as the sensation soaked me and left me hungry for more. *Can you taste the energy?*

Merlin stopped swimming. *Careful.*

I didn't want to slow. I slid out of his hold and went after Vane.

The very water had changed texture. It slid over and around me like a slimly film, but the cocoon wasn't safe and welcoming. This was darker. The water drenched my gills with the most powerful aphrodisiac. *Power.*

I CUT FAST THROUGH THE WATER TO THE PILLARS. WHEN I reached its base, Vane had already landed on a ledge just below the stone men. Merlin came up behind me as the rest followed behind him. Up close, they did look like giants—Herculean—and I got Merlin's reference.

Vane stood between the two men but there was nowhere else to go. The stone men marked a little alcove without any other sort of opening. He glanced around. Then, he stopped and pointed up.

I broke open a small flare attached to my wetsuit. Light pierced the dark. I swam up. The ledge just above the pillars had a hexagonal opening. An entrance and definitely not natural.

*Eowlyn, wait.* Merlin's anxious voice burst into my mind.

I went into the opening first. A vertical tunnel went up endlessly. I kept swimming. Below me, Vane and Merlin followed. After a short swim, I came out into a pool of water. Complete darkness filled the space. As I was still halfway in water, the small light on my wetsuit only lit the water. I swam to the edge of the pool.

Grabbing the light, I lifted it high in the air. It revealed only more black empty space.

Vane, Merlin, and Arthur popped up out of the water.

At the edge, I moved to heave myself out. Merlin stopped me.

"Wait," he said in exasperation. "Vane, get us a bigger light."

Vane flexed his hand and created a fireball. Light shone and cut through the dark.

I was in a cave. A small, dark cave.

"There's nothing here," I said.

"Look behind you," Vane whispered.

I turned in the pool and swam to the ledge where he pointed. Vane held up the fireball. Two columns just like we'd come through held a tall red door. A gold carving of a bull had been cut into its middle, and all of it lay built into a wall of black rock.

"I dreamt about this," Ryan said. Having just come up, she waded at the center of the pool. One by one, the rest of the team popped up out of the water.

Vane heaved himself out onto rock.

I moved to follow and hissed when my hand brushed the jagged rock that made up the edge of the pool. Ignoring the small cut, I pulled myself out. Merlin and Arthur did the same.

"Stop," Vane said.

"Why?" I asked.

He lowered his hand so his fireball shone on the floor.

I gasped. Nausea welled up inside me, but this time it wasn't motion sickness.

Ryan put a hand to her mouth. She said in a pained whisper, "How?"

Merlin put a hand on her shoulder to steady her.

A mass of casually tossed human bones littered the ground.

Beside me, Arthur let out a low breath. "This is unholy."

Unholy or not, I walked into the horror, closer to the lone bit of light from Vane's palm. Merlin broke open a crystal light stick. It hissed and sparked but filled the chamber with more light. He knelt on the floor and picked up a human femur bone. He traced the marks along its length.

"Ridges and sharp scrapings," he said. "These aren't battle wounds."

Vane knelt down and picked up another one. "These people were eaten."

"Gross," Gia muttered from the edge of the pool. She and

the other gargoyles and wizards had come out of the pool but remained at the edge.

"Gross," Ryan repeated. She pointed to the door. "The bones lead back to there."

Merlin and Vane stepped gingerly past the stones and went to the tall red door, which looked to be at least twice their height.

Merlin touched one of the columns. "I feel as if I've seen it before."

Vane floated his fireball in the air. Grotesque skulls, like laughing masks, covered the top of the door. The skulls formed a triangle and had been attached to a triangular slab of stone that extended over the top of the door.

"We've seen this," Ryan said.

"Yes," Grey, Blake, and Gia said simultaneously before coming up beside me.

"It's a trilithon," Blake added. "Two stones on the sides and one across the top. Like the structures at Stonehenge."

"Like the trial for Excalibur," I said.

Gia shuddered. "Except limbo didn't have any skulls."

"Triton's been modifying the original design." Vane moved to stand at the center of the door. He stared at the bull.

Arthur squinted at the structure. "Trilithon, you say? I have seen it before too. The standing stones existed in my time. We used them to determine the seasons."

"Wait." Merlin marched to the side of one column. "There is something off here."

He took a step...straight into rock.

"Merlin." I went to the column.

He came back out of the shadows. He grinned. "Miss me?"

I glared. "What was that?"

He poked his hand into the column. It disappeared.

"How did you do that?" Ryan demanded.

"It's an illusion," Merlin said. "A trick of the light. This door isn't built into the stone. There only empty space behind it."

"That can't be right," Vane said. "I don't remember all this from when I came to Aegae before but there has to be a reason for this." He waved a hand at the door. "This is Triton's doing. I can feel it. I can smell it in here."

I touched the golden bull. "The god Zeus had a bull. He turned into it to seduce the Queen of Minos."

"Minos?" Blake frowned. "Didn't he create the Minotaur?"

Ryan sucked in a breath. "That's what I saw in the caves in the dreamworld after Merlin took the snake blood. I saw a Minotaur."

"King Minos of Crete built a labyrinth to hold the Minotaur," Blake said.

Merlin came up to the bull. "Santorini is an outpost of Crete and the Minoans. It can't be a coincidence."

Vane held up his fireball high. "We need to open this door. C'mon, my dear Scoobys, any thoughts?"

"We are not your Scoobys," Ryan hissed. "And didn't the Minotaur eat people?"

Vane smirked. "You *are* a tasty morsel."

"Helpful, Vivane," Ryan retorted.

Merlin peered over the golden bull. "If the bull is the lock, we need a key."

"And we have it." Vane drew out a compacted trident and lengthened it.

Ryan pulled out Excalibur.

"Everyone else, get your sword," Vane said. "We may as well try this at once. We hit it with all the magic we have."

Blake, Gia, Grey, the gargoyles, and the wizards all pulled out knives. Merlin waved his hand. The knives instantly became swords.

"No." I put my hand on Vane's trident. "We don't need these. There is only one key. Remember the snake?"

"Ah," Merlin said. "The sword-bearer. Ryan?"

Sword in hand, Arthur stepped up to the bull. "I can help with this." He sliced his arm in a neat cut. He dripped his blade on the golden bull.

The bull's head twisted. Light formed around the door. The faint aria of music came from the other side.

Arthur yanked me back.

"What?" I stumbled against him.

A gust of wind blew as the door opened and the fireball blinked out. Blinding white light shone from the door, and with a small plink, the aria became a full-bodied wail.

The soundwave knocked me off my feet. I fell. Arthur flew backwards.

Merlin fell beside me.

Vane grabbed Ryan, cushioning her as they both fell to the ground.

Gia and Blake were knocked backwards.

Beside them, Grey and the gargoyles let out a roar as they were slammed down.

The wizards had slapped their hands to their ears and they fell to their knees, writhing.

The scream continued, though my ears bled from its relentless wave.

Merlin and I were pushed to our knees. Even fighting against the noise, I couldn't move. Through a haze of pain, I lay helpless as men streamed out of the gate with gold shields.

The men wore ancient Greek or Romanesque uniforms with armor-breasted tops, red leather skirt-bottoms, and armored leg plates. On their heads, golden helmets extended down over their cheeks. The top of the helmet sported a ridge from which a short line of thick red hair fanned out. In a glow of platinum and gold, the metal they wore could have blinded us with its brightness. It made their uniforms seem more futuristic than medieval.

Not only were their uniforms the same, but they also looked identical, like an army of bodybuilding barbarians. They could have given Arthur a run for his money. One bulky barbarian broke from the pack and marched toward us.

Like Vane and me, green tinged the scary Thor-sized man's skin. A long red cloak fluttered on his back. Keeping his shield in front of him, the barbarian stopped in front of us.

"These three are not asleep."

He spoke in a warbly language, one I'd never heard before, yet I could understand him. Though unable to move my head, my eyes flitted around the cave. He was right. Everyone including Ryan and Arthur lay on the floor passed out.

This was not good.

Another bulky soldier, this one older, came up beside the barbarian-in-charge. He wore a gold chain with a small emerald. "They have gills." He touched my head. "Yet you feel the power in them." He put a hand on Vane's head and raised a brow. He moved on and set a hand on Merlin. There he paused. "This one is hard to read. There is great power, but it is...empty somehow."

"Look at his blue skin, Theras," the barbarian-in-charge spat. "He is a wizard."

Merlin let out a breath.

"He's breaking through the paralyzing spell. We should behead him now." The barbarian-in-charge raised his sword to strike.

*No.* I struggled in my invisible hold.

The barbarian swung his sword.

# 22

# THE FISHER KING

The Dragon's Eye heated inside my wetsuit. Power surged through me. I catapulted myself in front of Merlin.

The barbarian-in-charge halted the sword mid-swing.

As I fell, my limbs became paralyzed again. My arm stretched wide I knocked Vane's trident from his hand as I fell. I landed on the ground with a hard thud.

Just behind me, Arthur made a small sound.

The muscular barbarian took an angry step toward me.

"Leonidas, wait," the older soldier said. He knelt on the floor and picked up the trident I'd knocked from Vane's hand. "Do you see this? This one is a son of Poseidon."

"Fine," the barbarian said unhappily. He knelt down by me. "I'll take the troublemaker. You get the rest."

He hauled me up into his arms. Dark green mermaid gills opened in little slits from both sides of his neck. As he leaned down to look at me curiously, his eyes were oddly bright in the dark cave. They were green in exactly the same shade as Vane's green eyes.

Another soldier ran up. "Sire, there are fourteen invaders. Five are gargoyles."

Leonidas's arms flexed, squeezing me. He grinned. "Really? This could be fun."

Leonidas turned, and over his shoulder, I spotted another barbarian, a young one, standing over Ryan. He picked up Excalibur. "Nice sword for a little girl." The boy reached down to play with Ryan's hair and pet her face.

"Her blood. Smells tasty," he said. "This one is mine."

The older one knocked the kneeling soldier over with a foot. "Look at her ears, fool. You cannot claim her. She will go to the king."

The fallen youngster growled. Scrambling up, he charged at the older man. Leonidas moved, managing to position me over one shoulder, and reached the boy. He blocked him and, in a blink, drove his sword through the boy's gullet.

The older soldier shook his head. "Sire, he came from a good family."

"He was a stupid whelp and I should have gutted him long ago." Leonidas slid his sword out of the boy. The blade ran red with blood. "How did this one get invited into the service?"

"He managed to make it through training," mumbled the older soldier. "He was a skilled thief. Fed himself well."

"That is the problem." Leonidas grunted. "But my father will not listen."

"He will have to eventually, my prince," the older soldier said.

"We shall see." Leonidas grabbed Excalibur and hooked the sword in his belt. He patted my backside with his hand and crossed to the red door. Oddly enough, his ears were also pointed.

The door shimmered.

It wasn't empty but some kind of portal. Close up, the

shimmer turned out to be blue-grey water, as if we were looking into an aquarium tank, but no glass held the water at bay. Some kind of molecular barrier did.

Leonidas stepped into the water. My gills flared and flapped as they gave me breath. Leonidas flipped me so I was tucked against his hip as he swam up. We swam to white light. Behind us, the other barbarians carried the rest of the crew.

We broke through the surface of the water.

An island loomed before me. I'd seen it before. Inside the Dragon's Eye. I'd reached the dark world.

UNDER MY WETSUIT, THE DRAGON'S EYE FLARED. IT WENT RED hot. As Leonidas pulled me along in the water toward a white beach, the Dragon's Eye worked at the paralyzing spell holding my body.

I moved my toes first. Then my fingers. Finally, a little bit of feeling returned as Leonidas dumped me on the beach. I could move my arms. I tried to wriggle. If my legs moved, I could break free and run.

The bulky barbarian put his hand on my neck and pressed. "Sleep."

My eyes closed.

I woke up first in a grand ballroom. My legs were shackled, and my hands were held together by gold handcuffs. I was chained to a sleeping Arthur, who was chained to a sleeping Ryan. Twelve of us were held together. I didn't see Merlin or Vane.

Blake, Gia, Clarence and the two other wizards among us wore a small yellow amulet. All of them except Gia had gone back to their regular skin. The wizards had been stripped of their rings and thus, their gills.

We sat in a rectangular ballroom. A long strip of red carpet ran up a stack of steps to a stage that featured an empty throne of gold. Behind the throne, on a marble wall, a replica of the red door with the bull had been painted.

Except for us, the ballroom remained empty. However, it was an unusual room. Other than the one behind the stage, it had no walls. Columns made up its four corners. Curtain rods attached from one column to the next ran the length of the room. On the wall opposite from us, deep red curtains billowed in the wind. However, behind us, the wall showed an awesome sight of an entire thriving city.

We'd been placed just inside an open terrace. The view from our height, at least three stories up, showed more levels above. The building was the tallest and probably the most central one. Its levels fanned out from narrowing at the top to a widening base below. I counted another four or five stories above our level.

Blue ocean surrounded the city.

We were on an island, in an open pyramid. Aegae. This was Triton's home. The city spread out from the pyramid and went as far as the closest hillside. I reached out with my foot and pushed at a vine that wound up the Grecian stone pillar next to me like a snake. From the top of the pillar, water spewed from a wide stone pipe and trickled down, creating a beautiful water-fall that emptied into the pool of water. More vines stretched into the pool of water that ringed the perimeter of the terrace. Bright flowers in deep reds and yellows framed the terrace.

Below us, a moat surrounded the base of the pyramid building we were in. Pipes branched from the moat and seemed to carry water throughout the city. Looking out across its length, I could see every building had a vertical garden and at least one waterfall.

"It's like we're in the Hanging Gardens of Babylon," Blake said in awe.

Beside him, Gia yawned. The others began waking.

Ryan sat up groggily. "It's beautiful."

"We're doomed," Grey said. With a hard tug at his chains, he pointed to a barren hill in his direct line of sight.

In a highly visible spot on the hill, like a gruesome billboard, twelve thick, twentyish-foot poles displayed twelve severed human heads.

*Severed human heads.* I stood up on my knees to peer at the horrific display. Dried blood ran down the poles in streaks. In that small spot on the fine green lawn, no grass grew. The head at the center looked back at the city, at anyone who dared defy it. By the amount of flesh, though torn and battered as if scavenger birds had been pecking at it, the head looked like a new kill.

Beside me, Arthur woke. "They mean to intimidate us."

"Not just us," I said. "Their own people too."

Ryan struggled in her handcuffs. "This isn't good."

"We've got to get out of here," Gia whispered.

Ryan glanced up at the sky. It was painted red with the oncoming sunset. "We don't even know where we are."

The trumpeting blare of a conch interrupted us.

"Emerson, magic us out of these," Grey hissed.

"I can't do any magic," Blake hissed. "These necklaces must be charms to dampen our powers."

The coordinated footsteps of a march sounded. A stream of longhaired warriors entered the room through a red curtain. They took position around the perimeter.

More people began streaming in, about a hundred or so people dressed in a rainbow of colors and accented with jewelry and gold. Green-skinned men wore ponytails and togas with tunics. The thin shirts lent elegance to the simple bolt of the toga's cloth.

"Mermaids," one of Grey's gargoyles hissed. "They exist."

*They sure do.* I tugged at my chains, which dug into my

wrist. Mermaid women entered. They wore shift-like gowns, also made from one bolt of cotton. The dresses crisscrossed over their cleavage and left their backs mostly bare. Heavy gold brooches and clips kept the clothing in place. Both men and women wore gold bangles and headbands.

"Some of the women have pointed ears," Gia whispered. "So do some of the men."

The conch sounded again.

Soldiers entered. These soldiers strode in with more precise movements and wore elaborate black-plumed helmets. All of the soldiers resembled each other in physique. In the middle, a man with a crown strode down a thin red carpet.

The older man had long dark hair highlighted by streaks of silver. He strolled forward at the center of all the soldiers, and he wore a stunningly white tunic and toga. His gold crown held the largest emerald I'd ever seen at its center, like a jeweled eye.

The crown's ends curled up in the shape of a fish. On each arm, he also wore gold armbands. One armband was shaped like it was eating its own tail. One armband had the traditional picture of a mermaid, with its half-fish body. The mermaid held a trident.

"A fish and a snake on the king," I hissed. "Why is that familiar?"

"The Fisher King," Blake whispered back.

"Or Poseidon, the sea god," Arthur said.

A cold shudder passed through me. We were one step closer to the gods. Possibly one step closer to Golden-Hainey. I glanced at Arthur. *Is he still alive?*

A commotion pulled me back to the mermaids. The pale-green-skinned king strode to the throne and sat down. Hard lines marred an otherwise handsome face. An odd gleam lit his eyes when he spotted us.

The king said something that sounded like Greek, but I couldn't understand him. We must have looked confused, because the king barked a word. The emerald on his crown glowed and warmth washed over me.

The Dragon's Eye heated in warning but subsided quickly.

"How did you find the gate?" the king demanded.

*Universal translator.* Magic had its uses.

"Release us," Grey said.

A soldier carrying a pointed spear came out of position from against the wall and cuffed him across the head.

The king faced the court. "Where is my son? Why has he called us here?"

"Father." Leonidas, aka the barbarian-in-charge, strode up through a sea of attendants. People parted for their prince. He stopped at the center of the room and pointed a finger at us. "I have brought you potentials for the blood moon."

"Blood moon?" I repeated.

"The last one didn't go so great," Ryan whispered.

The red moon had been in the sky the night of the trial for Excalibur.

The king squinted at the gargoyles. "The beasts will make for good sport but you cannot think there is a champion among the scrawny Terrans?"

Leonidas marched to me. He hauled me up. I kneed him, but he shifted and I got him in the stomach instead.

With a loud *oomph*, he bent slightly.

Ryan jumped up.

Guards from the back of the room rushed up and grabbed her.

Leonidas grabbed me by the back of the neck and hauled me in front of himself. He roughly pushed aside my hair to show my ears. "You see, she will make a beautiful champion."

The crowd murmured. A few licked their lips with a sly smile.

I had an eerie premonition that *champion* actually meant *sacrifice*.

The king laughed and clapped his hands. "We are impressed, son. This a rare find. Especially in Terrans."

Leonidas bowed his head. "I am glad you are pleased." He pointed to Gia and Ryan. "In fact, we found two more of them."

This time the crowd clapped too.

Leonidas bowed. He shoved me back with the others and a soldier grabbed my bound hands to keep me still.

"But there is more. I've found a particular gift for you father." Leonidas waved a hand and the older soldier from the cave emerged from the curtain, making a grand entrance. He brought two more bound prisoners—Vane and Merlin.

The king stood up.

Vane's green skin was gone. The mermaids had taken away the mermaid charm. He wore a much larger amulet than the wizards chained to me. Merlin was also bound with another large amulet around his neck, but they'd also tied a leather muzzle over his face. A mass of bruises covered his face.

The king strode to the two. He stopped in front of them and closed his eyes to sniff the air. He eyed Merlin. "Power sits in this one, but it's oddly blocked. Nevertheless, he will make a good meal."

*Meal?* Anxiety rose up my stomach.

"What?" Ryan cried.

Arthur let out a hiss.

Leonidas took the Medusa snake from his cloak. "We found this on the scrawny one."

The mermaid king grabbed the snake with greedy eyes. "I thought it only legend," he murmured. The king stalked to Merlin.

The older soldier holding him, kicked at the back of Merlin's knee. Merlin dropped to his knees on the stone floor.

The king put a hand on Merlin's head. The jewel in his crown glowed.

I shifted in place. *Like the Dragon's Eye.* The king had a magical charm.

The king squeezed the top of Merlin's head.

Merlin shuddered and gave a muffled cry.

The king began sweating. "He is stubborn."

The older solider, Theras, smiled. "Not a match for you, King Lelex."

Merlin's mouth stretched in the muzzle. The Dragon's Eye heated as it heard his silent scream.

Vane struggled in his chains. "Let him go."

"His name is Merlin. He is their most powerful wizard. I could not get more. The block on him is strong." Lelex gave a grunt. He let go of Merlin with a disgusted sigh. "There is much in his mind, but it is locked away. What shall we do with him? As he is, he's useless."

"Give him to me, sire," Theras said. "I have a few things I'd like to try."

"You will not break him," the king said in a near-pout.

"I will be as gentle as you wish me to be, your majesty," the older solider said with a sly smile.

The king crooked a finger to beckon two soldiers. "Take him to the holding rooms. I will try again later."

Leonidas grabbed Vane and pushed him toward the king. "But this one—you must see it to believe it."

The crown began to glow on its own. Lelex touched the jewel. His green eyes glittering, he locked his gaze on Vane. "Interesting."

Vane gave him a mutinous look.

"Why are you here, wizard?"

"Why should I tell you?" Vane spat.

The king waved at us. "I can start killing off your people."

Vane said coldly, "They are not my people."

"Ah. They are Merlin's." The king's eyes gleamed. "You do not like that."

"We found this on him." Leonidas beckoned a soldier. The soldier handed him the trident.

With a cry of delight, the mermaid king took the trident. "I do not believe it. I am showered with gifts today." One hand caressed the staff of the trident, while he turned the artifact over in his other. "It has found us again." Lelex walked up to Vane. "This belonged to you?"

Vane's lips tightened.

Actually, Ryan had gotten it. I didn't dare look at her.

Lelex held the trident in one hand and, closing his eyes, he held his other hand, palm out, at Vane.

Vane shuddered, even though Lelex hadn't touched him.

The trident jumped in the king's grip as if it wanted to return to Vane. Lelex's eyes snapped open. He dropped his outstretched hand. "How is this possible? The Fisher King has marked you."

Vane blinked. "I am not Bran of Pellam."

Beside me, Arthur shifted in place. He knew the name Bran.

Lelex chuckled. "Bran the Blessed? No, you are certainly not he. He came to us also. It happened over a thousand years ago, but I know our history well. After he lost his kingdom, he came to my ancestor." The king sneered, "Yet he was no longer the Blessed. He came to beg for help. He was weak. Wounded. Defeated. My ancestor gave him more of a chance than I would have. He only had to prove himself. He did not even survive one challenge. Why would we help a creature like him? We are Triton's descendants. Son and daughters of Poseidon." The king held up the trident triumphantly. "*We* are the Blessed."

His court cheered.

Lelex turned back to Vane. "Bran of Pellam was not the Fisher King. His kingdom meant nothing. But you are marked. It is most intriguing. By rights, Poseidon should only mark a child of Triton. But he has marked you—a lowly wizard. Why? Why are you here?"

"We seek a cure," Vane said.

Lelex's eyes widened. "The Immortal Healing Cup."

Under his muzzle, Merlin shifted.

Lelex's sharp eyes fixed on him. "Is this your true purpose? You want to live forever? There is no such thing. If there were, Bran would not have been defeated so easily."

"It was not easy, but I defeated him."

"*You* defeated him?" He took another step closer to Vane. Lelex's eyes gleamed. "But how could it be you? He came to my ancestor. It was ages ago. You cannot be so old."

"Magic," Vane said. "I was frozen in a cave. I woke only recently."

Lelex startled. He glanced up at the fading light in the sky. "If that is so, then the sleeper has woken. Time grows short for us all. The day of reckoning is near."

Leonidas bowed his head. "It is why this cycle's blood moon sacrifices must be our greatest."

"Sacrifice," the people in the court repeated. They whispered. "Sacrifice."

Several faces looked out at the sky with fear.

Lelex slammed the staff of the trident on the floor to get their attention. "You see, my people, our cause is just." He held his arms wide and addressed the crowd, "The trident of Poseidon has come to us in our hour of need. *He*, the all-powerful-one, has come." The king went up to Vane and peered at him. "Poseidon will be pleased with our offerings. We have been given this boon. We will not suffer their fate." Lelex pointed a finger at Vane's chest, hovering just over his shirt.

Vane held his face blank.

"The mark of the Fisher King is upon this wizard. But he is a son of Poseidon. He will do great things for us. And his companions"—Lelex turned back to us—"they will be a wonderful addition to the blood moon games. We will give Poseidon a true prize and he will favor us again."

"Here. Here." The room shook as the crowd stomped their feet.

"Sacrifice," the court whispered. "Sacrifice."

I glanced at the others, who wore equally horrified expressions. Considering our chains, certainly the sacrifice had to be us. What was a blood moon game?

# 23

## TAKE ME AND YOU WILL HAVE ONE

Leonidas marched up to me and grabbed me by the hand. "It is thirteenth night. The maiden will make a most auspicious offering."

Grey and the gargoyles surged up.

A soldier rushed them and pushed them back to the floor.

Ryan glared at Leonidas. "What a Prince Charming you are."

Leonidas frowned in confusion.

Gia giggled.

Leonidas scowled, realizing he was being insulted. He moved to backhand Ryan. I stepped in his path and he slammed into me, nearly knocking me down. He steadied himself and with a scowl and drew out his sword.

Sure I was about to be run through, I took a step back.

"Leonidas," Lelex said sharply. "Do not spoil—"

Vane jumped the king. Using the chain of his shackled hands, he slapped them over Lelex and pulled him into a choke hold. "Release us or I will break his neck."

Near me, Leonidas's hand tightened on his sword.

The king croaked out, "I am a descendant of Triton. I am

Aegae. I do not mind dying honorably. But your friends will not die so well. Aegae do not surrender."

The older soldier pointed a finger straight at Ryan. "He watches that one very closely."

I moved to block him again, but a soldier rushed me first.

Leonidas grabbed Ryan and thrust a sword at her neck. He snarled at Vane, "Do you seek her blood?"

Vane's grip tightened.

Lelex made choking sounds.

Leonidas thrust the sword tighter on Ryan, cutting into her skin. "I will make her the sacrifice right now. Poseidon will be pleased."

With a frustrated growl, Vane released the king.

Soldiers grabbed him. One punched him in the stomach. With a pained grunt, Vane doubled over.

Lelex rubbed his bruised throat. "I should take your head, but that would be too easy." He looked at us all chained together. A sly smile lit his face. "The maidens seem to matter a great deal. This is interesting. However, Poseidon will not be pleased with a mere beheading. We will make it a duel. Our champion against yours."

Leonidas's face turning red, he let go of Ryan. He stomped closer to the king. "But, Father, the duel is over."

"You have won every game. You are Aegae's true champion, but you have never had such worthy opponents. A true champion needs more than easy victory. We must show Poseidon a great game."

Leonidas scowled. "Look at their skin. None of them could possibly be a champion."

The king waved a dismissive hand. "I have decided. So it shall be."

The court chorused, "So it shall be."

Lelex rubbed his hands together. "A great gladiatorial match is just what this tired kingdom needs to revive us."

"Gladiatorial?" Ryan blurted out, "We're not going to slaughter some poor animals, are we?"

"You are the poor animals." Lelex grinned. He pointed to the spike with the beheaded corpses on the hill. "A champion and a sacrifice are chosen. If the champion loses or dies, the sacrifice is Poseidon's gift. We do this each day until the night of the blood moon."

The king walked back to his throne. He told the court, "We do this to pray to Poseidon. So he will protect us from the upcoming wrath. We are on the precipice of the last stage of the cycle. The end is at hand. We have the same mission. The same reason you seek the Cup is why we pray to Poseidon."

The end was at hand. I stilled. It was what Rawana's Eye had told us.

Lelex spoke with impassioned green eyes. "Our purpose is true. We seek to ensure the Aegae live. Our island is hidden from their world, with only a few gateways to connect us. We see their airships pass over us, but they've never seen us. We are hidden, but we are not immune. Their world will burn and so will ours. Both will be tested. We must survive."

Murmurs of agreement came from the crowd.

Vane pushed away from the soldiers holding him. "Do you know what is going to happen?"

"The gods have not revealed it to us." Lelex gave a grumpy sigh. "We just know the storm comes." The king straightened. He sat down in his throne and turned to Vane. "Night nears and the game begins. You must appoint one champion and one sacrifice. Whom do you choose?"

I opened my mouth to volunteer.

Arthur beat me to it. "I will be champion."

Ryan said, "No, I will be."

"Such conflict." Lelex gave a gleeful grin. "Leonidas, you choose."

Leonidas looked at me. "She will make a good match."

"No," Arthur said forcefully. "You want an exciting match. I will make it worth your while. How long can a little girl last?"

I scowled at the last sentence.

"I have chosen." Leonidas glowered.

"Are you afraid?" Arthur goaded.

Lelex laughed. "I like this one for next time, but tonight the girl will do."

A soldier came out from behind Vane. He took a conch hung at his side and blew into it. At the trumpeting sound, everyone in the court hurried to the sides of the room. Soldiers pushed Vane to the side of the throne. We stayed in place. Two men in trousers but no shirts, presumably servants, rolled up the red carpet.

Lelex waved his hand. The jewel on his crown glowed.

Marble slabs on the floor shifted and retracted. The floor opened to reveal a deep pit and stands already filled with people. Another crowd had been waiting on one of the lower floors. The ballroom was the roof of a stadium.

I stared into a pit. "This is happening now?"

Soldiers rushed forward and brought bench seats for the court, setting up the area like private boxes at a sports stadium. A soldier unchained me from the group. Arthur tried to charge them, but he was subdued by two other soldiers. My hands and legs still bound, a soldier shoved me forward.

Leonidas whined, "But the maiden should be a sacrifice, not champion."

As I neared the king, Lelex's eyes fixed on me. He held up a hand for the soldier to halt. He peered at me closely before barking, "Theras."

The older soldier left Merlin's side to hurry to the king. "Sire?"

"Why does the maiden reek of magic?"

Theras crossed to me. He put a hand to my chest. "She has a charm. We could not take it off her, Your Highness. It is too strong. By its signature, I would say it is tied to the wizard Merlin."

Lelex's eyes narrowed. "Can she fight?"

"We have her source under control." He pointed at Merlin. "Fighting will not be a problem."

"This will be a good test then. We shall see how strong this magic is when she is defeated." The king faced Ryan and the others. "We still need a sacrifice."

Arthur stepped forward. "I will sacrifice."

"We must have a maiden," Leonidas whined.

"I will do it." Mckenna took a step out of the circle of gargoyles. The girl gargoyle wore her human face. "If you require a girl, I offer myself."

Grey made a sound of protest.

"Check her ears," Leonidas commanded.

A soldier stepped forward and checked. He shook his head. "She is no maiden."

McKenna's cheeks flushed.

Self-consciously, I reached up to touch my pointy ears. *Unbelievable.* My eyes met Ryan's and Gia's. They wore the same look of realization. Wasn't it embarrassing enough to actually be a virgin? Did we really need a magical indicator?

Gia glared at Blake. "Even you?"

Blake flushed.

Ryan nudged Gia. She followed her gaze to Leonidas, who also had pointed ears. Gia smirked. He glowered at the girls.

I snuck a peek at Arthur's ears. *Yep, pointed.* He caught my gaze. While my cheeks heated, his expression remained unperturbed.

Arthur stepped forward. "I am a maiden. I will take the girl's place."

Lelex raised his eyebrows. His gaze traveled over Arthur. "You are eager to die. Yet you have the look of a champion. We may find you worthy yet. There are many days of the blood moon celebration to get through. We will take the gargoyle girl today."

"But the first day must set the example," Arthur stated. "Take me and you will have one."

"This is a day of firsts." Lelex flexed his fingers. "I suppose you are correct." The king waved his hand. "Very well. Soldiers, take the girl aside." He pointed a finger, adorned with an enormous jeweled ring, at Ryan.

"What?" Vane exploded.

Lelex arched an eyebrow. "The first sacrifice must be female. This girl does not matter more than the others, surely?"

Vane returned a stoic look.

Ryan stuck out her chin. "I will gladly take the place of anyone in my group."

Gia squeezed her shoulder.

McKenna couldn't quite mask the relief in her eyes.

"Ah, but I think not." Lelex pointed at Gia. "We will take the other one."

The king faced them. "Prince Leonidas will be the Aegae champion. Who will be his sacrifice?"

Soldiers parted and a young mermaid with pointy ears shuffled forward.

"Good," Lelex said. "Once you do this, child, your family's honor will be restored."

The mermaid lowered her head.

"We are settled," the king announced. "The champions will fight until one concedes. You must both agree on the same weapon."

"Knives," I said.

"Knives," Leonidas said in disgust. "What kind of battling weapon is that? We duel with swords."

Lelex's gaze raked me from head to toe, a grudging respect shown. "No one has ever requested a dagger. Not one in my sixty years." He turned back to the crowd. "Usually we allow a coin to decide the matter, but we will make an exception. We will do both."

Theras, the older soldier, came up to me. He held out his sword.

Ryan thrust Excalibur at me. "She will take mine."

The older soldier sighed. "This one is well made. Excellently, in fact. I think I will keep it."

"It is for her." Ryan said, "She wants this one—"

"She can fight with any sword," Vane interrupted from beside the throne.

He gave me a look that said, *Trust me.*

I took the older soldier's sword. He unsheathed a knife from his side and also gave it to me. As soon as my hand curled around the dagger, peace came over me. Hope survived the storm. This would be a big one.

Leonidas picked up his sword and ran a finger along its blade. He sneered at Gia. "Prepare yourself for death, gargoyle."

For once Gia's bubbly face didn't reveal her emotions. She bit her lip.

I took a hard breath and tested the weight of the sword in my hand. It moved smoothly and lightly in my grip. Hopefully training with Vane and Arthur would pay off.

***

I circled the pit, sword in hand and dagger in a makeshift cloth belt on my hip. I wore no armor, only the torn wetsuit.

Leonidas circled me. The crowd roared with approval. He did look stunning. Under a thin tunic, his tanned skin glistened with just a touch of glossy sweat. The hard lines of his regal face had a dangerous edge. Firm legs balanced as gracefully as a cat. His lips were curled in anticipation.

He'd taken off his armor breastplate before coming down

into the pit. He wore a nearly transparent tunic that showed off hard muscles. He wasn't all that old, but he'd been tested. I faced a true gladiator.

Leonidas charge me and the battle begun. Our blades met. He studied me, trying me out with simple moves. When I blocked those, he changed to more complex forms. I'd seen a few before. A few we'd all learned in training with Vane at Avalon Academy.

The school seemed so far away in the dank little pit where I fought not only for my life but also my teammate's.

He was the superior swordsman, but I didn't give up. Leonidas's green eyes lit with interest as soon as I continued to find ways to thwart him. In minutes, he lost his sneer and began actually concentrating. A slight smile played about Leonidas's lips as if he was enjoying himself.

I gritted my teeth. Two lives on the line and he wanted to play. These mermaids were nothing like the friendly half-fish ones who only wanted two legs and a kiss with their true love.

Another few minutes of sparring and the crowd clamored for more blood. They cheered when Leonidas began using things around the pit—a railing or rock formation or jumping over the moat that went around the perimeter of the pit.

Leonidas thrust the sword at my stomach.

I moved just in time to avoid a major injury, but the sword still sliced through skin and scraped my hip bone. I stumbled back.

Around us, the people roared, probably drunkenly, at the first blood.

I blocked Leonidas's attack and swung again. Ignoring the burning pain at my side, I went harder at him. One thing I could do well was be relentless. I hit my blade against his, again and again and again. Fury and pain rode me until they blocked out all the other noise.

Finally, Leonidas kicked at my feet and my foot slipped in

sand and mud. I went down. Leonidas leaped, intending to skewer me.

I rolled out of the way. I hit a wall of rock and scrambled behind it. When Leonidas neared, I climbed the short wall and leaped down at him with my sword aimed true.

Leonidas jerked out of the way.

I'd thrust hard but my sword only cut his shoulder.

As I fell forward past him, the crowd cheered, "Leonidas. Leonidas."

"Our prince, our champion," the crowd encouraged.

Leonidas whirled and came at me on the ground. He kicked the sword out of my hand. It flew across the pit.

With a grin, he swung his sword at my neck.

I rolled on the ground, barely avoiding the sword hacking down at me. With my feet, I hooked his ankle and pulled hard.

Leonidas stumbled.

I rose and grabbed his free hand. I yanked to bring him down. This I hadn't learned during sword training, but Vane knew all the dirty tricks of actually fighting.

*You can do this.* My body broke into a sweat with the effort of pulling down the big mermaid. The Dragon's Eye flared under my wetsuit. My eyes took a dark haze. Almost as if I'd stepped out of my body, I grabbed the dagger out of the belt and sliced the prince's sword arm.

Leonidas cried out and dropped his sword. With a quick thrust of my knees, I used his falling momentum to pull him down completely. His big body flopped down hard. My dagger slipped from my hands, but I rolled over on top of Leonidas. I grabbed his sword.

Noise erupted all around from the seats of the pit, most of it booing. My world, however, quieted. I picked up the sword and lifted it high to drive the sword at his neck. The ground shook and I went reeling back as a stampede of feet charged at me.

A white bull ran past. My entire world narrowed to the rampaging animal.

*White bull?* I leaped out of the way to avoid a death charge.

Leonidas scooted out of the way, too, as the animal ran between us, snorting and huffing in a flurry of clattering footsteps. Deep scars ran along the animal's sides. The poor thing had been used a lot in the pit.

Leonidas jumped to his feet. Just before the bull passed, he grabbed a leather strap tied around the animal's neck. He hoisted himself on top of the animal. The bull bucked but Leonidas held on with impressive skill.

Still holding his sword, I planted it in the ground and used it to stand.

Leonidas managed to get the animal to turn. He charged me.

*The only animal will be you,* Lelex had said. Apparently not.

The innocent animal approached with its horns angled forward, ready to gore me. My choices being limited, I let the bull get close.

I let Leonidas's sword fly like a spear, low at the beast. The white bull tried to turn to avoid the blade. Leonidas kept his hand tight on the bull's bridle and at the same time slid off the animal's back so he hung on its side. He knocked the sword out of the air, letting it scrape and cut deep into his arm.

I moved to get out of the way, but the bull clipped me.

The blow knocked me hard to the side. I went sprawling to the ground.

Leonidas didn't waste time. He grabbed his sword from the ground.

Spotting my dagger, I speed-crawled to it. Grabbing it, I rose on my feet but stayed crouched. My knees still tucked in and staying low to the ground, I turned.

It was too late.

Leonidas leaped at me with the sword. He punched my jaw.

Pain exploded on my face and cheek.

I fell back. Leonidas skewered me with the sword. The blade went into my chest, just above my breast. I cried out. He didn't stop. He pushed until he'd pinned me to the ground, digging the sword into the soft mud and pinning me like a caught butterfly.

I didn't stop either. I raised up my elbow, pushing against the sword and allowing it to tear up my shoulder as I rose up off the ground. My other hand swung with the dagger. I plunged it into Leonidas's throat.

Surprise lit his eyes. He'd forgotten about the small weapon. He fell back with a gurgle. His bottom met the ground and his hand pulled out the dagger. He put his hand against his torn throat to stem the blood.

I wanted to pass out. But I couldn't stop. I stabbed him again. If I could have been outside myself, I might have seen my own frenzy and stopped it. Inside the haze, however, I stabbed at him until he didn't move. He didn't twitch.

Finally, my own blood loss caught up. Unable to hold it, the dagger fell from my hand. I didn't move from my spot on the ground next to the broken prince.

The crowd stood. A cry sounded from within it.

*So much for your undefeated champion.*

Theras and a few soldiers jumped from the first level of the stadium into the pit. They ran to Leonidas. The old warrior put a hand on the prince's neck. The hand glowed. "Sleep. We will save you."

Leonidas went limp on the ground.

The stadium went completely quiet. I waited.

Theras turned to me, his lips curled in half-horror and half-fascination. "What kind of creature are you?"

# 24

# A GIRL IN A WHITE TOGA

A floating disc shot out from the top of the pit. Three girls in white toga gowns came down. They ran to Leonidas. Two of them put a makeshift bandage over his widening wound. The third girl, wearing a chain with a small emerald, rushed forward.

"Leonora," Lelex said from above. "Can you heal him?"

Theras answered for her. "My daughter will certainly try."

The girl, Leonora, put a shaky hand on the prince. "The wound is deep. But I will try." She began whispering. A sweat broke out on her forehead and a green glow formed around her hands.

As she continued to whisper, I drew out Leonidas's sword from my shoulder with a hiss.

The girl shook and trembled while the green glow overtook Leonidas.

Farther away, blood flowed freely down my front. Theras didn't move to help me with magical green healing.

Suddenly, the girl stopped whispering. Her eyes snapped open. The green glow around Leonidas's body disappeared.

However, the prince lay still.

Leonora gave a distressed cry. "I am not strong enough."

Theras signaled two soldiers. They leaned down and picked up the prince. They hurried to the floating disc.

"Careful," The old warrior barked. Leonora went after her father.

Theras walked by me. He hooked a thumb at me. "Bring her too. The king should decide if he wants to kill her."

Another soldier picked me up. I was carried to the disc.

With a low command, Theras directed the floating disc up.

On the disc, Leonora leaned down and touched my front. "This is a clean cut. I can stop the bleeding." Her hot hands touched me and I cried out. Tears streamed down my face as the pressure tried to make me black out. My entire right side burned. When she finished, I slumped on the disc, my body limp and unable to move.

We reached the top. Theras pointed to Vane. "Him. The wizard can be the strength Leonora needs."

"Why would I help you?" Vane asked.

Lelex got up off his throne. "This is my son. Do it or die."

Vane gave him a silent stubborn look. "He is also your only son. Let us go and I will save him."

"Get me an outsider," Lelex snarled at his shoulders.

One soldier grabbed Ryan.

"Your choice, wizard. How many of your friends will you have me sacrifice today?" Lelex walked to Ryan and touched her hair. "Or just this one in particular?"

In a swift move, Lelex took a sword from the soldier holding Ryan and stabbed her in the stomach.

"No," Vane bellowed. He rattled his shackles and tried to run to her. Soldiers held him back.

On the floating disc, I tried to get up. Pushing up on my arms, I only slammed back onto the metal disc.

Lelex smiled. "It is as I thought. You care a lot about this one, wizard."

With a gasp, Ryan clutched at the sword killing her. She drew it out. The heavy blade clattered to the ground. She stumbled and half-fell, half-sat on the floor.

"Impressive," Lelex commented.

Arthur tried to shuffle to her, despite the heavy leg chains. Another soldier yanked him back.

Vane took a deep breath. "Take this gemstone off me. I will heal your son. Then, you will let me heal her."

Theras moved to go to Vane.

"No." Lelex waved him off. "We cannot trust you, wizard."

Vane's eyes glittered. "I'll do whatever it takes."

"Will you?" the king asked. "I have a way to strip you of yourself. You have it in you. Since defeating Bran the Blessed, you have a touch of the divine. You took his power. You can be a true son of Poseidon. You will no longer be merely a wizard. You can be Aegae."

"Become one of you?" Vane frowned. "How?"

"Once I turn you, you will always hear the call of the sea. It will infect your soul. You will feel nothing. You will know no warmth or love. You will not yearn or lust. You will be as cold as the water, as dark as the ocean. You will not need emotion." Lelex put a hand on Ryan's cheek. He caressed her face. "Would you do that for her?"

Ryan croaked, "N-No, Vane!"

Vane's eyes locked on the king with hate. "I would do anything."

Lelex studied him with a small smile. "I believe you."

Vane faced him.

Lelex walked to Vane. "Theras, bring me the trident."

The older soldier complied. Lelex crossed to Vane on the dias. "Kneel," he ordered.

Vane bent down.

"Vane," Ryan called weakly. "Stop."

The crown on the king's head began to glow. He set the

trident at Vane's head. Lelex's eyes brightened with green light. A wave went through the room. Everything rattled. Vane dropped to all fours. The trident glowed with green light, becoming brighter and brighter until it turned into a burning glare. Lelex fired the trident at Vane.

Vane fell backwards, unconscious, onto the marble floor. The green light blinked out.

On the floor, Vane's eyes opened.

"Unchain him," the king said.

The older soldier took the chains off Vane's feet with a wary expression. Vane sat up, his face eerily calm, its pallor now firmly green. Hunter-green gills slashed across his neck.

"Who are you?" the king demanded.

Vane frowned. "Who am I?"

"You are a soldier of Aegae," Lelex pronounced. "You are a son of Poseidon. I am your king and you serve me."

Vane got up on one knee. He bowed his head to Lelex. "I am a soldier. You are my king."

Lelex touched the trident to Vane's shoulder as if he were anointing him. "Your name is Vane. Rise." The king pointed at Leonidas. "Help your prince."

Vane made his way to Leonidas. Leonora stood waiting. She dropped to her knees and put her hands on the prince. Vane put a hand on her. She began whispering but this time no sweat beaded her forehead.

Vane turned pale. His green hue almost glowed but he wore the same bland expression. After a few minutes of the whispered chanting, Leonora opened her eyes. She sank down off her knees and sat directly on the floor. Her shoulders drooped in exhausted lines.

Leonidas groaned.

Theras moved to help him up, but the prince waved his hand away and sat up on his own.

A cheer broke out. The crowd in the throne room stomped its feet, loud enough to make the room shake.

Vane stood quietly as Ryan bled on the ground.

With a Herculean effort, I pushed myself up on my knees. I stood up on shaky legs and said with more clarity than I felt, "Let him save her."

The crowd quieted. They looked up at their king.

LELEX GAVE A STARTLED LAUGH. HE RETURNED TO HIS THRONE and sat down. "Finally, a worthy champion for Leonidas. One able to give a child of Triton a challenge."

The crowd murmured uncertainly.

Lelex smiled. "We have been truly blessed. These games will please the gods." He nodded at Vane. "Save our new champion. I shall dub her the Little Savage." He waved his hand at Ryan. "And the other girl."

*The Little Savage.* My stomach churned. Vane moved toward me. I shook my head and pointed to Ryan. "Her first. The healer stopped my bleeding."

Vane crossed to Ryan. Leonora followed him.

Leonidas stood with effort. He waved at the pit.

They stood also and stomped their feet.

He turned to his father. He snarled, "Ready the sacrifice."

The king held up a hand. He addressed the pit. "People of Aegae, indeed, we are very pleased with the maiden's performance. She has made this a most exciting game. We are lucky our prince has been challenged. I have no doubt he will meet the challenge."

The crowd cheered in agreement.

Leonidas's sour expression softened.

"But we have a second champion tonight." The king waved Vane forward.

Leonora hovered over Ryan, whose chest rose and fell normally on the floor.

"Leonidas, bring your sword," the king commanded.

Theras handed him the sword he'd taken back from me in the pit.

Leonidas grabbed the hilt. He walked to the dais.

"Give our newest soldier your sword," the king said.

Leonidas looked at his father in surprise.

"His reward for saving you is to taste the sacrifice," the king declared.

Lelex turned a soft gaze on the mermaid girl. "Come."

The mermaid girl stood still. Soldiers came up behind her and not-so-subtly urged her forward.

"Submit or our laws demand the beheading of all your brethren," Lelex said.

The mermaid girl cried silently but began walking forward.

Arthur shook his shackles. "This isn't right."

The mermaid girl knelt in front of Vane. Two guards put a heavy block in front of her.

Leonidas handed Vane the sword.

Vane took it without a word.

The mermaid started to bend to place her head on the block. Vane held up a hand to stop her. His eyes held the girl's.

He lifted the blade.

The sword swung without mercy.

"Take her heart," Lelex commanded.

The girl's body fell to the floor. A gush of blood spewed from her severed neck and colored the white marble floor with macabre enthusiasm.

The mermaids didn't seem bothered by the sight. Leonidas leaned down and turned the girl's headless body with surprising gentleness. Vane sliced her torso. Leonidas reached in and pulled out the warm heart.

A girl in a white toga and bare feet brought the prince a gold platter. Leonidas put the still-beating heart on the smooth metal.

Lelex raised the trident and stabbed the air with it. "Poseidon will be pleased."

The court clapped in approval.

Lelex picked up the girl's head and held it up. Blood dripped down his hand. "One of your own has done you a great honor, the dearest sacrifice. We dedicate this feast to her. We offer her a minute of silence."

The crowd bowed their heads.

Lelex roared, "Let the banquet begin."

The girl with the gold platter rushed to the king. Lelex deposited the head.

The sadistic court cheered. Even barely conscious, my stomach turned. For once, I wanted to throw up. Maybe it would destroy the barbarically happy mood.

Vane and Leonora came up to me. Vane knelt beside me. Cold hands probed my festering wound. A shock of fresh pain hit me as the mermaid girl reopened the skin. She pulled torn muscle and tissue together, fiber by fiber, ligament by ligament.

I blinked hard, refusing to give in to the dark.

Vane put a hand to my temple. "Sleep."

My body complied with relief.

ONCE AGAIN, I FOUND MYSELF IN THE DARK WORLD. I SWAM ALONE IN THE water, facing dark cliffs. But this time a beach stretched out in the moonlight. Quick strokes in the gentle water put me on land. I walked on the cold beach. To my relief, I wasn't naked, though the mermaid toga I wore left little to the imagination.

A light came from the rock. I walked closer to the solid wall of rock that made up the cliffs. Light flickered deep within the dark. An opening in the cliffs showed a cave.

My heart skipped a beat. Was it the same cave Ryan had run from when she'd taken the snake artifact's blood—the one with the Minotaur?

"Eowlyn," a husky voice whispered.

I ran across the beach to the cave. Merlin called.

# 25

## TRYING NOT TO SCREAM

D AY TWO.

The mermaid girl died because of me. At the end of the day, I didn't care if she was a mermaid. No one deserved to be sacrificed. I pressed my hands to my head, trying to take it in that night while I lay in the morning light. Soldiers had separated me from the others and put me in some kind of a suite.

Mermaids dressed in simple cotton togas—not the heavy fabric ones I'd seen in the throne room—brought me food. I was led to a washroom. Two men mingled with women mermaids, but they didn't hesitate to assist in the bathing. After the bath, the mermaids—palace servants, I presumed—dried and dressed me. I spent some of the day reading a book from the grand suite's surprisingly large collection from all over the world, eating, training on a mat inside the room, and then being dressed in a gold bikini and toga to fight.

My wetsuit had disappeared. So had my regular bikini.

Lelex trotted out Arthur as the champion the next night. I got to watch from the mermaid king's side next to Leonidas.

Vane stood on the other side of the throne from me. He stared out at the pit without emotion.

Arthur fought another Aegean champion. It didn't surprise me Arthur won the night. I'd seen him fight in the pub. He was ruthless in the rink, cold and focused like Vane. Another mermaid paid the sacrifice and the Aegeans began to look unhappy. Lelex played it off with a hearty smile, but the sharp look in his eyes bespoke trouble.

After the fight, I was returned to the grand suite.

I startled when the doors swung open and soldiers shoved Arthur inside. He hissed, beaten and bruised from the fight. I ran to him.

His eyes widened on seeing me. "Eowlyn."

Vane came into the room. "Step back from him. We're here to heal him."

Leonora followed after Vane like a lost puppy.

Giving him a glare, I helped Arthur to the closest chaise. Leonora touched the diamond necklace the mermaids used to control Vane. She uttered a spell and removed the necklace. After that, Vane and Leonora made quick work of the worst of his cuts. Vane didn't speak at all, just moved methodically to give Leonora a power boost while she did the healing.

"He'll need to sleep," Leonora, the mermaid girl, said with shy grey eyes.

I nodded.

Leonora crossed to Vane and put the power-dampening necklace on him with an apologetic look. Vane accepted the necklace without question. The two headed to the door.

At the last minute, I ran to the door. "Vane, what should we do?"

The door shut in my face.

I glared at it, wanting to kick something, preferably Vane's backside.

Arthur moaned.

I walked back to him.

The blond giant's eyelashes fluttered open. He groaned. "I hurt all over."

As if they'd heard him, the door opened again and the team of servants who'd helped me bathe in the morning rushed in. Taking his arms, they ducked underneath his shoulders to support him into a large bathroom attached to the room. There was no door to the bathroom and the servants also didn't hesitate to begin peeling off his dirty clothes.

Arthur seemed to take it in stride, but I whirled away to another part of the suite, giving him some privacy.

After a few minutes of rustling, a hiss and plop told me he'd sunk into a bath.

"You can look now," he said.

I walked to the bathroom. His head rested against the top of the clawfoot tub. A rainwater showerhead trickled down and made pitter-patter splashes in the water. Most of his chest showed and water snaked down corded muscles. I took a hard swallow.

He looked completely relaxed. "It's almost worth a duel for this."

"Another innocent girl died tonight."

Sobering, he lifted his head. "The mermaid. I don't even know her name. You're right. I'm a scoundrel."

Scoundrel had to be much more of an insult in his time. The mermaids gestured for permission as they held out a bar of soap. Arthur took the soap with a gentle shake of the head as refusal. The mermaids stepped back, bowing their heads.

"You're used to this," I said.

He shrugged. "Being king did have benefits."

The mermaids left the bathroom and went to the lone bed in the room. They began to strip it and separate it to make two beds.

I leaned against a basin in the bathroom. "Where did they take you last night?"

"Nothing like this. I think this is the champion's room." Arthur waved a hand to the room. "They shoved all of us in a tiny little dungeon cell."

"Merlin?"

Arthur shook his head.

The anxiety knot in my stomach tightened. I crossed my arms around my middle. "The others are all right?"

"They're being fed. It's about the best you can expect," Arthur said. "Lelex wants to purge us without losing more of his own people."

"This will be the second night we haven't cooperated." I hugged myself. "How long is this supposed to go on?"

"Sixteen more days."

Sixteen days meant sixteen deaths. "No," I burst out. "I can't."

Arthur sighed. He began soaping himself. "How do we stop it?"

I paced across the bathroom marble. "We escape."

"Past the soldiers? Without any weapons? No wizards? No map? When you come up with a way, do inform me." He put his head back on the edge of the tub. "Meanwhile I'll be sleeping."

I stalked back to the room and flung myself on the bed. Though I tried to squelch it, a yawn escaped me. *No time for sleep. You have to find a way. You can't go in the pit again.*

*"Talking to yourself?"*

I frowned, half-asleep. *"Merlin?"*

No reply came. I reached up to close a hand around the Dragon's Eye. So far, the mermaids had been reluctant to mess with the necklace. I asked it, *"Where are you?"*

Another yawn escaped me. My eyes closed. Just for a minute.

 inside.

"Eowlyn," a whisper urged. It was Merlin.

Without another thought, I ran into the cave. The light guided me. Winding around, twists and turns, this way and that, I followed it. I didn't know what I chased, but my gut told me I had to find it. Finally, the tunnel opened into a cave, nearly identical to the one under the ocean. A pool of water stretched out and beyond stood a dark door, one similar to the red door that had led us to Triton's hell.

"Eowlyn." Merlin's voice reverberated around the cave. The yearning in it urged me to hurry.

I dove into the pool, not seeing another way around. I came out the other side, my toga sodden and clinging to me. I walked to the black door. It had a single doorknob.

A figure leaped out from the shadows. It landed in front of the door, blocking me. Four feet. Paws. A dark mane of hair. A black lion let out a roar.

He'd been a lion in Rawana's realm too.

"It's locked," Merlin whispered. "Just stay there. Talk to me."

Reaching up to my neck, I touched the Dragon's Eye. My gaze locked on the big cat with even bigger teeth and the door he guarded. What didn't he want me to see? I sat down. "Are you all right?"

"Tell me what happened."

So I did. He'd missed everything about the gladiator duels. The deaths. I took in a sharp breath of musty cave air. Bringing my knees up, I buried my head and rocked back and forth. I whispered, "How am I supposed to watch them die for sixteen days? I c-can't."

A click sounded. The red door unlocked and creaked ajar.

Nobody came out.

I stood and walked to it. Pushing the door open, I realized it led to a room. More like a cell. Maybe one of the dungeon cells Arthur had said the mermaids had dumped everyone into. However, Merlin was alone in this one. The cell was all walls with a tiny window on a door for outsiders to peer in.

He hung vertically from chains attached to the ceiling.

With a gasp, I crossed to him, only to stop abruptly when I reached him. Bruises and blood covered him from head to toe. A loincloth covered his privates, but he wore nothing else. Small cuts went up his legs and arms as if someone had played darts with him as the target.

I put a hand to my mouth. "What are they doing to you?"

He didn't answer. He didn't look up.

I waved a hand in front of his face. "Can you see me?"

Glazed eyes looked through me.

Another door to the cell opened. Lelex came in. He carried a whip. "Theras tells me the barrier in your mind is being very stubborn. But we cannot allow all that power to be wasted. There is a way to get to it. Unfortunately, it will break your mind." He unfurled the whip and drew it back. "But first, we must wear out your body. And that...I'm very good at doing."

The crack of a whip echoed in the room as Lelex swung the whip at Merlin's back. Merlin's head jerked as the fast-moving tip tore and ate skin.

I tried to grab the leather rope. My hand went straight through it. Lelex cracked it again. I tried to grab it again. The same thing happened. Stomping to him, I punched Lelex in the face. My hand went into his bulbous nose as if I was a ghost. Maybe I was. Looking up, I noticed the ceiling of the cell wasn't flat. It curved and bent...as if it wasn't really there.

"I'm in your head." My fingers touched the Dragon's Eye, which connected us. I walked around him.

He hissed as another lash struck his back. But he didn't look at me at all.

"You can't see me in here." I glanced around the cell. "This has to be some kind of construct in your mind. You're containing what's going on here." My eyes went to the door from where I'd entered. "You've fractured yourself. Your mind isn't here. It's hiding in the lion."

I touched his shaking shoulder. How long could he hold out like this? Even separating himself from the pain wouldn't last forever. What would Lelex do once he finally broke?

The Dragon's Eye went hot on Merlin's shoulder. He tensed. He glanced around blindly. I moved and he followed without his eyes really focusing.

He cried out as Lelex hit him again.

But my heart sped. Merlin couldn't see me, but he sensed me.

I moved a little again. This time when Lelex pulled back the whip and swung. The lash grazed me. I hissed as it connected. I jerked my hand away. A long welt showed on my arm. I couldn't grab the thing, but through the Dragon's Eye I was connected to Merlin. Not just his pain, but also him.

Lelex raised the whip.

This time I stepped up behind Merlin. The whip swung and came down. The lash hit me hard. The cloth of my toga tore. Unprepared for the magnitude of the strike, I cried out.

Merlin pulled at his chains in agitation. But he couldn't move. Couldn't stop me. Couldn't actually see me. He couldn't last, but maybe we could make it together.

I stayed. Another lash sliced my back. Unable to help it, I cried out again. My hands went around Merlin's waist, my fingers holding him tight as tears leaked out the sides of my eyes.

The whip snapped. Lelex hit my back again.

Merlin jerked in his chains, trying to throw me off him.

I held on.

DAY THREE.

"Wake up." Arthur shook me.

Pain exploded on my shoulder. I hissed as my eyes opened back in the champion's suite.

Dawn lightened the dark room.

"You were crying out," Arthur said. "Why is your sheet wet?" He peeled back the thin blanket I'd pulled up before falling asleep. He hissed. "Blood? What is this?"

I sat up. My back burned, on fire with pain. Unlike the wound from being skewered by the sword, which had been limited to one spot, my entire back, every tiny bit of skin, screamed in agony.

"How did this happen? You've been here all night." He jumped up. "Never mind. I'll get towels."

Trying not to scream, I sat up. When I turned to look at the white sheets on the bed, I nearly passed out again. Red streaked most of the bed. The dark world had been real.

The door opened. Arthur spoke to one of the servants bringing food. Ten minutes later, Leonora came in. Five excruciating minutes later, after the pulling and sewing of tissue and flesh as she healed my back, the mermaid girl turned with shaking fists to Arthur.

"What did you do to her?" she demanded.

Arthur raked uncertain fingers through his blond hair. Red streaked where he touched. Red from where he'd touched my back.

"He didn't," I told her. "This was your king."

Leonora's eye widened. "His Majesty, he would not be so cruel for no reason."

I resisted a snort. She didn't know her king at all.

"Sometimes the people closest to us have two faces," Arthur said. "One to their friends and one to everyone else."

Leonora's eyes flickered. "The champions shouldn't be disturbed. I will tell Leonidas."

"Leonidas cannot go against his father for an outsider,"

Arthur said. "You should not put him in such a position. However, we do thank you for your healing."

Leonora's shoulders eased. "This is true. I'm afraid Aegean do not trust outsiders."

Nor did they care about them.

"But we are not all like that," she said. "We are all creatures of this world, after all. Very well. I will not tell him but if you need me"—she took out a gem from her pocket and handed it to Arthur—"you may summon me through this. I have an identical one in my rooms and I will know it is you." She turned back to me and skimmed a hand over my back. "It will heal, but you should try to avoid using it strenuously."

I waited for her to leave before going to the other clean bed and collapsing on top of it.

"Eowlyn!" Arthur crossed the room to the bed quickly.

Tears streaked down my cheeks.

He kneeled next to the bed. A big palm smoothed my hair. "What happened?" he asked.

I choked out one word. "Merlin."

# 26

## THIS TIME I DIDN'T DREAM

Arthur touched my cheek. "What about Merlin? I don't understand."

My head rested against a soft pillow infused with the aromas of oak and earth—Arthur's scent. It oddly soothed. "The king is trying to break him to get to his powers."

"He doesn't have them. I thought he'd been drained."

"Lelex says they're blocked, not drained. That's what he's trying to fix. Have you seen his crown? It's like the Dragon's Eye, a powerful charm. Lelex will unblock Merlin and drain him again. And kill him."

"But what does that have to do with you?"

"The Dragon's Eye connects me to him and I was able to take his pain. I didn't think it would be physical." My mouth opened and I yawned. "I guess I was wrong."

Arthur's grey eyes flashed. "You need to take off the Dragon's Eye. You can't do this."

"They'll heal me." My eyes fluttered shut. "Anyway, after what I did in the pit, I deserve it."

I woke up later. Arthur forced me to do some training. That

night, in a twist, Lelex chose Arthur as Aegae's champion. He chose Ryan to go against Arthur.

"If at any time, I suspect you are not doing your best, outsider," Lelex told Arthur. "You will forfeit their sacrifice and their champion."

She nearly killed Arthur, but he managed to beat her, using the white bull against her. Arthur changed in the pit from wise king to battle-hardened warrior. He battled in a methodical, nearly unemotional way. Ryan fought with grace, wearing a mantel of honor which Arthur didn't possess. It was her downfall.

He won, but we lost.

Vane didn't show any emotion during the entire fight. But when McKenna bent her head down in front him and his sword flew, his grip tightened on the sword's hilt just a little. One thing I knew about Vane, his technique had been forged as a Roman soldier. He was absolutely flawless.

That night, I closed my eyes.

I WOKE UP ON THE DARK BEACH WITH MOONLIGHT STREAMING DOWN. I RAN into the cave and followed the light once more. A glimpse of a shadow on the walls, a half bull, half man, quickened my pace. The shadow followed me until I reached the inner chamber and swam across the pool. No lion waited. I ran up to the door. It was locked.

"Merlin." I pounded the door.

No sound came.

Had he locked me out? My heart raced with anxiety. Was he all right? Had Lelex broken him? I pounded the door again. "Come out." It didn't open. Panic churned in my stomach. I had to get to him. Before it was too late.

Behind me, water in the pool splashed. I whirled around. Was it the Minotaur? Had it come after me?

A figure emerged from the pool. A beast's head. But not the Minotaur. The black lion.

Merlin had shifted again. With a sob of relief, I ran to him. The black lion stiffened at my approach but this time I didn't hesitate. I knelt before the killer beast. Ignoring his massive jaw and teeth, I put my hands on his face and cradled it. "You're all right. I was worried."

The black lion's rigid stance softened. He leaned forward and nuzzled my nose with his. I grabbed his mane and touched my forehead to his. The beast let out a muffled sigh. He rested his giant head on my shoulder.

Behind me, the door clicked open.

The black lion lifted his head, letting me go. I crossed to the door and went inside.

Merlin lay on a cot in shackles. He wasn't moving. The knot in my stomach returned. I hurried to him and put my hand on his bared chest. His heart beat with unsteady rhythm, as if it were losing its hold on reality.

I crawled onto the cot and lay down against him. My head rested in the crook of his neck. "I'm here. You're not alone."

DAY FOUR.

Across from me, Arthur's eyes opened on the other bed. He yawned, mumbled, "Too early," and buried himself in the soft pillow. With a sigh, I flopped on my back and stared at the ceiling. There had to be a way out.

That night, Leonidas chose me again. Swords again. No dagger. As I swung the heavy metal, I searched the pit. There had to be a weakness I could exploit. Arthur stood at the top next to Vane on the king's dais. Lelex stayed on his throne. The sacrifices watched their life being decided from the edge of the throne room. Tonight, it was one of the wizards and another girl.

Leonidas surprised me with a jab to the arm that sliced deep, tearing flesh and muscle. As I hissed, he kicked me in the kneecap. My entire leg crunched as my knee blew out. I went stumbling to the ground. Leonidas backed up, swung his sword down for the kill. My fingers closed around dirt. I threw bits of it at his face. The prince stumbled. I grabbed his ankle, bones crunching worse on my leg, and pulled to bring him down. The pit released the white bull. I leaped up on one leg. This time I rode the raging animal. Leonidas stood. It was exactly the wrong move. I drove the bull and gored Leonidas. Then, I leaped on top of him, broken leg and all, and gutted him with the sword for good measure.

The crowd stood mostly silent, fearful for their prince. A few whispered, "Little Savage."

A mermaid died.

I wanted to throw up. Instead, I collapsed, my shattered knee screaming in pain.

Vane and Leonora sprang into action.

After sliding off the bull, I sat on a half wall in the pit, completely dazed. My leg hurt but so did the phantom pain on my chest and the lashes I'd suffered on my back. It was as if my mind couldn't reconcile the pain and the healing.

Soldiers carried me out of the pit. A stairwell showed stairs descending even farther down. I was led up stone steps. The champion's room wasn't too far from the pit entrance.

The doors opened and Arthur burst in. His escort of guards pulled the door closed. He crossed to where I lay on a bed bleeding.

"They've really got to stop giving us white sheets," I joked.

Arthur winced at the mess made of my leg. Taking my hand, he held it tenderly. "You were amazing."

His tenderness was almost too much to bear. I resisted an urge to sob uncontrollably.

Luckily, the doors opened, and Leonora and Vane entered. Vane wore one of the diamond necklaces that dampened a wizard's power. Considering what I'd seen happen to him during the Roman times with Septimus, Vane had to be chafing at being bound again.

Arthur let me go.

I bit my tongue from screaming as Leonora reformed the bones. Her fingers shook as she worked. "You aren't afraid to kill Leonidas."

My eyebrows rose. "It's either him or one of my friends."

"But the way you do it. As if you have nothing to lose."

My eyes lowered. I whispered, "I can't stop myself."

Leonora's hand trembled against my leg. "And what if we can't heal him?"

I ground my teeth. They didn't even try to heal the sacrifices. "When he steps into the pit, Leonidas knows the risks. He must crave the fight."

The fair-haired healer paled. "You are wrong!"

I hissed. Sharp pain went through my knee where she healed it.

She blinked and the pain stopped. She concentrated on the knee. "It's not his fault. His father orders the games. They've been necessary only since His Majesty returned with magic from his travels."

My ears perked. "Lelex didn't always have magic?"

Leonora shook her head. "He gained it when he left the kingdom to explore the outside world. Leonidas and I were very little. It was before he ascended to the throne. The power protects us, this island, but we pay a price. The power must be fed."

"Fed with the games and the sacrifices," I said.

"You see, it is not in Leonidas's nature. He does it for his kingdom." She let go of my leg. She went to Vane. Emitting a soft word that made the wind whirl in the room, Leonora took the diamond necklace off Vane. Vane didn't react to the necklace being removed. He crossed to me and put his hands on my leg to heal it. I studied him as he worked in a methodical and detached manner. The green sat deep on his skin. Had we completely lost him? The red glow of magic subsided as he finished healing, and I put my hand over his before he could leave.

"Is Ryan all right?" I asked.

"She's been placed in another room for champions. The king doesn't want too many in one place."

My lips curved up. "Is he afraid of a little rebellion?"

Vane's demeanor turned cold. "The king isn't afraid. His Majesty is wise."

The pair left, leaving only me and Arthur in the suite.

*Dammit, Vane.* Had they completely robbed him of his identity? I slammed my hand down on the bed and let out all the pain riding me. My hand stung, but I didn't care. With a choked sob, I tried to lay down. My head bonked against the wall.

Arthur came up to the bed. "Can I help?"

I shook my head. "I just need to think for a while."

"I'm going to get cleaned up," he said. "The pit leaves one feeling most foul."

I didn't reply as he walked to the bathroom. A gush of water sounded as he filled the tub. In the darkening room, the shadows began creeping out of the corners. Unable to hold all my jumbled thoughts, I forced myself up. I walked to the bathroom.

Arthur lay with his eyes closed. My breath was becoming shorter and shorter and I struggled to pull in air. I sank down onto the bathroom floor and leaned back against the nearest support, the stand of a basin. "I can't do this for twelve more days," I said into the quiet room.

Pulling up my knees, I went into a fetal position, and buried my head. "I c-can't watch them all die."

Water moved. Drips splattered the floor as Arthur left the tub and padded across the floor. "Gwenhwyfar."

"I'm not her," I wailed, sniffling a little as tears leaked from my eyes.

"I know you're not her. But you're still Gwenhwyfar. It means champion." He sat on the floor and pulled me into his arms. Two strong arms engulfed me in a bear hug. He squeezed tightly as if he could drive out the pain just by squeezing. He whispered in my ear, "Not savage."

Burying my face in his neck, I let out a muffled cry. "It is who I am."

"Who you are is what you've been trained to be—a warrior."

"Does a warrior do what I do in the pit?"

"They do what they have to do to defend what and who they love."

I softened. He made me sound noble. I almost believed him. I sniffled some more. *At least he put on a towel.* "Why do you have to look like Thor?"

Arthur stiffened. "I am no Viking, Gwenhwyfar."

I gave a watery chuckle into his neck. "My bad."

He kept holding me. I don't know how long we stayed there, but eventually I found myself deposited in one of the two beds. Mind and body exhausted, I closed my eyes.

I didn't dream that night.

DAY FIVE. Arthur and Ryan fought again. Arthur won. A gargoyle died.

DAY SIX. Leonidas battled Ryan. Ryan won. A mermaid died.

DAY SEVEN. The pit keepers handed me a bow and arrow. Leonidas didn't stand a chance. I had him pinned within the first minute of the fight. I drove an arrow into his chest. Soldiers surrounded me immediately. Theras rushed Vane and Leonora down to him. The crowd booed at the short duel. But I surrendered the weapon with relief. No sword. No dagger. No bloodlust. At least on my part.

A mermaid died.

In the night, the Dragon's Eye took me to the dark world.

In the night, I found Merlin.

~

DAY EIGHT.

I faced Leonidas again. I had to admit I'd learned to move quicker, to think quicker. With each game, Leonidas grew more adept. At first, I thought he'd begun echoing my attack forms, then I realized they were Vane's forms. Vane was training him. A sinking feeling of despair went through me. Vane had gone fully mermaid.

I beat Leonidas with a spear.

Lelex declared the games would be held with swords only. Another mermaid became sacrifice.

Back at the room, I slipped into sleep.

~

I WOKE IN THE DARK WORLD. ON THE BEACH IN MOONLIGHT. MY FEET carried me deep into the cave where the black lion waited. The Minotaur chased me but didn't get close. He seemed merely curious. One time I sensed his eyes on me as the black lion nuzzled my face in greeting. The door unlocked and I found Merlin in chains.

This was the first night since the night I let Lelex whip me.

In just a few days, Merlin's body had thinned from abuse. Another door opened; Lelex came into the room again.

"Your friends will not take another mermaid," he declared. "Your power will be mine. Then, I will have enough strength to protect us from what's coming."

What was coming?

"Triton cannot help us in this war. We must help him," he fumed as he drew out the whip again. "It's in there in you. All the power, I can almost taste it. You will succumb."

The whip flew. I stepped up behind Merlin again.

I held on for as long as I could. Then, I sank to the floor, clutching Merlin's legs. Lelex swung the whip again.

Merlin let out a hiss.

Lelex dropped the whip. "Maybe you're ready now." He went around until he faced Merlin and reached up to grab his head. The jewel on Lelex's crown glowed. He squeezed Merlin's skull. The legs I held shuddered. Merlin screamed.

I woke up, screaming.

Arthur scrambled out of bed and hurried to me. In the dark, he touched the blood on my back. "Merlin again."

I nodded.

After giving my shoulder a gentle pat, he went to the door. He pounded on it for a while, but no one came. Throbbing pain consumed my back and I buried my head in the pillow. A rush of water came from the bathroom. Arthur came back and peeled back the sheets. "This is how we did it in my day. It will be better cleaned up."

I doubted it but I didn't protest as he cleaned me with the warm water.

Under the gentle care, my eyes shut again. I fell asleep. This time I didn't dream.

Day Nine. Day Ten. Day Thirteen.

They all blurred together in a picture of blood, pain, and death. We lost a gargoyle and two mermaids. Arthur and Ryan fought again. Ryan lost again. She fought Leonidas three times and won twice. During one duel, Lelex flooded the pit with water. Leonidas won.

Clarence was the sacrifice.

I watched with stunned eyes as a mermaid beheaded the older wizard.

Every night, the Dragon's Eye took me to the dark world.

Every night, I found Merlin.

DAY FOURTEEN.

The bull gored me. I lost against Leonidas. The wound refused to stop bleeding. Vane jumped onto a floating disc. Leonora jumped on eagerly behind him. *Don't fall for him, girl. He's taken*, I thought before I passed out.

I WOKE UP IN THE DARK WORLD ON THE BEACH. MOONLIGHT STREAMED down but I couldn't move. I lay in the water, my limbs frozen. Shrouded in darkness, I touched my belly, but I couldn't feel it.

Trying not freak, I crawled backwards, scooching along in the sand. I didn't get far, just a little above the touch of the water and its gentle waves. I don't know how long I lay there. The pounding of footsteps called my attention from the water. The black lion stalked me on the beach. He'd left the cave. He looked worried.

I grabbed his head when he came close and nuzzled it. "Am I dying?"

The black lion let out a disgruntled growl.

Letting him go, I lay back on the sand. "It's not a bad place to go."

The black lion growled louder. He lay down, his head resting on the crook of my shoulder. His lips pressed against the side of my neck.

I startled. Lips?

My gaze jerked from the moon back down to earth.

Merlin's head rose. A human head. He studied me with judgment. "You're hurt."

"You're not safe as a human. It's too risky. If Lelex—"

Merlin put a hand to my lips. "There are some risks worth taking. Going into the lion state makes things clearer, easier to see. Also, Lelex can't find me because I've fundamentally changed. But there is one thing that is stronger." Lifting up, he put both hands on my cheeks and cradled my face. "You do not have permission to die."

My eyebrows rose. "I need permission?"

"Absolutely." His lips swooped down on mine. He played with me with his tongue. I moaned, pressing closer to him. He pushed back my hair so it splayed on the sand. "You do have some strength left."

Some.

The wind shifted. A rustling came from the cave. The Minotaur.

"I don't know what it is," Merlin said.

"Lelex?"

Merlin shook his head. "Something else." He glanced at the cave. "Maybe what we came for."

The sky rumbled, marring the perfect night.

Tears leaked out of the sides of my eyes. I still couldn't move. I whispered, "Why can't I move?"

"You're broken in the real world." Merlin lowered his head to nuzzle my neck. He bit softly at my jawline. His hand found the hem of the dress I wore. My uniform in the duel was always the same—a white toga-style shift over a gold bikini. He pulled up the fabric. "But not in here."

Cold wind against bare skin made goose bumps rise. I shivered. "What are you doing?"

"Distracting you," he said, his hand sliding up and down my thigh.

"What are you still doing?"

Handsome lips curved up into a grin. "Trying to round those ears."

My pointed mermaid ears. I blushed in the dark.

His hand stilled on my hip, at the knot of the bikini string. One tug and the entire bottom would unravel. He asked, "Will you allow it?"

Wind carried his scent. Amber and a hint of sandalwood. Deep with a hint of mystery. My hands went up and I ran my fingers through his brown wavy hair. I pulled his face close. "Kiss me again."

Merlin smiled against my lips and slowly tugged down the bikini string.

## 27

### YOU NEED TO TEACH ME THAT TRICK

"Argh." I jerked awake.

Vane looked down at me blandly. He sat in a chair by the bed. "Welcome back. That was a difficult healing. You've been out for hours. But by the smile on your face, I'd say you had a good dream."

My cheeks flamed. Self-consciously, my hand went up to my ears. Nope, still pointed.

"You are still connected to Merlin." A hint of amusement crossed Vane's expression before he masked it. He fiddled with the diamond necklace he couldn't take off. "This is good. Very good."

My eyes narrowed. "Where is Arthur?"

He pointed to the other bed. "I put a sleep spell on him."

"Why?"

"Because we're going to escape and you're going to help me."

I gasped. My legs went over the side of the bed. I tried to jump up only to stumble.

"You're still recovering," Vane said in a cold manner.

I wasn't buying it. I stumbled over to him and, collapsing a little on top of him, I gave him a bear hug. "You're fixed."

Vane stood, supporting me. He ushered me back to the bed. He shook his head. "I'll never be fixed. What the king did can't be undone. But I have been remembering."

"How long?" I demanded.

"Since the first few days."

I hit his shoulder. "That long. You've been playing robot-Vane for that long and you remembered weeks ago?"

"It took me awhile and I'm still unclear. It's like I remember bits and pieces of a dream."

I lay back on the pillow. "Why now?"

"Tonight is the fifteenth night, the night before the blood moon. It's our last chance to take Lelex. After that he'll be too powerful. The blood moon restores his energy. But tomorrow night, thanks to my brother holding out for so long, he'll be at his weakest."

My eyebrow cocked up. "How does Ryan feel about this?"

For the first time, a hint of uncertainty flashed in his green eyes. He said, "I'm about to find out."

*Day Fifteen.*

That night, soldiers walked us through a long tunnel. As soon as we entered the pit, Lelex threw us for a loop. He declared I face off against Arthur.

Arthur laid down the spear he'd been handed. "I will not fight her."

An erratic Lelex screamed, "You would sacrifice an innocent without giving her a chance."

"Take me instead."

"No. You are the champion. Not the sacrifice."

Arthur didn't move. He stoically repeated, "You may kill me. You may kill anyone. But I will not fight her."

I tried to catch his eye. He knew the plan. This would be

easy. All he had to do was to kill me. But Arthur refused to look at me. I hissed, "Arthur—"

"Bring the girl," Lelex shouted.

Standing next to his father, Leonidas looked down at me in confusion.

A soldier came out of the tunnels. He dragged Ryan along with him. The soldier unshackled her and shoved her at us.

"The Little Savage will be the mermaid champion today," Lelex said. "The other maiden plays for the outsiders."

"Little Savage. Little Savage. Little Savage," the crowd chanted.

I cursed. *Little Savage.* Would I ever let go of that moniker? My entire life it haunted me. I'd denied it so long. Now, on Triton's Island, the truth had revealed itself—I'd been lying to myself all along.

"Little Savage," the crowd cried. The circle of faces went up three levels and all them looked eagerly down on the match.

Ryan crossed the bridge over the short moat and we faced each other. So much for Vane's plan to have me lose tonight. I glanced up at the sacrifice if Ryan lost. Unwittingly, Lelex had chosen the one closest to Ryan. A handcuffed and leg-shackled Grey stood at the top of the pit.

The ding-dong of a bell began the match. A shock went through me as Ryan's spear struck cleanly, slicing open my arm. We battled back and forth with the spear. She had better technique, but I was quicker. I took a hard hit from her as another set of doors opened. The white bull came charging into the pit.

Throwing Ryan off, I ran to the half wall and grabbed the strap of the bull as it passed. Its soft hide tickled my arm and, leaving one hand on the strap, I dropped to the bull's side. Ryan biggest weakness was the bull. I ran at her. As she watched it, I fashioned the strap on the bull to make a quasi-bowstring. Pulling back my spear like an arrow, I let it fly.

It hit its mark. It hit Leonidas, who peered over the edge of the pit. The spear pierced his stomach. He cried out and began tumbling.

Soldiers rushed forward and managed to catch him before he fell into the pit.

The crowd stood up but remained eerily silent. I got off the bull and strained to see what was happening at the top.

Lelex came off the dais, close to the edge where the soldiers laid Leonidas. He yelled, "Get the prince the healer."

Leonora rushed up. "I need Vane."

Theras beckoned him. "Come."

Two soldiers escorted him. Vane stopped just in front of Lelex.

With a soft magical command, Theras removed the necklace that dampened his power. He told Vane, "Help her heal him."

As soon as the necklace was removed, Vane grabbed a sword from the older soldier's side. He shot a fireball at Theras, sending him flying backwards, and pulled the king into a choke hold with the sword. "Let us go or die."

Lelex laughed. "You've tried this once before, wizard. What makes you think it will work this time?"

Vane grabbed Lelex's crown. He threw it down into the pit. "Your charm is gone, Majesty." With his free hand, he threw two fireballs at the soldiers holding Grey. "*Agni.*" Vane thrust the sword against Lelex's skin. "Time to go."

Theras coughed. On the floor, he clutched his singed chest. "Don't do anything foolish."

"You don't know me very well." Vane knocked Lelex on the head.

The king went limp.

Leonora let out a cry.

While still bound, Grey grabbed a fallen sword. Grey ran to Vane. Blasting his shackles, Vane handed him the king. "Take him to the pit."

Theras pushed up. He grabbed a sword and faced Vane.

Vane pointed to the bleeding Leonidas. "You can fight me and I can kill you. Or you can help your daughter try to save her prince. Which will it be?"

After a brief moment of hesitation, Theras straightened. He moved backwards toward Leonidas. "I will come after you," he promised. "You will die for your treachery, Vane."

"You will have to find me first." Vane laughed. He blasted more soldiers and ran to the floating disc, which had already started going down with Grey holding Lelex. Vane jumped off the edge and landed on a floating disc. Green glowed below the floating stone and, instead of coming down, it stayed up in the air. Vane used his own magic to keep it afloat.

*Someday, you need to teach me that trick.* As soldiers rushed the pit, my attention turned to fighting them.

Ryan attacked the two soldiers guarding her and knocked them unconscious. She ran up, her spear in hand. She shoved me aside and got on the bull.

On the floating disc, Vane put out his hands and aimed down at the stadium. "*Uksati agni.*"

Fireballs, one after another, like a machine gun, hit the sides of the stadium. The crowd screamed.

I leaped into action and used the spear to begin disarming the mermaid soldiers in the pit. Arthur grabbed a fallen sword and did the same. Ryan rode the bull, taking out soldiers. Rocks crumbled from the walls of the pit as Vane fired two giant fireballs directly at the waterfalls that fed the moat.

The mechanism that controlled the waterfall disintegrated and water began to gush out of the wall, flooding the pit again. Vane blasted two more fireballs at the source of the water. The explosion caused the roof to groan and creak. It started to collapse.

Falling rock stopped the gushing waterfalls. However, since the blocked up pipeline began to strain and the walls began to bulge. Blocking the flow of water was most likely going to flood the palace.

The air thickened with smoke and dirt all around us.

The white bull whined at the foul air. Ryan patted its head and soothed the beast. I had to admire how it quieted under her care. Vane and Grey landed with Lelex. Ryan rode the bull to them. The animal went straight to Vane. He snorted in a friendly way and licked Vane's face. He grimaced and patted the bull's head awkwardly.

"Does Vane have a widdle puppy?" Grey laughed.

With a grunt, Vane threw Lelex on top of the bull.

The bull hurried across the bridge into the tunnel. We trailed behind it. As soon as we got past the moat, a skeleton crew of guards attacked. Vane waved his hand and knocked them all out against the wall.

"You're no fun," Grey said.

"We don't have time to play." Vane shot a fireball behind us. Rocks collapsed and closed off the tunnel from the pit.

"Where's everyone? Merlin?" I asked.

"On the level above us," Vane said. "The others are near where he's being kept."

The bull whined. Ryan pointed to a gash on the bull's side. "You need to heal the bull."

"I've promised him more than that," Vane said grimly. He moved to put a hand on the beast. Green magic flowed out. It healed the gash but Vane didn't stop. "Don't worry. You'll be free soon, as I promised."

"Free?" Ryan knocked Vane's hands away from the bull. "You're not killing him."

"We need him still, for now," Vane said. "But it's what he's asked. He's been through enough. You, of all people, should know that."

Ryan's eyes narrowed. "You can talk to him?"

"They call me *silvertongue*, remember? I promised him an end if he'd help us today."

"This is not the end." Ryan put a hand on its wet nose and stared at him with determination.

Vane cursed. "We'll talk about it later. Let's go."

The bull shadowed Grey as we went around this way and that through the labyrinth of the palace. Ryan traded a spear for a sword and I found a bow and arrows. The bow fit like a third arm on my shoulder.

Arthur grinned when he saw my choice.

"What?" I asked him.

"I don't know if I should say it," he said.

My grip tightened on the bow. "Gwenhwyfar?"

"She wielded it as if it were an instrument of magic."

Vane led us swiftly through the tunnels. Despite sounds of chaos and water flooding the floors, we made it to the next level without running into any soldiers. The farther we got from the pit, the quieter it became. The pit's collapse had been a good way to empty the hall of soldiers. The second level lay mostly empty except for the rising water level, which reached past our ankles. We went up to the third level and Vane stopped in the middle of a crossroad of hallways.

"Grey." Vane pointed down a yellow-painted hallway. "Get Excalibur. Then get the gargoyles. They are in one of the cells. Then come back here. If we're not here, get the wizards." He pointed to green-painted hallway. "We're going to get Merlin first."

I shook my head. "Arthur and I can get Merlin. You and Ryan get the others."

Vane's hand tightened on the bull. "No, Merlin's been down here for fifteen days. Who knows what Lelex has done to him?" He patted the unconscious king. "We might need the king to get him out and neither one of you has magic."

Arthur nodded. "I'll go with Ryan and Grey. Vane, you should go after Merlin."

I nodded.

Vane and I hurried down the white hallway. We rounded a corner. Vane pulled me back. A group of five soldiers stood guard at a door with a slit on its top.

Vane touched my shoulder. "You're not going to like what you see."

"I've already seen him," I said, my hand going up to touch the Dragon's Eye. "I know."

Vane's brows rose in surprise. He studied my pointed ears for a long minute. Finally, he said, "I'll take care of the soldiers. You get Merlin."

Without waiting for my reply, he ran out of the shadows at the guards. He shot a fireball at them and one at the door. The guards scattered. The door flew open. My heart racing with adrenaline, I sprinted to the door. With my bow and arrow, I nailed a soldier to the wall.

I stopped just inside the cell.

It was exactly as in the dark world dream. A lone cot. Merlin strung up in chains nailed to the ceiling. Except he'd looked normal in the dreams. A lone light flickered over Merlin.

Not wanting to frighten him, I took a small step toward him.

Merlin's head jerked up at the tiny sound.

He gazed at me from an emaciated blue and black face. Gaunt haunted eyes opened through bloodied swollen eyelids. His ribs stuck out from his skin, and he hung like a puppet with a bit of hide and skin left on him.

I took an arrow from my quiver. I shot one chain.

Merlin flopped forward.

I took out another arrow, my last one. I shot the other chain.

I ran forward to catch him before he collapsed.

He fell into my arms.

# 28

# NOT BY A LONG SHOT

"Merlin." My hands cupped his face.

He lay on the floor where I'd lowered him, unmoving.

The Dragon's Eye heated.

Leaning down, I gently put my lips on his bruised ones. "Wake up."

His body trembled. I pressed deeper.

Behind the backs of my eyelids, the dark world stood waiting.

*I could see him on the beach. The black lion paced back and forth, looking out at the water. He waited. For me.*

*"I'm here," I whispered in the real world. "Come to me."*

*The black lion plunged in the water.*

Merlin's hand came up. He pulled my mouth against his. The kiss consumed me. Gently at first and then all-encompassing as he fed on me. My body shuddered. The Dragon's Eye glowed, draining me and giving my energy to him.

A hand jerked us apart.

Vane stood above me. "Not too much. He'll kill you."

I blinked. "He wouldn't." He could drive me to the brink,

but he would know when to stop. I brushed back sweat-damp-ened hair. The emaciated look had lessened but his gaunt face still held deep grooves. "He's still unconscious."

Vane laid his palms on Merlin's chest. "He needs more. It's his mind. He's probably done the same thing I did. He's locked himself inside a box. However, while I've spent the last weeks digging myself out of mine, he's spent the same time digging himself in deeper." Green magic drifted from Vane to his brother. When Merlin didn't move, Vane grabbed the Dragon's Eye. Red heat flowed from Vane to the dark gem. "I'll connect you. Go to him. Get him out."

I went back into the dark world.

INTO THE WATER. INTO THE NIGHT. I SWAM TOWARD THE BEACH. THE LION was gone. Merlin lay on the sand. A figure hovered over him. It turned and its shadowy profile silhouetted against the moonlight. A half bull, half man.

It looked at me. "I wait."

I stood in the water. It reached my thighs. I walked closer. "For who?"

"We are protected, but the time has come to free us. One who can hold the power is coming," its raspy voice said.

My legs cleared the water. "I must take him."

The Minotaur let out a low snort. "I will make a bargain."

I stopped. "Bargain?"

"A race," he said. "In the cave."

"Then you'll leave?"

The Minotaur's bull head gave a soft nod.

I cleared my throat. "Fine."

"Yes?"

I glanced up at the moonlight. What was I getting myself into? "Yes."

The Minotaur made a low, guttural growl of triumph. He leaned down and put a hand on Merlin's chest. The moonlight became brighter and it shone down on Merlin. He floated up to hover above the sand. The Minotaur snatched him out of the air. He carried a rag-doll Merlin held easily in his hands. He put Merlin in the water.

Merlin spluttered. He jerked awake.

The Minotaur stepped away from Merlin. "Take him."

"What about the race?"

The Minotaur smiled. "Watch for me. I will collect it later." In a blink, the Minotaur disappeared, as if he'd winked out of existence.

Merlin turned to me in the water. "What did you do?"

I woke to Merlin sitting up on the prison cell floor. He stared at me.

Vane patted my back, sighing in relief. "You did it, Patience." He turned to his brother. "We have to hurry. Soldiers will be coming."

The white bull trotted through the door, carrying Lelex.

Merlin stood. He strode to Lelex. "Wake him up."

Vane whispered, "*Jagara.*"

Lelex snapped awake. The white bull shrugged him off and the stout king landed on his feet. He grinned at Merlin. "They fixed you."

"Why haven't you been able to restore my powers?" he demanded.

Lelex shrugged. "It is like a door in your mind. I hoped to soften your barriers enough so I could slip through the door. Breaking you down weakened the walls of you mind, but I needed more time."

"More time and he would be dead," I spat.

"It was a risk," Lelex acknowledged, without any more feeling than a rancher had for prize cattle.

"What is the Minotaur?" I asked him.

Lelex hissed in surprise. "You saw the creature."

I nodded. "You are connected to it."

"We are not merely on Aegae because we are Triton's children. We are here because we are its protectors."

"Protectors of what?" Vane asked.

"Within Aegae lies the realm of the Earth-Shaker. Those who seek him shall be consumed by him." Lelex looked at Vane. "Only the Fisher King may control him. Why do you think we made you one of us? You are the Fisher King, Vivane."

Vane paled. "What does that mean?"

Lelex giggled. "You should have stayed Aegaen if you wanted to fulfill your destiny. Now, we are sworn to stop you."

"We seek only knowledge," Merlin said.

"You seek power," Lelex spat. "They are coming. There will be a war. We must all save ourselves."

"War against whom?"

Lelex smiled slyly. He glanced at me. "The golden one has chosen his champion."

I paled. "G-Golden one?"

Lelex began whispering. A green shimmer grew around his body. Merlin walked up to Lelex. He grabbed the crown and its jeweled charm.

"No." Lelex leaped at Merlin.

"*Nidra*," Merlin whispered.

The green jewel on the crown went dark.

Lelex slumped, going unconscious. Vane caught the king and dumped him on the bull.

A weakness stole over my entire body, and my legs folded underneath me. Merlin crossed to me in two steps and caught me.

He buried his face in my hair and took a deep breath. "I'm sorry."

"You siphoned the Dragon's Eye," Vane said slowly. He gave

his brother an impressed look. "You stole her energy to take Lelex's magic. I didn't think you had it in you."

"I've learned a few things," he murmured, sweat breaking out on his forehead as he held me.

"You used Eowlyn," Vane pointed out.

Leaning on Merlin, I pushed myself up to stand. "Can we not do that again?"

Merlin stood too. "I used almost all my strength. I'm going to need help getting out of here."

Vane hooked a thumb at the white bull. The animal was chewing something in his mouth, completely unconcerned. Vane brought the bull close and helped Merlin get on the bull's back. Merlin didn't meet my gaze as he rode behind Lelex's limp body.

The bull took Merlin out of the small, gruesome room. Merlin didn't look back. Neither did I as I followed them. We met the others in the hallway.

"Merlin," Ryan said happily. She came up to his leg, dangling off the bull, and squeezed his ankle. "You're all right."

*Not by a long shot.* But I didn't correct her.

"We have to go," Grey said, out of breath. He pointed behind, the way they'd come. "Soldiers are searching the hallways. It's Leonidas."

"Let's go," Vane directed us. "We need to get to Lelex's chamber."

# THE WHIRLPOOL RODE LIKE A WET SLIDE AT A WATERPARK

I stayed close to the bull, wanting, but not daring to glance at Merlin.

He kept his face forward as Vane led us up a wide staircase to the top level of the palace.

"Think I can get my wetsuit back?" Grey tugged at the toga the mermaids had dressed him in, as befitting the sacrifice

Ryan grinned. "You don't like wearing a skirt?"

"It's better than being smelly," Gia scratched at her wetsuit. "At least you got a bath."

Arthur glanced at me guiltily and I shook my head, not wanting to tell her we'd been getting baths every day. He glanced at Merlin before turning to me, "Are you alright?"

My hand tightened on the bull's hide. "It's not me you should be worried about."

"At least you got a cell to yourself, *maiden*," Blake said. "The rest of us were packed into one."

Gia stuck out her tongue at him. Only ten out of fourteen remained. We'd lost two gargoyles and two wizards.

"I'm so ready to get out of this hellhole," Grey said.

A rustling turned my attention back to the bull. On top of

him, Merlin's shoulders drooped and he struggled to stay upright. Surprisingly, the animal picked its way up the staircase with graceful agility.

Vane led us without faltering. We snuck down abandoned corridors. Many had flooded. The strange echo of music, an aria, floated up from the middle of the palace.

"What is that?" Ryan asked.

"Whatever it is, it's keeping them busy," Vane said.

"Where are we going?" I hooked a thumb at Lelex who hung like a saddlebag behind Merlin on the bull. "Because I don't love having the evil dictator with us."

"We need him, so don't try to get rid of him. I'll take care of him soon enough." Vane led us to a corridor lined with portraits in ornate gold frames and rich red tapestries depicting battle scenes. "The palace is built into the side of a hill. Which I find interesting. I've learned there are two frescoes of the red doors we came through. One is in the throne room. One is in Lelex's bedchamber—"

"How do you know what's in his bedchamber?"

Vane smiled wolfishly. "I have my ways."

"You would," Merlin said.

"The bull will throw you if I ask him," Vane said mildly.

In another corridor, soldiers found us. Our little group of gargoyles and wizards easily took care of them. While I didn't particularly feel a need to fight, the others itched to get some revenge after weeks of isolation.

Finally, the last corridor ended. We reached a part of the palace which looked like a branch cut off from the main building. A covered walkway led to an isolated bedchamber with huge double doors. We hurried along the marble floor of the walkway. Glass showed stunning vistas of Aegae. The setting sun and its approaching dark echoed the heaviness in my chest. Would we ever get out of the long dark of the past few weeks?

The chamber had been ideally situated into the side of the

hill and had the added benefit of being protected by it. We reached the doors. Ryan took out Excalibur. The rest of us readied our stolen swords for what lay within.

Vane flung open the gold doors.

The chamber lay completely empty. On the far wall, a massive bed with a golden canopy had been put against the rock and stone of the side of the hill. Embroidered on the canopy was the crest of the mermaids and a winding snake.

"Lelex's room," Vane confirmed. As we all streamed in, he crossed to a big armoire and flung it open. Along with clothes, an array of weapons hung inside. After grabbing a tunic, he slammed the armoire closed. He tossed the tunic to Merlin, who put it on over his bare chest. Vane punched the armoire and cursed. "The trident isn't here."

"That is because I have it," Leonidas declared from the door. "Give me my father."

He stood in the hallway. Soldiers stretched out behind him all the way down the entire length of the bridge. Theras stood at his side, Leonora hiding behind him.

At the side of Lelex's massive bed, Ryan and Arthur crouched down into battle position with Excalibur. Grey, Colin, and the last gargoyle raised their swords. The wizards outstretched their hands. The ten of us against a hundred of them—our chances were good.

Leonidas looked at Vane with a furious expression. "You have betrayed us most grievously, Vane. For this I shall make your death slow."

"Get in line." Merlin slid off the bull. He came down unsteadily but righted himself.

"*Jagara.*" Vane waved his hand at the sleeping king.

Lelex stirred. I pulled him off the bull before he could fully wake. Standing at his side, I put my blade against his throat.

Lelex stretched as he woke. He grinned, completely unperturbed by the sword at his neck. "Did you get yourself trapped, Vivane?"

I dug the blade against Lelex's throat.

"Where is the red door?" Vane demanded.

Eyes widening in surprise, Lelex's eyes shifted right before he smiled slyly. "What door?"

"The bed," I told Vane. "It's there."

Vane commanded, "*Kavas.*"

The emerald gemstone glowed. The massive bed creaked. Vane parted his hands and the furniture split in a loud squeal of splitting wood. Those standing by the bed moved quickly.

Underneath, an image of a red door had been painted into stone. The stone also had two sides and a third top, just like in the cave.

"A trilithon," Blake said with wide eyes.

A golden bull had been painted in the middle of the red door.

"What is that?" Leonidas demanded.

My grip tightened on the blade on Lelex's neck. "How do we open it?"

Merlin held out Lelex's crown. He tore the jewel from it and tossed the useless gold. "With this."

"That does not belong to you. You won't be able to use it," Lelex snarled, putting out his hand. The jewel in Merlin's hand glowed bright green.

A piercing wail went through the room. It tore at my ears and the room swam before me. I struggled to stay awake.

"I think I've heard enough. For a lifetime." Merlin stepped toward me. He grabbed the sword, and without warning, he pulled the sword back and swung. Lelex's eyes went wide with surprise just before blood began spewing from the direct hit to the neck.

The wail cut off.

He fell forward on his knees, clutching at his neck.

"No," Leonidas cried. He charged forward. Chaos reigned as he, Theras, and the mermaid soldiers pressed in through the door.

Merlin didn't hesitate. He got behind Lelex and hacked at the king's neck again and again to finish the job. Lelex's severed head rolled on the floor. Blood spewed from the body as it fell on the white marble. It was not a clean kill, but Merlin's lips curled tight as if he'd preferred it that way.

There was no time to dwell as soldiers swarmed the room. Grabbing the bloodied sword from Merlin, I tangled with an attacking soldier.

Merlin ran to the door. The bull trotted after him. He tossed the crown jewel to Vane. "Open the door."

"Eowlyn," Ryan shouted. "Form a line, cover them."

I ran to join a formation of wizards and gargoyles across the door. Leonidas's mermaids attacked. We held the line.

Behind us, Vane held the green jewel over the painting on the floor. "*Vivrnothi.*"

The green jewel glowed brightly. A green wave blasted the room. It blew through me like an angry breeze. The mermaid I dueled faltered. I used the opening to skewer his stomach. He fell back. Anther mermaid took his place.

A whoosh sounded, followed by the swirl of raging water.

I glanced back. The door had been opened and it was a whirlpool. In the middle of the floor.

Ryan made a sound of fury as Leonidas disarmed her.

"Leonidas," Vane said. "Stop or lose the crown jewel."

Leonidas stilled.

Vane dangled the jewel over the whirlpool. "Tell your soldiers to stand down."

Leonidas put up a hand. The soldiers stepped back but held their swords ready.

I edged to the whirlpool.

"Let us go and you get this back," Vane said.

Theras stood on alert. "It's a trick—"

"No trick. We go. You get this." Vane waved the crown jewel. He tossed it carelessly over the whirlpool to Merlin.

Leonidas paled.

Leonora came up beside Leonidas. "To be king, you will need the jewel."

"Go," he said.

Vane nodded at Ryan. She jumped first with the white bull. The others followed her, jumping in groups. Arthur grabbed my hand and we ran to the whirlpool.

"Here you go." Vane tossed the jewel to Leonidas.

Startled, Leonidas reached out to catch it. He dropped the trident. Vane waved a hand and the trident flew to him.

Arthur grabbed my hand. He yanked me into the whirlpool. The last thing I saw was Merlin and Vane jumping.

Leonidas shouted, "Follow them."

Blackness surrounded me as I submerged. The whirlpool rode like a wet slide at a waterpark. I twisted and turned, all the while speeding down. I came out of the dark and got dumped into a pool of water.

Luckily, I still had gills. A bit of yellow light shone, and I swam up to the surface of the water. Blake had lit a few fireballs and it exposed another cave-like cavern, only this one was much bigger than the one filled with gruesome bones and skulls. Musty air and undisturbed moss on boulders throughout the cavern whispered no one had been here in a long time.

Vane hauled himself out of the pool.

Merlin came out next. He looked at the gathered group. Besides him and his brother, all who remained were me, Arthur, Gia, Blake, Ryan, Grey, Colin, and another gargoyle.

"Your gills are gone." Vane pointed at Gia's hand. "The pond stripped our spells."

Gia's ring had gone black

Merlin shook his head. "The whirlpool did something to the charms. But our natural magic seems to be intact."

I touched the Dragon's Eye.

*It's too closely tied to me,* Merlin mind-spoke. *It would take more powerful magic to break it.*

"What do we do now?" Blake asked.

Grey pointed to a path in the boulders. "I'm thinking we follow that."

"We follow you, sire," the remaining gargoyle told Grey.

He grimaced and walked away.

Ryan frowned after him. Gia walked to her. "They drew straws to be the sacrifices, but Grey tried to cheat so he would draw the short straw—"

"He what?" she exploded.

"He's becoming their leader. Their king."

Ryan put her arm around Gia's shoulder and leaned on her.

Vane glanced at her with a tight, unhappy expression.

I walked after Grey. Through the boulders, Grey stopped before a tunnel.

Ryan gasped. "I've seen this before."

*The cave from the dark world.* I let out a breath. "It's real."

A splash came from behind us in the pond. Leonidas's head popped up from the water.

"Move!" Vane dragged Ryan into the tunnel.

We all hurried inside.

"Blake, Gia," Vane shouted, "blast the entrance."

Fireballs flew. The tunnel rumbled loudly. Boulders collapsed to block the opening.

"*Vicarati,*" Vane commanded, pointing the trident at the rocks. Red magic mingled with bright green and it fluttered across the rocks before it sank into them and disappeared.

"It won't hold them," Merlin said. "If Leonidas has the jewel, he'll break through magic."

"He doesn't know how to use it well enough yet." Vane's

eyes glittered green in the dark. He touched the trident with reverence. "We may not have your power but this has enough strength to at least delay them."

"Look at this." Blake shot a fireball up at the rock. It lit an ancient sconce of straw and burning oil. He shot another one a few meters down the tunnel.

Vane patted his back. "At least we're in the right place."

"Let's hurry," Ryan said.

We ran down the passageway for nearly an hour. We stopped, huffing and puffing, when the passageway ended in another cavern. A long, narrow stone bridge stretched across a river of murky water.

Vane pointed to a boulder with a painting of a golden bull. "Definitely the right place."

Grey put one foot on the bridge.

"Wait." Colin put a hand on Grey's chest. He picked up a loose rock from the ground and threw it out over the bridge. Gigantic tentacles sprang from both sides of the bridge like snapping jaws. Suction cups lined with sharp spikes on the tentacles caught and crushed the rock with ease.

"Fun," said Blake.

"We could have used Lelex's charm about now," Merlin said.

Vane's eyes gleamed. "I didn't think you had it in you to kill him."

"He was about to kill us."

Vane snorted. "If that's what you want to tell yourself."

"What would you call it?"

"Revenge," Arthur said quietly.

"Agreed. Maybe there's hope for you yet," Vane said, but he wasn't looking at Merlin. He was looking at me.

I shifted in place. *What do you want me to do?*

Vane turned back to the bridge. He threw another rock.

When the tentacles flew up, he shouted a spell. "Blake, Gia, you two are the only other wizards left. Help me."

Blake and Gia did the same. A roar filled the chamber and the whole cavern shook. Water lapped over the bridge. The river started rising, trying to bury the bridge.

"What now?" Arthur said.

"We need to try this from the bridge." Without warning, Blake ran onto the bridge.

"No," Gia screamed. "Vane, do something."

She moved to go after him.

Vane put out a hand to stop her. "Trust him. See what he has in mind."

The tentacles appeared. Blake shouted a spell and ran through it. The bridge shook. A giant female head on a long, slim neck rose out of a hole at the other end of the bridge. The Medusa head had snakes instead of hair squirming out from its follicles. On its face sat one giant eye and a mouth with three rows of teeth.

The creature emitted a shrill, rolling scream.

"A gift from the Gorgons," Merlin said.

"Blake," Vane shouted, "don't look at it."

The creature smiled.

Blake dove into the water.

Gia let out a mewling sound of grief.

# 30

# LABYRINTH

"I'm getting him." Grey jumped into the water.

Colin's face went ashen and then he did the same.

Merlin cursed. "It's a Medusa. We have to cut off its head."

Ryan said, "We just passed Charybdis."

"If it is, then this could be Scylla. Cutting off its head would only grow back two."

The bull snorted beside Vane. It stomped on the golden carving in the rock.

Vane put his hand on my shoulder and put his other hand on the bull's bridle. His voice changed and he began speaking in a short, gruff voice. *"I will run across. I am fast. You keep your eyes closed. I will tell you when to strike. Then I will be champion. I go to the great fields. I was saved for this. It is my time, sire—"*

"It's the bull speaking," Merlin murmured.

Ryan shook her head. "No, we can't."

Taking one step, she grabbed the bull's stirrup and jumped onto the animal.

"Ryan," Vane cried. "Don't—"

Ryan raced the bull across the bridge. Tentacles rose once

again. She maneuvered the bull easily through the suctioned menaces. They reached the hole just as the creature's head rose from the water, snakes writhing. The bull jumped over the snakes. It landed on the other side right as the creature's head fully surfaced. The creature screamed.

"Take its eye," Vane shouted into the chamber. "Leave the head."

The creature whirled to face the bull, but Ryan was already swinging her blade.

She got its eye. Closing her eyes, she stabbed the other one.

The head screamed again.

Vane ran forward. "Take the head now."

Excalibur swung in her hand.

I ran down the bridge. The others followed.

Vane blasted the head of the creature with the trident. Green light covered him, just as if he still had Lelex's jewel.

I reached out, but the white bull had already turned to stone.

Vane shook Ryan. He barked, "How could you be so reckless? You are the sword-bearer."

"Exactly. This is why I am here." Ryan put a hand on the stone statue. She traced the bull's scars, which ran along its side. She blinked but tears still spilled down her cheeks. "We never even asked him his name."

"*Mahoksa*," Vane said. "It means Great bull."

Colin's, Grey's, and Blake's heads surfaced from the water. Blake hung between Colin and Grey.

Ryan faced Vane. "Why did you take out the eye instead of the head?"

Vane's lips twisted into a tight smile. He was still furious. He bit out, "When it screamed, I understood it."

Merlin frowned. "This is beyond a wizard. A creature as rare as this you could only understand if you were a mermaid—"

"I *am* a mermaid...sort of. Lelex changed me." Vane lifted the hair off his neck. "You don't have gills, but I will always have them. Do you understand?" He spoke to us, but he looked at Ryan.

She bit her lip.

His pupils flared green. "Do they disgust you?"

"Of course not," she said quickly. Worry lined her face.

"Good." Vane turned back to the bull. "We should put the creature to rest." He raised his hand at the bull statue. "*Antyakriya atasa.*"

A sharp wind whittled away the stone statue and ground it into fine dust.

A rough doorway showed beyond the bridge. Beyond it, we emerged onto another ledge. This time, there was no river. We stood on a cliff. In the valley below lay an enormous and winding maze.

"The labyrinth of the Minotaur," I said.

Merlin grimaced. "Endless walls of dark rock and some kind of black vegetation on top. I already don't like this."

Vane lit a fireball. He pointed a path off the cliff. "Steps going down. We need to keep moving."

I went to the top of the path. It spiraled down, going steep and long.

Grey groaned. "Why? It's going to take us days to figure this out."

Vane made a sound of impatience. "Do you not think Leonidas is coming after us, Ragnar? We don't have days. Either we seize the power that is down here or he will." He waved a hand at us. "We've already lost four. I *killed* one of you myself. I have to live with it. But I don't have to live with more of you dying."

Merlin raised a brow. "Are you all right, Vane?"

"I'm not all right. I'm a mermaid."

"You're not one of them," Ryan crossed to him and put a hand on his arm.

To my shock, he shrugged her off. "Yes, I am. I always will be." Vane waved the trident in jerky moves. "That's how I know to do this."

Ryan stepped back with a startled look.

A green map appeared in the air.

Blake cleared his throat. "Maybe I could double-check?" He muttered a magical command. A burst of wind buzzed around my ears. Yellow overlaid green light, turning it brighter. It matched perfectly.

Vane arched a look. "Good. You'll hold the map."

"I can do it," Ryan said.

"Are you willing to go shirtless?" he bit out. "The map needs to be put on skin."

She blushed.

"I'll do it." Grey slid off his tunic, leaving the toga. "I don't want Emerson completely nude."

Blake still wore his wetsuit.

Vane flicked his hand and the map lay over Grey's back. It sank in like a tattoo, a green one.

"What are we waiting for?" I started down the steps.

The rest followed. On my neck, the Dragon's Eye pulsed.

*The Minotaur wants you. He is at the center of this. What will you say when he asks for more than you're ready to give?"* Merlin spoke in my head.

Aloud, I replied softly, "I'll say I'm already taken."

"WHAT MAKES YOU THINK THE ANSWERS ARE AT THE CENTER OF the maze?" Ryan asked. "You've been to Avalon and you didn't heal. You didn't bring back anything that could cure Rourke."

"While Lelex rooted around in my mind, I did the same to

his," Merlin said. "There is something down here that is very important. I got the sense it was related to the blood moon."

"And the blood moon is related to stars." I sighed. Lying back against a boulder, I looked up into the darkness. Since we were deep underground, I had to try to imagine a canopy of stars against the pitch dark ceiling we found ourselves under.

Colin had built the small campfire.

Usually, Vane liked those kinds of tasks, but the deeper we got into the cave, the more brooding he became. As if the weight of the world rested on his shoulders. Almost as if he were channeling his brother.

We were several hours into the maze. The entrance had been made from an arch of three giant stone slabs—a trilithon. We'd been walking through at a breakneck pace, until we reached a clearing with a small pond. Blake lit a few torches around us. Vane surprised us by pulling rations from the skirt of his futuristic mermaid uniform. I had a sudden vision of him as the Roman soldier he used to be.

When everyone exclaimed with shock, Blake explained about spells and matter displacement, but I didn't really care. I was just happy to have something more substantial than slimy black vines to eat. Colin constructed makeshift pallets out of huge fronds that canopied the maze.

The clearing contained tall hedges that marked off private areas. Gia, Ryan, and I picked one for the girls to refresh themselves. Blake, Grey, and the gargoyles took another. Arthur went with them. Vane carried his pallet off to a secluded area at the very edge of the clearing.

"Guess he doesn't like us," Blake said.

After several yawns, Gia went off to the girls' spot. Ryan pulled Blake aside and did a fair bit of whispering before she went after Gia. Looking glum and tired, she lifted her hand in a weak wave as she passed.

"Something is going on between her and Vane," I told Merlin.

He leaned back against a boulder, watching the fire. "How do you know?"

"Ever since the bull, he's been avoiding her. Now, he's gone off on his own." I chewed my lip. "Ever since the pit, he's been pushing us hard. I don't think he's as accepting of being turned as he says."

"That's good."

I gaped at him. "What?"

"He's finally taking something seriously. This is a good thing."

"No." I shook my head. "It's not like Vane. Not like the Vane we know anyway. You of all people know what a monster Lelex was." I pointed to the dark spot in the trees where Vane had disappeared. "He took the trident with him. He cradled it like Excalibur." I picked up a twig from the ground and threw it into the fire. "You weren't there, but you should understand. None of us will be the same after coming down here."

Merlin studied me. "Is this about Vane or is this about you and the pit?"

I blinked, pushing back a sudden sting of tears. "What do you know about it?"

"We are connected. You saw the black lion. What do you think I saw?"

I bit my lip. A girl on a beach who'd gone a little too far?

"You are the balance, Eowlyn. Between light and dark. You kept me sane at great cost to yourself."

"Not so great a cost. I had healers."

"At *great* cost. Only someone like that could let go of Excalibur. Arthur couldn't. Ryan couldn't. You fought a god and won."

"I suppose that is something." My eyes went up to the dark

ceiling. Another cavern. Another secret quest. "What is it about you that has me following you inside obscure hills?"

"Or getting tortured by mermaids?" he asked lightly. Sitting up, he reached out and weaved his fingers into my hair. He cradled my scalp and ran a thumb over my ears. "I liked those ears."

My cheeks heating, I picked up a twig from the ground and threw it into the fire. I watched it dance and burn. Past the lump in my throat, I whispered, "Are we going to talk about it?"

His fingers stilled. "About what?"

I turned my face so his palm cradled my cheek. "What happened the last night in the dark world?"

His eyes becoming hooded, he said, "The last night?"

I could strangle him. I let out a little huff. "You're going to make me say it, aren't you?"

He sat up straight. "Yes."

At least he didn't deny it. The Dragon's Eye sat quiet. Almost too quiet. I touched it.

Merlin pushed my hand away. "I want you say it out loud. *We* need this to be out loud."

"We were...together," I said, wanting to die at my own awkwardness. "But we were in a dream."

"It was very real," he said flatly. "What you did by taking the lashing for me was very real. What happened on the beach was very real. Maybe we weren't there physically but what happened wasn't some fantasy. I wanted you." He took a breath and scooched closer to me. Sitting cross-legged, he pulled me into his lap. His hand found my back and pushed lightly against my spine. "I want you still."

I straddled him. My hands found his shoulder and wound around his neck. "Then tell me the truth."

Brown eyes crinkled. "Truth?"

"What happened with Lelex? Why did you kill him?"

Merlin's eyes shuttered. His fingers tightened in my hair

until he was almost pulling at the strands. "You of all people should understand bloodlust. He deserved what he got."

"Did you deserve it?" My hands wound tighter around his neck, and I pressed closer to him. "What he did to you physically was bad enough, but you held him off. Now you have to live with his death."

"That's just it. I didn't hold him off." Merlin put his head in the crook of my neck. He confessed, "He got in." His voice dropped even lower until I could barely hear him. "He preyed on me and he won."

"I don't understand," I whispered into his ear. "Help me understand."

The Dragon's Eye heated.

I FOUND MYSELF IN THE DARK WORLD. IN THE OCEAN WITH TURBULENT waves that raged and spat. Fighting their onslaught, I swam hard to the beach. A shadowy figure paced the sand at the edge of the water. He stalked out to meet me and yanked me from the grasping arms of the water. It was Merlin. Brown hair. Lean face. Naked chest.

He pulled me down so we were both on our knees. I wore the same toga and gold bikini. He yanked the toga off and then laid me back on the sand. His body covered mine and his head dipped to find my mouth. Not in a gentle onslaught but in rough possession, much like the manic waves of the dark ocean. And all I could do was to ride out the rage. I let him consume me, feeding without care or thought. Taking without remorse. Finally, he lifted his head. Brown eyes glowed gold.

WITH A GASP, I WOKE. MY LIPS UNLOCKING FROM HIS, MY HANDS

dropped to hang on to his shoulders as I absorbed what I'd seen. *Golden-Merlin?* My nails dug into his tunic. "But how? I saw Arthur before."

Merlin's lips flattened. "Lelex. He has a connection to the gods. He used the trident. He planted the connection inside me. Like an infection."

"The trident is a tool of the gods." I glanced at the hedges where Vane had disappeared. My nerves jangled. "What if you weren't the only one infected?"

"It's hard to tell with him. He's always been so volatile. But inside me...I can feel it. Like a disease, it grows. It waits."

My fingers gripped his tunic tighter. *Lelex's tunic.* The king's mark wasn't only on the outside but inside as well. "No. We won before. We can win again. We can't let them in."

"The gods want something from us. They've put three of us in play in this game."

"Arthur, Vane, and you," I said. "But what for?"

"You mean what do they intend for us to win?" Merlin looked to the black passageway out of the clearing. "My instincts tell me we're about to find out." His hand tightened on me. "But I need you to promise something."

I swallowed, my stomach hard and in knots.

Merlin cradled my face. "Whoever the victor is in this little game, you will show him no mercy."

# 31

## THE NIGHT OF THE BLOOD MOON

I couldn't do it again. I couldn't sacrifice him again. My mind reeled as I went to find Ryan and Gia. I didn't see them in the girls' spot. Voices came from another spot, a small clearing behind a wall of thin vine-ridden trees, and I wandered over to it. I stopped short when I came upon Blake with Ryan and Gia.

Ryan sat on Vane's sleeping pallet. Tears ran down her cheeks and all she wore was a champion's gold bikini. Her tunic lay on Vane's pallet. Her body trembled from head to toe.

I touched the Dragon's Eye. *Merlin. We need you.* "What happened?"

"He's gone," she said.

Merlin came running up. He stopped abruptly when he spotted Ryan. He cursed. "Vane." He glanced around. "Where is Excalibur?"

Ryan jerked aside her tunic. She picked up Excalibur and slammed it down in front of Merlin. "Happy? Your precious sword is safe." She stood up. "Is that all we are to you? Instruments? Do you even care about anything but the all-important quest?"

"The all-important apocalypse," Merlin said calmly. "Let's not forget we have the lives of everyone on this planet in our hands."

Ryan's lip stuck out in a sulky manner. "He took the trident. He's been obsessed with it. He has this scar on his chest—"

Merlin nodded. "He got several scars from his time with the Romans."

"But this is different. It's not so much as a scar but an infection. Lelex did something to him when he turned him into a mermaid. It's fed all his insecurities and it has grown." She gestured over her front. "The scar's grown like a spiderweb all over his chest."

"He said he felt changed. This must be what he meant." Merlin raked his hand through his hair. "How could you let him go?"

Ryan scowled. "I didn't know he was going to run off. I didn't know he was going to ask me—" She blushed furiously. "Never mind."

My eyebrows rose. "Let me guess. You turned him down and he didn't take it well."

"Is this my fault?" she asked quietly.

"No," I said quickly, my gaze going to the sleeping pallet. Going to her, I took her hands in mine. "Whatever you feel about him, *any intimacy* is your choice for when you are ready. Not when he's ready."

Blake cleared his throat. "What do you think he's doing?"

"He's going to the center of the maze." Arthur came through the thin trees. "It calls to us."

I got up. "The Minotaur."

Merlin sighed. "We should go now. We can't let him get there ahead of us. Who knows what he'll do." He muttered, "At least he doesn't have a map."

Another rustle sounded. Grey wandered into the secluded spot. "I'm not sure he needs one. I noticed when we walked here, he seemed to know the path before you picked it out on the map."

"Whatever is at the center is most important."

"Vane is important," Ryan said.

Merlin ground his teeth. "I'm doing what is best for everyone. Not just for one person."

Ryan gave a bitter snort. "How's that working out for you?"

"There is always a middle ground to be had," Arthur said. "I do not believe this is any different. But we will come to that when we need to. It's useless to speculate now."

"He's right. We don't have time to argue about this," I said. "Let's shut the camp down and go."

Colin, Grey, and Arthur made quick work of the camp. Looking longingly at my pallet, I resisted a yawn as we began walking. Hungover from a lack of sleep, I trudged beside Merlin. I had to admire his perseverance. He kept his focus on the mission. Maybe a little too much. I nudged him with my shoulder. "He is your brother. I know you care."

"The gods are playing him, Eowlyn. Just like they're playing me. Maybe to them we are just a silly game, but to us, to this world, this is all very real."

I put my hand on his arm. "Winning isn't enough if it costs you everything."

Merlin shook his head. "That's just it. I've been prepared for the day it costs me everything. It's the price you pay to do something great."

Blake kept a few small fireballs afloat to light the way. Behind us, everyone held hands to stop from falling over. After endless twists and turns, the air changed. Goose bumps on my arms rose. Adrenaline hit like a drug to wake me.

"Do you feel that?" I whispered.

Merlin nodded. The passageway ended at a large opening. Another set of columns topped by a triangular slab of stone framed the exit. A sheen of green light shone beyond it. I moved to step through the columns.

Arthur grabbed my hand. "Wait. Shouldn't a wizard test it?"

Merlin made an impatient sound. "Vane is ahead of us. We need to get there before he destroys anything." He stalked past us and through the columns. "Consider me the test."

The others followed.

Arthur stopped me. "We are nearing the end, I can feel it. Whatever we find, I need to know something first."

I looked at him curiously.

He ducked his head. Gold hair fell over his eyes. "The air carries much in the labyrinth. I heard you and Merlin conversing. I think I understand how close you've become to him in this dark world you share through the Dragon's Eye."

In the dim tunnel, I blushed. *Close* was an understatement. Yet, there wasn't time to really understand what close meant. "What are you asking, Arthur?"

His hand on my wrist tightened. "He cannot be what you want." He gestured at the tunnel. "This is his purpose."

I put my hand on his. "This is our purpose."

"I do not think you can fully envision what that entails." Arthur let go of my hand.

"Let's find out." I stepped through the entrance to the center of the maze and its waiting destiny.

I caught up to Merlin and the others at the foot of a small hill. Arthur stopped beside me.

The Parthenon, or a replica of it, stood on top of the hill. Perfectly symmetrical Doric columns and a white triangular top crowned the Grecian temple. Unlike the Parthenon in Athens, this temple remained untouched and in perfect condition.

Merlin pointed to the triangular top of the temple. Different Olympians had been carved in the marble. "Zeus takes the center with Poseidon and Hades beside him."

"I thought we were here for the Lady, not the gods," Ryan said.

"The Lady of the Lake is one of them," I said.

"Look at the top of the triangle," Blake said. "Poseidon holds the trident that goes up to the center point."

"The Parthenon in Athens celebrates Athena, the goddess of wisdom. This must be Poseidon's temple. He's one of the three most powerful gods."

"Why are we standing around?" Gia said. "Didn't we come into this nightmare to see what's inside?"

Merlin put a hand on my shoulder. "Remember, we'll always be asked for more than we can give. You are one of the few people who can do just that. If I fail, I need you to carry the weight."

But could I do it? I wasn't such a selfless creature. I let out a slow breath. I gripped a sword in sweat-slicked hands. We went up the hill. A short set of marble steps led onto a veranda surrounded by marble columns.

At the center, a small door led inside.

Blake floated a fireball to light the way. Torches hung on another rectangular set of columns that held up the roof inside. Blake lit them.

Inside the temple, four giant marble statues formed a square in the middle of a long room. The statues went from floor to ceiling.

Blake nodded at a statue in the back. "Hades with a serpent."

"Poseidon with the trident and the conch." Ryan pointed to the one next to it.

I looked at the third, which stood at the front of the square. "Zeus and his lightning bolt."

Merlin went to the last statue, a woman with a crown on her head. "The Lady of the Lake."

I walked up beside him. She was beautiful, a regal face carved with caring lines.

"The red door." Blake pointed to a spot behind the statues.

Two slabs made up the sides of the doors. Another slab covered the top. "Another trilithon," I said.

Ryan squinted. "There is no golden bull on the door."

She walked to the square and stumbled at its edge. "Whoa."

I walked up and stopped short. The floor was deceptive because there was none. The statues lined a pit. Unlike the Aegae pit, this one went only one level deep. At the bottom of the pit, another creature had been painted in red.

"The bull," Ryan said.

"The Minotaur," I corrected. Its bull face was painted in red. A mask of gold had been laid over its face. Two emeralds gleamed from its eye sockets.

Merlin stared at the Minotaur. "Lelex."

"Just like Lelex's crown," I said.

"Wait, I see something." Blake jumped down into the pit.

"Blake," Gia said. "Don't die."

He smiled. "I don't plan to."

I moved to go into the pit. Merlin put a hand on my arm to stop me.

"Columns go all around the pit," Blake called out.

Merlin let out a breath. "It's a ceremonial stage."

"To do what?" I asked.

"You need the blood of the sword-bearer," a voice came from the shadows. "And Poseidon's trident." Faster than I could blink, Vane moved out of the shadows near the door and grabbed Gia.

"Gia," Blake cried from down below in the pit.

Vane held a sword to Gia's throat. "Drop your swords."

"Do it," Merlin said.

We dropped our swords. Vane waved with his free hand and sent the swords flying into the pit.

Grey yelled at the door. "Colin—"

"Oh, he and his friend are quite incapacitated," said Vane.

"What did you do to them?" Grey raged. "They fought at your side."

Vane shrugged.

Merlin stepped toward him. "What do you want, Vane?"

"What we all want." Vane crooked a finger at Ryan. "I need the sword-bearers to go down into the pit."

"Sword-bearers?"

"All three of them. Ryan, Eowlyn, Arthur, get down there."

"You can't win," Merlin said. "We outnumber you."

"Actually, we outnumber you." Leonidas stalked inside.

Theras followed close behind him. He pushed Colin and the other gargoyle into the room. The older warrior's eyes locked on Vane holding Gia hostage. "Interesting."

"I thought I lost you lot in the maze." Vane sighed.

Leonidas pointed to his head. He wore his father's crown. "You cannot hope to beat us."

Ryan's eyes fixed on Colin and the other gargoyle, still very much alive. "You didn't kill them."

Vane gave a twisted smile. "Yet you so easily believed I had."

"I don't have a problem killing any of you," Leonidas commented.

"Do you want Aegea to survive?" Merlin said. "Your father has been coming here to recharge the crown with magic whenever you needed. That much I saw in his mind. The magic is charged with whatever lies here. He couldn't have known its effects. I believe exposure to it has turned the mermaids into something...harsh. But your father did it because he glimpsed the future, a future where this island is in grave danger. That's why he wanted to break me. I used to have visions of the future." Merlin stepped closer to Leonidas. "Will you lose it now he's gone?"

"He's gone because you killed him." Leonidas shot out a hand. Green fire streamed from his hand.

Vane released Gia and fired the trident at the green fire. The trident shot another blast and deflected Leonidas's green fire. However, its wake still hit Merlin. He went flying backwards into the statue of the Lady.

Green fire went wide and hit the statue of Zeus, exploding a hole in the middle of the column.

Arthur rushed Leonidas. Theras and another guard attacked him.

The Zeus statue cracked. The ceiling rumbled as it caved a little.

Gia elbowed Vane hard in the stomach and hurried to Ryan.

"Stop," Merlin bellowed. "The four statues are pillars. If you destroy them, you'll bring down this temple."

No one slowed. A mermaid fired an arrow at Arthur. It hit him in the stomach.

"Arthur." I hurried to him, taking out a dagger. I threw it at Theras.

It landed hard into the older warrior's shoulder. He hissed.

Leonidas put up a hand to fire again.

"Stop." Vane pointed his trident at Leonidas. "If you die, who will save your people?"

The ceiling rumbled.

But this time it wasn't another hit. Merlin got up, rubbing his head. Blood smeared his hand.

"My dear boy." An odd light hit the statue of the Lady. The marble face moved. "My own blood. I have been waiting a long time."

"Lady?" Vane said in shock.

The statue laughed. "Not quite, Vivane. We left your shores long ago. However, I left this memory for when the time was right—during the final days, when you would find me again. The day of reckoning."

"Why lead us here?" Merlin asked.

The statue laughed. "This is one of my earlier homes. I was protected by my son and grandson."

"Who are you? A god?"

"I am a Guide, a guardian sent to protect the flock. You have called us many names throughout your time, but you will know me most as Rhea."

"Poseidon's mother?" Vane said. "The mother of Zeus and Hades? The Titan Rhea?"

My mind reeled. The Lady of the Lake was originally the Titan Rhea?

"Why are you here?"

"I fostered this world. I helped it grow. Then our time passed. You did not need us anymore. But I did not leave you alone. I knew the day would come when you would need my guidance. On that day, I have left them you, my champions."

"Champions?" Vane said.

The statue nodded. "The Earth-Shaker's power is stored here. The Destroyer. Poseidon or Neptune. He has been called all these things. I left a piece of us, of him, tied to this world. One of you can wield it. By taking on the mantle of the Earth-Shaker, you will become the protector—the Fisher King."

"What is the price for waking the Earth-Shaker?" Merlin asked.

"The Earth-Shaker is part of this world's core. He has become part of its life force. Separate him and the world will tremble."

"Tsunamis." Merlin rubbed his head. "I saw this."

Vane's hands fisted. "How can you demand such a price?"

The statue bowed its head. "It was not our intention to be spiteful. It was the only way to keep the Earth-Shaker's power intact for you through the ages. You must step back and see the whole. Those you lose will be but a small part. On the longest day of the sun, on the day of reckoning, the trial to prove your humanity begins—"

Green fire hit the statue. It cracked the statue of the Lady.

A rumble shook the ceiling.

"You idiot," Vane shouted at Leonidas.

"Falsehoods," Leonidas cried. "This is some wizard's trick."

I stomped up to face Leonidas. "Listen to it. We are all here for the same reason. Your father said you are the protectors of the Minotaur. You have been protecting it for just such a day. It is coming. The end is coming. Your father also called it the day of reckoning."

Leonidas stilled. "Is this true?"

I clutched Arthur. "Your father talked to Theras. Ask him."

Leaning on me, Arthur yanked out the arrow from his side with a hiss.

Leonidas faced Theras. "Is it true? Did my father speak of the day of reckoning?"

"Yes." Theras winced and took out the dagger I'd stuck in him. "Your father dreaded its coming. It's why he kept pushing for more and more power."

"Tonight is the night of the blood moon. The veil between us and them is thin. Lelex must have known this." Vane held up the trident. "I've been driven to Aegae for a reason. I have been here before. I was meant to be here again." He pointed the trident to the pit. "Where Poseidon rests."

"Do not move," Leonidas spat. "Your tongue is smooth, betrayer. Your words like honey, but you are a snake. You cannot be trusted."

"Let us show you," Merlin said, getting up. He reached into his pocket and took out Rawana's Eye. "This will show you all."

Vane gave him a long look that said, *Are you serious?*

Merlin turned to the pit. "This place is special. This is the temple of the Lady. All our answers lie here."

Leonidas hesitated.

"Use your crown." Vane pointed to the pit. "Try to summon Poseidon."

Leonidas blanched. "He will talk to me?"

"In the pit." Vane strode to its edge.

Leonidas glanced at Theras, who gave a slight nod. Leonidas strode to the pit. He put out a hand. The emerald on the crown glowed green. The emeralds on the golden bull's head also lit. His hand shook. Leonidas's eyes widened. "There is so much power."

"This the source of your magic." Merlin went to the edge of the pit and looked down. He held out Rawana's Eye. "Vane, you are one of them. Use the trident. Between you and Leonidas, you can open this."

Vane pointed the trident at the Eye. It floated in the air in front of Merlin.

Leonidas stared at the floating organ. A green sheen came over the Eye. The bull's head glowed but nothing showed.

"Wait, you're missing one thing." I squeezed Arthur's shoulder.

He winced and held the side where he'd been hit.

I walked to the Eye and took out a dagger. I sliced my hand and poured blood on the dismembered flesh.

Vane shot it with the trident. Leonidas's green light shimmered.

Wind shot through the temple. It grew, echoing and howling. The torches winked out. The temple went dark.

The Eye glowed like a beacon.

We were all plunged to the stars. The Eye encompassed everyone in the same celestial event Merlin and I had witnessed. The explosion of a distant star. Its wave reaching our sun and causing a superflare. The earth burned, leaving the sky scorched with fire and brimstone.

The end of the world.

## 32

# THE MINOTAUR

The vision ended and I found myself in the dark. Rawana's Eye dimmed. It floated down and Merlin put out a hand to catch it.

A vomiting sound came from the pit, where Blake was.

Gia threw up too. So did the gargoyles—all three of them, including Grey.

Ryan and Arthur looked ashen.

On the floor, Arthur's body shook.

Vane leaned on the trident, sweating.

Leonidas had fallen to his knees. Theras walked to him and helped him up.

The army of mermaids had tears running down their cheeks.

Theras turned to Vane. "How will you save us from the reckoning?"

A cold smile echoed a chill of green that flashed in Vane's eyes. "To answer, I will need the maiden." He pointed at Ryan.

Ryan walked to the edge of the pit. She jumped down. "What do you need?"

Vane followed her.

From beside Arthur, my gaze caught Merlin's. "Help me get him down to Blake."

Merlin crossed to us and helped Arthur up. We went to the edge.

Merlin held out a hand to Arthur. "Hold on and I'll lower you."

Arthur shook his head. "I can make it." He lowered himself to sit on the edge and slip-slided down.

Merlin and I landed before he did. Arthur's feet hit the floor and he stumbled. I caught him and the blond giant leaned on my shoulder. Gia, Grey, and the gargoyles jumped into the pit.

Leonidas and the mermaids peered down from above.

"Blake," I called. "Can you heal Arthur?" I doubted Vane would.

Blake hurried to us.

Merlin left my side to stride to the bull's face. "The Minotaur in your dreams is a warning."

As Blake worked on his side, Arthur said in a weakened voice, "If there is something resting here, are you certain you want to wake it?"

Vane pointed the trident at the emeralds. "Ryan—"

"I know." She walked to the bull and knelt to the floor. She took out Excalibur. She sliced her forearm and dripped blood over the bull's emerald eyes.

Vane fired a shot at the bull's head.

The bull glowed.

Between the columns which made up the perimeter of the pit, a stone section slid up and a hole opened. Water began to pour out from the spout. It ran to the bull's head and pooled into the grooves surrounding the painting. The water completely covered the bull's head.

Merlin walked to the water. He put a finger on it. His finger didn't get soaked. Instead, the water shifted underneath his touch like silicone gel. He put a fist into it. His hand pierced the delicate film and became drenched. "This is Lake water."

Holding Arthur, Blake hissed, "He isn't healing."

Arthur began to tremble. I touched his forehead. He was burning up. My head jerked to Leonidas. "Was the arrow poisoned?"

Leonidas grinned. "It's fatal."

Anger quickly followed shock. But I jerked my head to the shower of Lake water.

The water continued to spew.

"We need to leave the pit," Ryan said. "The water is flooding it."

"Go," Merlin said. "Everyone out."

Gia, Grey, and the gargoyles ran to the wall to climb out of the pit.

Vane stepped in front of Ryan. "Not yet." His face softened. "Stay. Trust me."

Ryan hesitated.

I tugged Arthur toward the bull.

Blake blanched. "What are you doing?"

"Get out of the pit, Blake," I told him. "Go after Gia."

Up on the front edge of the pit, Leonidas yelled, "Wake the bull, Vivane. The Earth-Shaker will save us."

"No one is waking anything," Merlin declared from beside the bull. Foot-deep water covered the bull. He stood protectively over it. "We are not going to unleash anything that causes such destruction."

"If a sacrifice is asked, it is what will be paid," Theras said.

"If you are too weak too stomach it, we have no more need of you." Leonidas jumped into the pit.

Taking Ryan by the hand, Vane strode to Merlin and the bull, which was now covered with knee-deep water. "Take out Excalibur."

Arthur began to droop on me. I waded through the rushing

water, hauling Arthur with all the strength I had, to the spewing center of the Lake water.

Merlin turned to me. He said in alarm, "Eowlyn, wait. You don't know what it'll do."

Ryan held Excalibur, her face confused.

Vane let her hand go. Turning on her, he pulled up the trident and blasted the sword.

Ryan gasped. She dropped to her knees, but held onto the sword.

Merlin's head whipped back to them. "No, Ryan, drop the sword."

He tried to leap at his brother, but Vane pushed out a hand.

Merlin went flying back to the floor.

Vane continued to shoot green blasts at the sword.

Torn between who to help, I set Arthur under the spigot of water, intending to sit him down and run to help.

Water drenched Arthur.

Arthur pulled me under.

# 33

## THE EARTH RUMBLED

Arthur's blood spilled into the Lake water.

The Dragon's Eye heated as water touched it.

With a gasp, Merlin fell to his knees.

Inside, I screamed.

I LANDED IN THE DARK WORLD ON ALL FOURS. ON THE BEACH. THE WATER rippled behind me but I couldn't move. The Dragon's Eye glowed hot and bright. I fought to breathe. Arthur walked up from the ocean. Golden eyes shone, emphasizing the brightness of his hair in the moonlight.

The low growl of a beast sounded from behind me. My head jerked to the sound. The black lion jumped off the rocks. Its eyes glittered with gold too.

Out of the cave, the Minotaur emerged.

It walked calmly onto the beach. Behind him, the cave trembled. A tinge of green shone from the rocks.

Arthur came up onto the beach.

I stood in the middle of all three—lion, Minotaur, and Arthur. The

Dragon's Eye became hotter and my lungs struggled to take in air. I dropped to my knees.

The black lion jumped in front of me.

Arthur held out a gold coin. "Choose, wizard. Her or the coin. You can only do one."

Behind the Minotaur, rocks tumbled as the cave began to collapse.

"Hurry," Arthur said. "Or you will lose both."

The black lion gave me one last look before it lunged and snatched the gold coin from Arthur's hand. It tried to savage the hand, but Arthur sent the lion sprawling to the ground with a soft blow of air from his mouth. The lion whined as it landed hard on the ground. It wriggled up quickly, however. It sprinted past the Minotaur and into the cave.

I gasped, as the Dragon's Eye began suffocating me.

Arthur smiled. His sturdy legs, bared from the knee down, neared. He wore a long white tunic, which was tied with a gold belt and stopped just above the knees. He held out his hand. "Reach for it, Gwenhwyfar."

Hot pain shot through me from the Dragon's Eye, but I hesitated.

"The lion chose. He didn't choose you," Arthur said. "But I do."

I slapped my hand into his.

Arthur pulled me up.

Out of the dark world, I blinked and I'd returned to the Minotaur's pit.

Merlin stood behind Ryan. She trembled under Vane's attack as she tried to hold Excalibur upright. He shot blue fire from his hand. Merlin's magic healed.

Vane stumbled back in surprise.

Arthur strode to Ryan. He took Excalibur in a deft move.

The Dragon's Eye sat on my neck like a mountain-sized anchor around my neck, but I fought through waist-high water to Arthur.

Merlin turned his blue fire onto Arthur, trying to blast him.

Arthur held up Excalibur and the magic merely deflected off him. Getting to the bull, he plunged Excalibur into the water.

The second Excalibur pierced the bull, the Dragon's Eye shot with cold. Exactly the opposite of the dark world. I froze in place, unable to move.

Light radiated out from Excalibur. The ring of columns surrounding the pit stirred with life. They started spinning as if we were in the middle of a centrifuge. Under the water, the floor cracked.

Merlin, Vane, and Ryan were thrown to one side as the floor opened like a giant's jaws. Lake water receded rapidly into the crack. From the floor, the Minotaur's golden head floated up. It hung in the air. Beside Arthur.

"Arthur," I croaked.

His eyes turned to me. For a moment, the gold inside them dimmed.

The cold eased and the Dragon's Eye calmed. Freed, I hurried to him. "Wait. Don't take the mask."

"Ah, Gwenhwyfar." His hand reached out. A finger slipped out of the Dragon's Eye chain from where it lay against my heart and he gripped the gem. "But that is why I am here. By design."

On the other side of the crack beside Ryan and Vane, Merlin made a choking sound.

"P-Please," I asked. "You are more than someone's design. You are my friend."

Sorrow flashed in Arthur's eyes. "I wanted more."

He let the necklace go. Arthur caught the floating Minotaur's head. He put on the bull's mask.

The earth rumbled and came to life.

Water from the spigot stopped, every bit of it disappearing into the crack in the floor. A great wave blasted the room. The whole building, whole world shook. Walls thundered. Green fire flowed from the floor into Arthur. His entire body glowed green for a few seconds. The Dragon's Eye fluttered nervously.

The shadow of the Minotaur hung on Arthur like a cloak. Emeralds no longer filled the mask's sockets. Instead, Arthur's eyes stared back at me. They glowed gold.

*"I am returned. We meet again, Gwenhwyfar."*

My entire being stilled. Fear made my heart race, the deer facing the predator.

Merlin leaped from the other side of the crack. So did Vane. Ryan followed. She held Excalibur.

Arthur faced the trio with an amused expression. He waved a hand and Excalibur flew from Ryan to him. He played with the sword, testing its weight in the air. "It really is beautiful. But far too much trouble. I can take care of that."

He snapped Excalibur in two.

Ryan paled and stumbled back. "No."

The pit rumbled again. Red fire bubbled underneath the bull's painting. A sinkhole formed and the floor began to collapse. It started to pull us down. Columns of the ring around the pit began to crack. One column fell like a tree trunk.

The mask wobbled on Arthur. But the gold in his irises remained bright.

Vane shot him with the trident.

Arthur stumbled, retreating a few steps. He tripped on broken stone and fell backwards. As the pit collapsed, Arthur pushed himself up on the trembling floor and held up a hand.

The trident flew out of Vane's hands and slapped against Arthur's palm.

Merlin grabbed my hand and jumped up onto the fallen column. "We have to leave. The red door opened as soon as he took the mask."

He tugged me up.

"We can't just leave him," I shouted as I scrambled up on the wide column. We went toward the red door.

On the other side of the shaking pit, near the temple entrance, the mermaids backed away.

I hurried along the column with Merlin. Vane and Ryan followed.

Behind us, Arthur lifted a long column like a missile and floated it in the air.

The mermaids watched with awe. He rose above the pit. With the trident in his hand, he radiated raw golden power.

He'd become a god.

"Hurry." Merlin tugged me faster down the narrow column. Only the trilithon showed. The red door had disappeared, and in its place, there lay an open mist.

"The Fisher King rises," a mermaid cried.

With a small cry, the mermaid beside him dropped to his knees. The other mermaids followed.

Gia, Blake, Grey, and the others weaved through the kneeling mermaids. They skirted around the edge of the pit toward us.

Leonidas and Theras hit Arthur with arrows. He knocked the arrows away with barely a wave. His attention caught, Golden-Arthur turned and landed on the other side of the pit with a thud. The ground shook where he landed. Theras let out a silent war cry. Arthur sliced at him with the trident. Theras's head fell to the floor, severed from his body.

Leonidas stopped abruptly.

Arthur strode to the new Aegean king.

Leonidas dropped to his knee.

Golden-Arthur aimed the trident. He blasted them all, and a wave of golden-green fire swept over the mermaids.

Merlin pulled me out of the pit. The remaining columns fell as the temple collapsed. Stone pieces from the ceiling began to fall.

"Get to the mist," Merlin yelled at Gia and the others. "Now."

Gia, Grey, and the gargoyles hurried past falling stone blocks and ran into the trilithon gateway.

Golden-Arthur turned from the fallen mermaids. His voice traveled across the pit. "Gwenhwyfar."

Merlin grabbed my hand. He yelled, "Vane, take Ryan. Go."

Arthur rose in the air. Although lacking his supervillain cloak, he flew across the pit.

Merlin and Blake began shooting fireballs.

The Dragon's Eye heated against my neck. Syphoning off me, Merlin began blasting bigger fireballs at Golden-Arthur.

The barrage slowed him.

Vane grabbed Ryan as he hurled fireballs and hauled her into the mist.

"Go, Blake," I yelled.

Blake ran, still firing fireballs. He went into the mist. Merlin and I reached the trilithon. We smacked into silent grey stone.

The mist cut off.

I whirled around.

Arthur landed right in front of me.

Broken stone fell on him, but he waved it away as if the stone were bubbles.

Merlin held out a hand. "Stop."

Golden-Arthur waved and Merlin flew to the side as if an invisible hand swept him aside.

Golden-Arthur advanced on me. He grabbed my chin. Gold

glowing eyes locked on me. "Why leave with him? He has betrayed you. He chose to save her."

"I did," Merlin said quietly.

Golden-Arthur's lips curved up. "You will always choose her."

Merlin didn't say anything.

Golden-Arthur wagged a finger at him. "Speak the truth."

"Yes," Merlin ground out. "Ryan is the sword-bearer. She is necessary."

His words stabbed something deep in my heart.

"Ah, Merlin." He reached out and grabbed the Dragon's Eye. "All this power you've restored, but you still haven't learned. Sometimes I forget how primitive you still are."

Grunting with effort, Merlin put up a hand, intending to blast him.

"Do not test me, wizard." Golden-Arthur snapped his fingers and Merlin's hand slammed down and lay flat against the wall. Reaching out, he took a strand of my hair and tugged at it. "I expected as much from him. But you, Gwenhwyfar, you have let me down. Still, you brought me my favored vessel."

Clawing past my fear, I choked out, "This has all been a trap. You needed us to bring Arthur to the temple."

"I needed the power Poseidon placed in this temple." Golden-Arthur smiled. "Such is the irony. *She* went to so much trouble to keep it hidden. She intended to use against it me. Instead, I used it to return."

"That's why you woke Arthur. He is your vessel."

"*Perfect* vessel." Golden-Arthur slid his fingers along the strands of hair until he reached the end. He let my hair fall. "It would be easy to end you, Gwenhwyar, but he loves you. Which makes you worth the trouble. Therefore, I'm going to give you a gentle reminder. I am afraid you have forgotten who you are."

Behind me, the mist opened again.

My fingers dug into my palms. With one single whim, he could end me. I whispered, "Who are you?"

"Finally, a good question." The god's lips curved up. "I am the beginning. The end. And everything in between. You will never have enough of me. I am thing that devours all."

My eyes widened. I knew the riddle. "I know your name."

Golden-Arthur pushed me backwards.

"No." Merlin cried. He ran at me. "Lady, if you can hear me at all. Please." The Dragon's Eye carried Merlin's final plea. *I've been ready to pay the price. Ready for battle. To die. Until now. I need more time.*

But it was too late. I'd already fallen through. The mist swallowed me.

34

## MERLIN

I landed in the middle of a busy street. Two cows barreled down the dirt lane.

A man rode atop one. He shook his fist at me and yelled, "Watch it, boy."

A young boy yelled, "Oaf, don't you recognize him? It's Master Merlin."

*They know me.* In a daze, I moved to the side into a gutter of mud. Passersby wore tunics and leggings. Cottages with straw roofs lined a busy street, maybe the only main street. Above the village, in the distance, loomed high walls containing a castle that reminded one of a stone swan.

*Camelot.*

I was home.

A horse rode up from behind me, from outside the city. The horse wore a fine saddle. A familiar face, one I hadn't seen in ages, steered the animal. I squinted up at him. "Perceval?"

He grinned. "Merlin, what are you doing out of the castle gates? I thought Lady Guinevere had you busy. The wedding is in less than a week. You know how she relies on you."

Arthur's wedding? Why had Golden-Arthur dumped Eowlyn here?

A knot twisted my stomach. I closed my eyes and reached out for the presence of the Dragon's Eye. *Eowlyn, where are you?*

"I am truly happy to have run into you." Perceval jumped down off his horse. He lowered his voice. "Eowlyn's still unsure about getting married. But maybe you can talk some sense into her. I don't want to interfere, but who wouldn't want his sister to marry King Arthur?"

# AUTHOR'S NOTE

**I hope you have enjoyed Kings of Merlin!**

This book brings together the old and the new. If you enjoyed My Merlin Awakening and Ever My Merlin you'll see a lot of familiar faces. In a new way! This book bridges the My Merlin series with the Gods of Merlin series. Look toward the battle of the Gods in the final chapter of Gods of Merlin!
Which is why I need your help. Please support this book by **leaving a review** at your favorite retailer. Your review keeps this writer writing!

Look for more information on upcoming books, read deleted scenes, articles, and listen to the soundtrack, or sign up for notifications of new releases on my author website. (HTTP://WWW.PRIYAARDIS.COM).

Talk to me at the following hangouts!
Facebook: HTTP://WWW.FACEBOOK.COM/PRIYAARDIS
Goodreads: HTTP://WWW.GOODREADS.COM/PRIYAARDIS
INSTAGRAM: HTTP://WWW.INSTAGRAM.COM/PRIYAARDIS
Twitter: HTTP://WWW.TWITTER.COM/PRIYAARDIS
PINTEREST: HTTP://WWW.PINTEREST.COM/PRIYAARDIS
YOUTUBE: HTTP://WWW.YOUTUBE.COM/PRIYAARDIS

# SNEAK PEEK! LEGACY OF MERLIN

Coming Soon...

**LEGACY OF MERLIN**

**Gods of Merlin, 3**

Dive into the past to the world of Arthur and Camelot. See it anew as the final battle between Merlin and the Greek Gods decides the fate of the future.

Available Summer 2020

Sign up for notifications of new releases on my author website.
(HTTP://WWW.PRIYAARDIS.COM)

# SNEAK PEEK! PRINCESS THREE EYES

**Coming Soon...**

A sweeping tale of power, intrigue, and betrayal, in the court of the Raj, the Third Kingdom. A young girl has a third eye which opens and closes at will on her forehead, but the useless appendage does nothing. Or does it?

Available Summer 2020

Sign up for notifications of new releases on my author website. (HTTP://WWW.PRIYAARDIS.COM)

# MY BOYFRIEND MERLIN, BOOK 1

**Read the original bestselling trilogy!**

**Before the Gods meddled, there was Ryan...**

17 year-old Boston high schooler, Ryan DuLac just found out the guy she's been crushing on, hot biker Matt, is a little older than he was letting on. By a few eons... In fact, he is really Merlin--the Merlin, King Arthur's Merlin, the greatest wizard who ever lived. Frozen in a cave for over fifteen hundred years, he's woken for a purpose. But Ryan's not impressed. Tired of being a relationship loser, she'd rather kick his legendary behind.

Sure, the world has been crazy ever since the sword and the stone fell out of the sky like a meteor. But despite gruesome gargoyles, a deadly new world of magic, and the guy driving her crazy, Ryan knows that family is everything. Will Merlin sacrifice hers to save the world? Will she be able to stop him?

# ABOUT THE AUTHOR

PRIYA ARDIS loves books of all kinds—especially the ones which let your chai get cold. Her novels come from a childhood of playing too much She-Ra and watching too much Spock. She started writing in notebooks on long train rides during a hot summer vacation. Her favorite Arthurian piece is *The Lady of Shalott,* a poem by Lord Alfred Tennyson.

Please support this book by **leaving a review** at your favorite retailer. Your review keeps this writer writing!

Look for more information on upcoming books, stay connected at the following sites, or sign up for notifications of new releases on the author's website (HTTP://WWW.PRIYAARDIS.COM)